CRAZY OVER YOU

YOU

TAMING THE PACK

WENDY SPARROW

Entangled Publishing, LLC
2614 South Timberline Road
Suite 109
Fort Collins, CO 80525
Visit our website at www.entangledpublishing.com.

Select Otherworld is an imprint of Entangled Publishing, LLC.

Edited by Lewis Pollak
Cover design by Fiona Jayde Media
Cover art by iStock

Manufactured in the United States of America

First Edition July 2015

To Stephanie—
I'm always willing to take on the responsibility of being the craziest person in the room when you're there to make me laugh and be my friend.

Chapter One

Some days were best forgotten.

As he sat on the edge of his bed, Travis Flynn was hard-pressed to decide if these last few days were among them. True, they'd removed the threat of poachers that had been hanging over the Lycan community for nearly a dozen years. He'd lost some pack members, including Ross, who'd arranged a genocide of his people.

Also, he'd started his courtship of Alanna, despite there being only mild sexual interest between them. She was alpha material. He needed a mate. She was the most logical choice. It was hard to say what he'd feel for her when he'd achieved this goal.

He'd presided over a marriage today. That had been... interesting.

Maybe that was it. He was settling for a mating partner instead of a scent-match. Some Lycans never scent-matched. And he'd been Alpha for a year, and there were expectations.

The Alpha was meant to contribute to the continuation of their species. After so many years of poachers taking their toll, their species could use a few Lycans getting it on. Besides, you never knew when someone like Ross would come along and destroy the monotonous routine you'd worked hard to achieve by killing you and using your innards to lay a false trail. He could wind up a bag of guts in someone's fridge like their pack member Colby had.

In that light, mating with Alanna sounded much better. Anything was better than ending up with no one caring you were dead. Alanna would be a good alpha female. And she wasn't exactly hard on the eyes. It would be fine. It would be good. And claiming a mate was part of his life plan—a meticulously constructed timeline he couldn't suspend indefinitely while awaiting a scent-match that might never occur.

Travis wiped both hands down his face. He needed sleep.

He lay back on his bed and turned off the light. He'd fought hard today. He shouldn't have the energy to stare at the ceiling and worry about his pack. His right leg hurt like hell—even if Alanna had stitched it up. He'd carry a scar from the bullet wound he'd received in today's battle.

Closing his eyes, Travis willed himself to go to sleep. He had a lengthy day ahead of him tomorrow. He needed to go in and function as the local sheriff. He couldn't take more time off. The threat was terminated. Things were satisfactory. Life was acceptable.

He should try counting sheep.

A wolf counting sheep.

He laughed to himself.

Okay, seriously, he needed sleep.

Finally, exhaustion dragged him under.

The sharp sting to his neck and the pressure of someone crouching on top of him, pinning his arms, woke him up. Travis gasped in a breath, and his heart went wild as he frantically tried to assess the situation. *Friend or foe? Is this even real? If it isn't, is this a nightmare...or a very good fantasy?* He blinked. *Damn. Maybe both.*

It wasn't every night you woke up with a naked female on top of you and one of your kitchen knives at your throat. *This is...unexpected.* His pulse kept up its pace despite his mental reminder to "stay calm"—pulses didn't listen to such things, dammit. This was fine. He was in control. Well, he wasn't, but he soon would be.

He inhaled, trying not to move...and it hit him. His mouth went dry as his forehead started to sweat. Hormones rushed through his system like he was a teenage boy with a crush—not a grown-ass man, a sheriff, with a genius IQ and a gun somewhere around. Now? Here? Of all the...oh, she smelled good enough to eat...dammit, seriously? Damn was it inconvenient to scent-match to someone wanting to kill you. And in the middle of the night? He didn't even know her.

He drew in a ragged breath. *You can do this.* If he played his part right, he could get the upper hand.

Logic.

Ignoring his hormones. And her very naked body. Her naked body with gorgeous curves that made his fingertips tingle with the desire to trace them. If only his arms weren't pinned.

A wrinkle formed between her eyebrows, and her mouth firmed just as the sting of the knife blade brought him back to reality.

Ease up on the devouring her with your eyes, moron!

Fantastic night vision was a huge liability right now.

"Hello, what can I do for you?" He blinked forcefully and tried to imbue the right amount of lazy, nonthreatening drawl into his voice.

"Where is my brother?" she asked, slowly enunciating each word as if dealing with an idiot. Her voice was sexy and deep, and his body didn't care about the knife at his throat. Focusing on the pain helped him leash the animal inside.

Inhaling again, he mentally groaned. Siblings smelled close enough that you could peg a relation.

Just go ahead and kill me.

"Can we discuss this without the knife?" She wasn't going to take the news regarding her brother well. Who would? *Honey, your brother was a traitor to our kind and tried to wipe out an entire population of Lycans. He was ripped to shreds. There weren't enough pieces of him to bring back in a box to bury.*

Narrowing her gorgeous blue eyes, his captor said, "You've all been over at his place and taken things and gone through his stuff. The place has been picked through like a crime scene. I want to know why and where he is. I know you're his Alpha. I know you know where he is."

Travis was, and he did…but he wasn't about to blurt that out. "I didn't know Ross had a sister. You didn't live with him." He'd known Ross for years, and she looked around the same age. Ross had never acted as if he had family, and his mother had died when he was an infant. But this woman smelled like she was family of some sort.

She frowned at him.

Warmth flushed his skin. He was burning up with

wanting her. Okay, obviously there wasn't going to be a lot of small talk. Even her frowns were a turn-on.

Concentrate, Travis. Focus. Clear your head. She has a damn knife at your throat. Hell, her legs were long—all sinewy smooth muscle and…dammit.

She inhaled to speak, and then she stopped and blinked…and her pupils dilated. Her breath hitched as she released it. Her frown deepened. "What…just…happened?"

Apparently, the scent-match had hit her, too. Hopefully she wouldn't kill her soul mate.

Her voice deepened as she said, "He was my half brother. My mom moved away, and he didn't find out about me until… Why do you smell like…?" She moaned and closed her eyes.

He felt the same way.

Kill me now.

No one could be worse for him to scent-match with. No one.

Unless it was Ross himself. His muscles twitched in a repressed shudder.

And Ross was dead.

Travis had an IQ of 163, and he couldn't think of anything beyond the scent of her skin and the touch of her brown hair as it brushed the side of his face. Even the knife at his neck wasn't feeling like much of a deterrent.

She panted out a breath as she opened her eyes. "You smell like everything I've ever wanted."

"If you put the knife down…we can talk about that."

Sometimes, you had to make the best of a bad thing. And considering the naked body hovering above his—the best might be very good. She was gorgeous. At least she was a Lycan. There was that. The last couple of scent-matches he knew of had been to humans. Judging from the fact that she'd shed her clothes to go into form, she was definitely a Lycan. And while nakedness wasn't as big a deal among Lycans, that was possibly only because their hormones weren't normally this front-and-center. Was this what it was like being in heat? He blinked and tried to concentrate. And if he could breathe less, that would be great.

"I'm not moving. I'm not a threat to you. Just put down the knife." Because if she had a knife at his throat even before she found out her brother was dead, things would be much worse after.

She licked her lips, still breathing faster. At least she was considering it. This might not go as unfavorably as he'd first thought. Maybe they were estranged. Hell, maybe they hated each other and she was looking for her brother so she could put a knife at his throat, too.

Hopefully not while she was naked.

"My name is Travis," he said slowly.

She narrowed her eyes. "Don't treat me like I'm crazy."

Whoa, he hadn't even begun to treat her like she was crazy—which she was. Normally, he wasn't attracted to crazy women.

"What's your name?" he asked.

She inhaled to speak and then started blinking rapidly again and let all the air out of her lungs raggedly. Yeah, this scent-match thing was powerful. It made you overlook things like incompatibility—one of you being a local sheriff, the other being a head case with a knife in her hand. She yanked the knife from his throat and set her hand on the pillow beside his head before leaning down and pressing her mouth against his. Firecrackers went off in his chest, and he closed his eyes as he lifted his head. It was a damn good thing she'd moved the knife, or he might have lopped his whole head off trying to get closer.

Of the million and one things he might have expected—that wasn't one of them.

But he was willing to go along with it.

This was the quickest he'd ever kissed a woman after meeting her. Definitely the soonest he'd had his tongue in someone's mouth as she made soft moaning noises. Plus, she was naked. This didn't happen. Not in the real world. If only she hadn't trapped his arms at his sides with her legs. One of her hands—the one not holding the knife—came up to cup his head so she could deepen the kiss.

Okay, he was definitely willing to put up with crazy.

She pulled back slowly, her teeth scraping across his lower lip. "LeAnn." She wiped her mouth—that heavenly mouth—with her free hand.

"LeAnn." It suited her. "If you'll let me up, we can keep talking about this." And by "talking" he meant he'd have her on her back, moaning out his name rather rapidly. His very long stretch of abstinence was about to end.

She licked her lips and wrinkled up her nose. "First, tell me where my brother is."

Well, that would ruin any "talking." "First, let me up."

Raising her eyebrows, she leaned forward and put the knife back at his throat. "First, tell me where Ross is."

He sighed. "Well, you've heard of the poachers, I'm sure." Whichever pack she'd formerly belonged to would have mentioned them.

She studied his face with narrowed eyes. "What? You

mean like animal poachers?"

"No, I mean… Wait, what pack were you a member of?" She was now in the Rainier pack by virtue of being his mate, but this was all happening unbelievably fast for him to process that.

"I wasn't in a…pack." She said the word like it was bizarre and foreign.

So she'd simply roamed. But any of the packs she'd been in touch with in the last decade would have mentioned poachers. "Well, in the packs you've met with, I'm sure they've brought up poachers." Maybe if she had her memory jogged as to the abhorrent nature of her brother's crime, she'd be less upset.

"I've never met with a pack. Why would I? I mean, I know what my brother was. He showed me on a trip—that's how I knew about you, but he didn't take me to any meetings."

Her brother let her handle being a Lycan all on her own? That was nearly criminal in and of itself. No wonder she was crazy. Being a Lycan was fairly all-encompassing in the way of lifestyles.

"Well, okay, so there are…well, *were* these individuals who hunted down Lycans for their organs. There is a black market for Lycan organs."

Her mouth dropped open, and the knife left his throat again. "That's horrible."

"Yes." He cleared his throat. Normally, he'd adopt his dim-witted persona to set someone at ease, but he couldn't seem to dredge up that side to him. He didn't want to. He wanted LeAnn to see him as an Alpha. "So, they've been hunting our kind for around twelve years and wiping out our population."

She nodded. Her mouth was pursed in this adorable way that made him want to kiss her again…and they were talking about poachers and the extinction of his species. There was something quantifiably wrong with him. Seriously.

"Now can you let me up?"

She considered this for a second, but then shook her head. "What if you call the police?"

"I am the police. I'm the sheriff."

She frowned. "Well, that's unfortunate."

"But I'm not planning on doing anything." Not anything as a sheriff, anyway.

With a shrug, she scooted backward—freeing up his arms. He could at least stop her from going for his throat when he broke the news about her brother.

He got up on his elbows. "So, we thought poachers had killed someone in my pack last week, but it turned out to be a trap for a nearby pack where…uhh…someone had notified the poachers of the identities of the entire pack. They'd basically sent out an extermination order. Men. Women. Children. The poachers killed an elderly woman before we got there to help."

"That's awful." She scooted farther back and got off his bed, holding the knife in front of her. "What does this have to do with my brother?"

He could lie to her, but she'd need to know soon enough, and there wasn't a gray area to what Ross had done. "Ross was the one who notified the poachers of their identities."

She shook her head. "No. No, I'm sorry. You're wrong."

He sat up. Time to lay all the cards on the table and work back from there. "When I arrived there, your brother was holding a woman for ransom as part of the trap…this was yesterday."

LeAnn continued to shake her head. "No. You're wrong. Ross said that someone had it out for him. That I shouldn't be surprised if he went off the grid for a while. But…no. He didn't do that. You're wrong…or you're lying…or…"

"I'm not. I'm sorry. Your brother is dead. Another pack killed him after he attacked the Alpha of Glacier Peak. We lost a lot of Lycans yesterday because of your brother." They had effectively ended the threat of the poachers, but he wasn't going to offer her that silver lining.

She frowned. "He's not dead. I'd know if he was dead, and besides, he's been around here. He was here tonight. That's why I figured you'd know."

He'd seen denial, but that was taking it further than expected. "He's dead. Really. Honey, I'm sorry, but…"

"No!" she said, pointing at him with the knife. "No. You're wrong. You're wrong." She backed up slowly, breathing faster, and he could see the sheen of tears in her eyes.

He got up from the bed—an inch at a time—maintaining eye contact. This *could* be going better, but at least she hadn't sliced his throat, and he'd told her without her going ballistic and knifing him. Now he just had to get her to believe him. "LeAnn, it's okay. Stay where you are, and we can talk about this. This isn't your fault."

"No. He's not dead. I can smell things really well, and he's not dead. He was outside your house earlier tonight."

"All Lycans can smell things well, and trust me, he's dead." And her brother should have helped her find a pack so she'd be more aware of the Lycan way of life. He wanted to kill Ross all over again for that. What kind of brother would let his sister deal with this all by herself? Ass.

"Well, good for you guys, but I can smell my brother's scent, and he's alive. And he didn't do anything to your...people or species or whatever like you're saying. He wouldn't."

Travis stood up and stared at her. Okay, the hormones might be messing with his head and, yes, he was tired, and he wasn't handling this optimally, but... "LeAnn, you do know that you're a Lycan, right?" Even if the naked thing hadn't tipped him off, she smelled like a Lycan now that she was as aroused as he was. There was a wild aspect to the sweet musk she was putting off. It was making him insane. Knife or no knife...crazy or sane...he wanted to drag her back to bed with him.

She laughed, and for a moment, he was relieved... because of course she knew.

Then she shook her head and said, "No, I'm not."

His mouth fell open.

What?

"And Ross isn't dead."

Chapter Two

Seriously, why did all the hot ones have to be freaking out of their minds? And wow, was he hot. It was just as well she'd gotten that kiss out of her system and gotten the hell out of there. Now she could have a rational conversation with the local sheriff. Well, rational on her end, anyway. She knew he was wrong—about so many things. All his crazy accusations had rattled around her brain last night keeping her awake. She blinked forcefully. There was not enough caffeine in the world for mornings like this and the man who'd just arrived.

LeAnn wrapped her fingers around her warm mug as she watched him get out of his truck and head toward Ross's front door.

He is so wrong. She'd tell herself that every few minutes. LeAnn tilted her head, considering. *Wrong in all the right ways.*

Opening the door, she left the screen door shut between them as he approached. *Mm-mm.* Travis was worth watching.

That sandy-blond hair of his had felt so good against her hand. And not once had those hazel eyes looked panicked despite the fact that he had a knife at his neck. It looked like she'd managed to nick him a bit. Oops.

He caught sight of her and stopped at the bottom of the stairs. He was wary today. He shouldn't be. With him being able to turn into a wolf, he really had the upper hand. He could tear right through this screen door.

She leaned casually against the doorframe and sipped from her mug.

"Are you feeling more reasonable today?" he asked. Hell, even his voice was sexy. He talked slowly, like he had all the time in the world for conversation…like it was a lazy morning and they'd woken up in bed together.

Blinking slowly, she shook her head to rid it of that image. She'd never gone zero to sixty with a guy like this. She wanted him—*really* wanted him—like attack-and-take-no-prisoners sort of want.

He took her head shake as an answer and muttered, "I didn't figure so."

"I can hear really well, too." She had remarkable hearing, actually. She could hear crazy well.

"Of course you can—you're a Lycan!"

Whatever. She'd have noticed if she turned into a wolf. Her brother apparently lucked out on the good genes. The wolf genes.

Travis must've decided she didn't bite and took a tentative step up onto the porch. *Hah! He was wrong again.* She loved biting. She'd really love to bite him. Instead, she took another sip from her mug.

"How do you explain being naked at my house last

night?" Travis tilted his head and narrowed his eyes.

He was adorable. It was a shame they were at cross-purposes here. She inhaled as his scent reached her. How could one man smell so much better than every other man on the planet?

Mm. It was too bad he was insane. "I sometimes run naked, and I ran to your place from here." It was a bizarre exhibitionist side of her that surfaced occasionally. She cleared her throat and hid her heated cheeks behind her mug as she took another sip. One minute she was dressed and then the next she was looking down at her stark-naked limbs and wanting to scream that it had happened again. At least she'd been out in the wilderness this time.

He scowled. "Because you're a damn wolf. Of course you run naked."

"Whatever. Do you have any real news about my brother?"

"Just the same as last night." He stared hard at her. "Your brother was a murdering bastard who is now dead."

Hm. "I see you're pouring on the charm this morning."

"I tried to be nice and gentle with it last night, but you seem to need things blunt and with a hard edge, and even then you apparently won't believe them." He folded his arms.

"I'm not the one who thinks he's dead when he's clearly been around here." She sniffed. "Can't you smell him? He went from here to your place last night."

"He's lived here—of course his scent is around. That's all it is. That's all it *can* be."

Typical. He didn't even try to pick up Ross's scent. Maybe it was just as well. It sounded like wolf-man had a bone to pick with her brother, anyway. She'd be on her own trying to find Ross—which was fine. It was how she preferred things. You couldn't trust anyone but yourself. A lesson she'd learned and relearned.

"I tried to look you up. I couldn't find any connection between you and Ross."

She shrugged. "His dad didn't acknowledge my mom... partly because he was still married at the time, and I was born right before Ross's mom died. He never even told Ross about us. I got a hold of Ross about five years ago when my mom finally fessed up. I get the sense that she didn't necessarily want to explain that she'd gotten freaky with a werewolf at one point in her life, let alone admit that he was married. Ross didn't want to believe his dad had an affair and then wrote us off. Then we met, and he knew."

They'd finally made progress two years ago when he came to visit. He'd talked about this girl he liked who didn't seem to want him as more than a friend. LeAnn had been ditching out of a bad relationship. He'd helped her finally end that relationship. Helping her had seemed to help him. He needed to be needed. He was a good guy. He'd even said that she shouldn't be with someone who didn't treat her right. That she deserved to be treated right. There was no way he'd done what Travis said he had.

"What's your last name?"

"It's none of your damn business," she said calmly as she took another sip. This was fun. It was only fun because her brother was alive, though.

"Maybe I'll take you in for trespassing."

"Maybe you'll need to find my brother and ask him if I'm trespassing."

He took a deep breath and then kept his eyes closed for

an extra-long blink. When he met her eyes again, she could see the wolf in his eyes, and she had the feeling she was on a very short leash. Ironic. Since she wasn't the one here more likely to be leashed. Well, maybe recreationally.

"So, what are you intending to do here?"

"Track down my brother and find out the truth of what's going on."

"Trust me, you don't want to go down that road. It ends in a cabin surrounded by a lot of death that your brother caused."

For an instant...just an instant...she doubted herself. She hadn't spent as much time with her brother since that visit two years ago. The phone call last week was out of the blue. But this was Ross. Ross who'd taught her how to track on one of her trips to visit. Ross who'd beaten the tar out of her ex, Clayton, when he'd shown up and tried to hurt her. She only had a handful of memories of her brother, but they were all good.

And he was alive. His trail from here to Travis's place was fresh. It couldn't have been more than a few hours old. That was how she'd ended up on this man's doorstep...and in his bed...and reading his mail. He was paying way too much for internet.

Travis cleared his throat. "Now, on to the other thing we need to talk about."

She raised both her eyebrows at that. The other thing? He sounded the tiniest bit arrogant there.

He gave her a long look. It probably intimidated the idiot girls he was used to dealing with. He probably dated pretty airheads. At least she knew he wasn't married; the only other scent around his house had been another male's in the guest bedroom. But she shouldn't have kissed him. Even if he'd been irresistible. She was resisting him today just fine. Well, sure, her grip on the mug was a smidge tighter, and she fought the urge to shift around uncomfortably or run through the screen door, but she could fight her urges. She wasn't an animal.

"What other thing?" she asked when he appeared to be waiting for it. She was going to be able to fight these urges for only so long. Hopefully he'd stay right where he was, too.

He gestured between them. "Us. We've scent-matched. It means we're mates."

So...she wasn't expecting *that*. She stood there blinking stupidly. He'd said *that*. Mates. Her mouth opened and closed. It was insane. Sure, there was this primitive sort of connection between them—she didn't just kiss anyone— but this pull...this brain-frying lust...it'd fade. They weren't mates. "Does that line work often?"

"You know it's not a line. You can feel it. That's why you kissed me. It's either that or you're really..."

"Slutty?"

"I was going to say friendly."

She shrugged. "I'd had a long flight. Plus, there'd been a bit of an adrenaline spike. I was wired." *Which explained last night. How are you justifying wanting to curl yourself around him today, LeAnn?*

"Uh-huh."

"You kissed me back." It had to be said. She'd had his enthusiastic agreement there.

"That's because I know we're scent-matched and meant to be together." The corner of his mouth lifted in a half smile. "Also, typically when a naked woman starts kissing me — there's not a downside."

Oh, there was a downside. They were up against it today. "Trust me, we're not meant to be together. If you knew anything about me, you'd realize that."

"It can't be helped. We're not going to scent-match with anyone else. It's you and me — or no one. Once we've accepted the scent-match, we're considered married by the pack."

Married? Her eyes widened. She swallowed thickly and starting mentally preparing an exit strategy. *Okay, deep breaths. Deep breaths.* That was nuts. Married was tied down. Married was trapped. Guys cheated. Guys left you. Married was opening yourself up to having your heart ripped out. He had to be joking. "Have you noticed everything out of your mouth seems to be more and more ridiculous?"

"You can deny a lot of things, LeAnn, and believe me, you're the last person I'd want to scent-match to, but this thing between us isn't going away."

The swift pain that followed that remark stole her breath for a moment. Not that she believed in soul mates or love at first sight, but she was the last person he'd want to be with? The last person? There was a whole world of people out there. She wasn't *that* bad.

"Yeah, you're really not charming, are you?" In fact, he'd just about charmed himself into a kick in the nads, and she wasn't buying this scent-match crap. It was good that her anger was nixing this girlie need to cry...even if she still felt sick inside.

The last person. If he knew her, that'd be different. He could get in digs like that — he was the damn sheriff. But he didn't even know her. What a bastard. She rounded her shoulders, tucking into a smaller target before she recognized she was doing it and stiffened her spine. *No. No one tears me down like that. Not anymore.*

He clenched his teeth. "I didn't mean that the way it came out. I only meant that this isn't something we can ignore and hope it fades. It won't. And this whole thing with your brother puts us in an…awkward position."

It wasn't much of a recovery. Nothing was quite as romantic as him settling for her because he thought she smelled nice. *Scent-match, my ass.*

"I don't feel anything for you," she lied. In her lifetime of lies, this was a small one, and it was all about self-preservation. She wasn't about to show weakness. She'd been weak for a guy before. Never again.

"Yes. You do." He took a step closer.

"No. I don't."

"You can't resist me." He took another step toward her.

She sipped from her mug. Hm. It seemed like she could. Today. Which was especially good since she was the *last* person he wanted to be with. Last night, resisting him had been impossible. When he was all warm and drowsy in a room that smelled like him. Her grip tightened again. Okay, she had to steer clear of the local sheriff and then get out of here as fast as she could.

He started unbuttoning his shirt.

Her eyebrows shot up, and her mouth went dry. Oh wow. It was like he'd peeked inside her head.

He kept going.

"What are you doing?" Hopefully he couldn't hear the panic in her voice. She'd smothered it pretty well, but…holy hell, he had a nice chest.

His uniform's shirt and undershirt hit the front porch.

Oh, his abs were about the best she'd seen. Where was a bucket of ice when she needed it? It felt like she was running a fever. A fever for the local sheriff. This was so not good.

Unlacing his shoes, he shoved one off and then the other. His hands went to his pants.

Whoa. "Uhh, seriously, what are you doing?"

"Proving to you that you won't be able to resist my scent and this whole thing is futile." And off went the pants.

She felt light-headed, and her knees went weak. It was too much. She huffed out a breath. Okay, no. He wanted to play dirty. They could play dirty.

She went to get her phone. He wasn't kidding…he smelled amazing…and he had on paisley boxers…or he had. They were off, too.

Her brother had a few numbers and business cards on the fridge, including one she'd memorized and dialed now as he was taking off his socks.

She really shouldn't breathe. Her eyes kept wanting to roll back in her head while she moaned. He was…wow…but she could resist. For a very short window of time. A window that was shrinking.

"Hello. Sheriff's department. How can I help you?" a woman's sweet voice answered on the phone.

"Yeah, my name is LeAnn, and I have a naked man on my front porch claiming to be your sheriff."

"You do?"

Yes, she did, and he was standing there as naked as the day he was born, and he was right—he was irresistible. Her grip on the phone and the mug were near shattering them.

"Are you sure?" the woman asked.

"Yes, would you like a description?"

"Um. Maybe. I don't know. Are you sure it's Sheriff Flynn?"

Travis had his arms folded and was shaking his head back and forth. He also seemed to be fighting a smile. He'd asked for this.

"Well, let's see, shall we? He's well-built." It was hard not to inflate his ego while still being honest. "Looks like he lifts free weights. Definitely a runner. Nice ass. Real six-pack abs. He's got the whole…uhh…package. Oh, also, he's got a sweet tattoo. I don't know how you feel about tattoos, but this is some sexy ink. Looks like an *R*, but also a wolf." It figured a Lycan would have a wolf tattoo.

Grinning, Travis bent down and grabbed his clothes… and not a moment too soon. She was seconds from tossing the phone and the mug and jumping through the screen door.

"Hm, looks like he's getting dressed again. Never mind."

"Did you want to file a complaint?"

"Oh, there's definitely nothing to complain about." Well, it was a shame he was getting dressed, but it was really just as well.

"Are you sure it's our sheriff?" The poor woman sounded halfway between scandalized and titillated.

"Yep. He'll be a little late getting in to work," LeAnn said, hanging up.

"This isn't going away," Travis said as he buttoned his pants.

"I don't know. A cold shower. Maybe a nice, long run. That should make it go away."

He laughed outright. Then he settled a somber gaze on her. "I'm serious, LeAnn. You and me were meant to be together. First, you accept the scent-match and the fact that your brother was not the man you thought he was. Then we can start figuring out our future together." He'd ticked them off on his fingers like he had a mental list going.

How clinical he sounded about it. *First, recognize that I'm the new god of your world and your only family was a genocidal maniac. Second, we have sex.* No, "have sex" still sounded too casual. Procreate. No. Participate in sexual congress with an aim of reproduction. Something like that.

"And if I don't?"

He shook his head again. "The pack will accept you. You can stay here. We protect our own. We may not be your brother, but we can be your new family."

She held back a sigh at his words so he wouldn't guess that this was the most seductive moment yet. But a sheriff with her? No. Hell no. Besides, as he'd said, she was the last person he wanted to be with, and he didn't know how right he was. She'd find her brother and the truth—then she'd get the hell out of here.

"I won't accept them," she said. It was for the best. She really wasn't the right person for him. He hadn't needed to say it out loud, but it was still the truth.

The stark…naked…truth. Damn, it was a shame he'd put his clothes back on. Her knuckles were white where she was gripping the phone and her mug. If he stayed here much longer, she'd turn into an animal—which she never did, despite what he thought. LeAnn clenched her teeth.

How did he manage to smell like sex without smelling like sex? He smelled like raw, savage passion. Like going at it under the sun in the middle of a field. Or stripping down in the backseat of a car because there was no way you were making it all the way home. Travis Flynn smelled like your best time about to happen—when everything turned white behind your eyelids and a scream caught in your throat. That was him—all wrapped up in muscles and now in a uniform. And this bad, bad girl had always had a thing for a guy in a uniform.

He scowled and turned away.

Her shoulders slacked and she huffed out a breath. *Hell, that was close.*

Striding away, Travis called over his shoulder, "I wouldn't put anything in his fridge. He used to keep dead body parts in the freezer."

"Yeah, right," she muttered. At least she could loosen her death grip on the phone and the mug now that he'd moved away.

He raised a hand. "Honest truth."

She looked over her shoulder at the fridge. Eww.

• • •

He had less than no hope of concentrating on anything at work. When he'd walked in, late as LeAnn had mentioned, he and Betty had opted not to make eye contact for the day. Hiding out in his office should have given him ample time to catch up…but for two details—two items.

Item one being his scent-matched source of frustration. He'd seen her naked, and he couldn't unsee that…and, honestly, he didn't want to. But the image of her leaning over him was burned into his retinas. Even when he closed his eyes, LeAnn was there. She was gorgeous. She was like a wall pinup in his brain for the day.

Item two was all the crazy assertions she'd made. He rubbed both his hands down his face. This was asinine. Anything she said was insane ramblings from a mentally unstable, albeit very hot, woman. There was no reason to suppose that Ross was still alive. None. He based his actions on logic and reason and… He called Miller anyway—on his cellphone—after he'd closed the door to his office.

"Well, hell, Travis, I didn't realize we'd be chatting every day now. I knew it was a mistake to let you see me naked."

Normally he'd have some response, but he couldn't seem to keep his mind on anything. Well, not anything without blue eyes and satiny brown hair and a body that wouldn't quit.

"How sure are you that you killed Ross?" Travis asked the Alpha of the Black Tusk pack.

"Pretty damn," Miller said with a snort of disbelief. "You don't really recover from being torn to pieces. My pack didn't exactly take kindly to what he did to one of our own—beyond bringing the poachers. Colby was pack to us."

"And you're sure it was him—not the wolf he let loose." Jordan had mentioned Ross had released an actual wolf that looked just like him.

There was a telltale pause before Miller said, "Yeah, of course it was him."

"You saw his tattoo?"

"Tattoo?"

"All of Rainier has phosphorous tattoos that you can see in both forms. You might have been able to see it somewhat with the shade of the trees."

"I didn't notice a tattoo, but it happened fast. Once we caught him…well, it was over quick. A pack killing isn't pretty. We don't stop and shake hands and check out each other's ink."

That's what he figured. It had to have been Ross. An actual wolf wouldn't behave the same or smell the same. Then again, pack thinking sometimes overrode rational thought. If they'd seen a wolf that looked like Ross, the Black Tusk pack might have convinced themselves it was him. Hell. This was a pain. LeAnn had made him doubt himself.

"What's all this about?"

He might as well get it out. It was bound to spread rapidly when he told his pack—which he'd have to do, for several reasons. "Ross's sister came looking for him."

The other man hissed out a breath.

"She has no idea what he was doing, and she wasn't involved," Travis said quickly.

"You're sure?"

"One hundred percent." He might doubt a lot of the rest of what she thought, but she had no idea what Ross had been up to. "She thinks I'm crazy for even suggesting it." Which was funny…if anything was funny.

"So you wanted to check to make sure or she wants his body or what?"

It didn't sound like there was a body to give her—which he didn't like to think on, even if Ross had deserved it. "She swears she could smell his scent around his place and my place last night."

"She's Lycan?"

He paused. "I think so."

"You think so?"

Yeah, that sounded stupid. How else would she recognize a scent? Why else would she have been naked at his place? She was a Lycan. Travis clenched his teeth and started lining up items on his desk down to the millimeter. Who ran naked? No one ran naked. Barefoot, sure. In very little clothing, okay. But naked? He put his pencils one inch apart. She was a Lycan.

Miller was still waiting for his answer. "Yeah. I mean, yes, she is."

"Did *you* smell Ross around?" Miller had to ask that.

Dragging his hand through his hair as he leaned back in his seat, Travis said, "I don't know. Her scent is close enough to his that it was probably her I'm smelling." There had been something out there, but it had to have been her. Ross *had* to be dead. Anything else wasn't logical. Anything else was absurd.

"She's probably chasing her tail." There was a pause before Miller asked, "You're sure she had nothing to do with what he did?"

"Yeah, she's not even from around here." She'd mentioned a flight, but he should really find out where she was from…and a last name. Not that she'd have it for very long if she accepted the scent-match. Scent-matched was as good as married.

"Well, good. And that makes me sound like a hard-ass, but yesterday is still fresh in my mind. She should get the hell out of here. Even if Ross helped us finally get rid of those bastards, he's not winning any popularity contests anytime soon. Any kin of his isn't welcome."

Travis saw red and clenched his teeth. If Miller were in the room, he'd have torn into him. She couldn't leave.

Miller cleared his throat after Travis's continued silence. "You don't want anyone in your pack getting any ideas—

thinking they're doing something for the good of the pack."

"There's one problem with that."

"Her leaving?"

"Yup."

"What?" Miller asked.

He picked up a pencil, twirling it between his fingers. Travis'd always been the careful one in his family. His only sibling had been reckless and carefree. One day, he'd run out and enlisted on a whim. Just done it. When Josh had been killed overseas a dozen years ago, the senselessness of it— He'd died dragging a friend's dead body out of an ambush. They'd called his brother a hero, and he was, but there had to have been a way for Josh to still be alive. His brother had rushed in before he could analyze the logistics. He'd run headlong into the fight like he always had.

He'd always looked up to Josh—trying to be like him. Josh had let him follow him everywhere despite their age difference. No one was as much fun to shadow as his brother. And everybody loved him. He was easygoing. Josh'd always tried to get his little brother to loosen up and go with the flow.

As an adult, he saw that for the mistake it was.

Travis had loved Josh, but his brother had always lacked self-control, and it'd gotten him killed. Travis chose what happened. He did. Or he had. It was all about to go to hell. He was about to lose control of everything, and he'd always had control.

"I scent-matched on her. She's pack." The pencil in his hand snapped. He threw both pieces away. He'd finally said it out loud. That made it real somehow. He was scent-matched to the sister of his pack's enemy.

Miller exhaled slowly. "Damn."

His thoughts exactly.

"Just…damn."

Yup.

"Your pack knows?"

"Not yet."

"Did any of your alpha contenders die yesterday? Hell, that sounds cold, but…staying Alpha in that pack is like working with live wires."

It didn't surprise him that the other Alpha recognized this pack had the potential to be difficult to maintain. It was a surprise he'd managed this long. If any of the females in the pack had wanted to be Alpha, he'd have been challenged over and over by the males wanting to be with them. "I wish. I lost Eli and Tom. The rest of us have enough injuries that I'm hoping they'll think twice about challenging me immediately."

"I wouldn't count on that. The two I'm thinking of—the ones snarling at you and refusing to follow directions in the middle of yesterday's fight…"

"Troy and Liam."

When they'd split off from Glacier Peak pack to form their own pack with Travis as Alpha, he'd known those two were going to be a problem. There'd been Lycans who'd joined from other packs who were arrogant with something to prove, but none compared to the two he'd brought with him from his old pack. As a whole, the pack was gaining a reputation for being the "frat pack," and their careless audacity yesterday had only entrenched the belief.

In particular, Liam and Troy had stubbornly wanted to be reckless and boneheaded. If Travis hadn't forced the issue—in snarling fury—they'd both be dead today. Instead, he had two wolves who were pissed at him for saving their lives.

"Yeah. Troy and Liam. Hotheaded jackasses," Miller said. "I was tempted to use them as shields in the fight so we could get closer to the damn poachers in the trees—that's about when you went all badass and ran across the clearing. Seeing as how you'd risked your life in a stupid way, I figured they might be worth something to you."

"Pack is pack. You can't always pick the morons you'd give your life for." But he wouldn't squander it like his brother had. The shortest distance between two points had been straight through the clearing, and the poachers had been distracted by the firefight. It'd been a reasonable decision. He could think fast on his feet—logically—and the end result of his being in control was more people lived. It weighed on him that he'd lost two yesterday, even if it was a realistic cost.

"Not your mate either, apparently."

He recalled her face when he'd said she was the last person he'd want as a mate. For a second, that bravado of hers had fallen in a wince as she broke eye contact with him. It had been her first show of weakness in front of him, and it hadn't made him feel more powerful. He'd felt like a bastard for shooting his mouth off like that.

LeAnn was gorgeous and feisty and she gave as good as she got.

But the timing of the scent-match was hell. Fate had a sick sense of humor. Last night he'd been thinking about how waiting on a scent-match didn't fit his life plan, but this couldn't have happened at a worse time.

And Troy and Liam might capitalize on it.

"Not that we needed any more dead Lycans yesterday, but you better watch your back." Miller sighed. "It's a shame. I've really enjoyed dealing with you and not one of those morons. Even when you pull your I'm-an-idiot act, you're still better than them."

"Thanks," Travis said drily. He typically dropped the act around other Alphas, but Miller had stayed with Jordan for a few weeks before he'd been made Alpha.

Miller laughed. "You know, seeing Jordan and Christa yesterday almost had me wishing I would scent-match, but…"

Pinching the bridge of his nose, Travis gritted his teeth. Why couldn't this have happened in a year or even a month? Why now? He still had the stitches in his leg from yesterday's battle. He'd been hunting Colby's killer for the week before that. He needed sleep and to heal. Not to be chasing a damn ghost, hiding his knives, and waiting for his first challenge.

"Hopefully, she's hot."

Well, there was that. If he kept thinking about *that*, maybe the rest of his world being turned on its ass wouldn't be as bad. "Smoking. Crazy as hell, but you can't have everything."

"Sometimes the crazy ones are the most fun."

She'd sure made the morning interesting. He'd never get bored when she was that unpredictable. She could be fun…in so many ways. As long as he didn't die in the first challenge.

• • •

Things weren't adding up. Either the entire pack, including its Alpha, was guilty as hell or her brother was. Why had they searched Ross's place and taken his computer?

"What did you do?" she muttered to herself as she moved around his house. She was so accustomed to leaving no trace behind her that it was strange to not mentally stockpile locations of items. She could move the address book to a different spot on the counter. She didn't have to leave a stack of bills fanned precisely as it had been. Geez, did everyone pay too much for utilities around here? Rural living apparently wasn't all it was cracked up to be.

Wiping tired hands down her face, she leaned against the counter. Travis and his pack had probably removed anything of value to her. Anything they knew about. Movement outside caught her attention, and she stared at a large bush just inside the copse of trees behind her brother's house. Something was in that bush, staring right back at her.

Clenching her teeth, LeAnn went to the door and opened it. She could almost see a set of eyes slightly below waist level. One of the pack was here. She inhaled. Not Travis. His scent made her body feel superheated and sensitive...and like she had an itch that needed scratching. It was going to be hard to leave here when she did. Despite the fact that this new welcoming committee had sharp teeth and didn't appear to be so welcoming.

"If you want to come in and talk, we can. Otherwise you should get out of here before I go for a gun."

No movement.

Nice try.

"I know you're out there." She inhaled again. Great. Female. Nothing like starting off the day with a girl fight. So this was the pack that Travis had mentioned. Her new family. Uh-huh, they'd sure love to welcome her with open arms.

Especially if any of what Travis said was true — and he genuinely seemed to believe it.

It didn't matter. She really didn't deserve nice things. Things like belonging and love were for people who hadn't done what she'd done.

Her new…sister was still staring her down. Waiting for her to show fear. She was feeling the love.

She sat down on the steps and leaned against the porch railing. No way was she backing down, but bravado could be so exhausting.

The breeze now carried the scent of heightened emotions…anger possibly? It didn't smell like fear…no fear had a scent all its own.

Her mother slammed her palm down on the counter, making her daughter jump. "You were a mistake, LeAnn. Your father, that bastard, took everything from me when he got me pregnant with you. And you — you're just like him. Do you have any idea how much I've given up for you? And do you appreciate it? No. The school called again. You've been hours late to school all week and your teachers say you look so dazed that they're sure you're on drugs."

"At least I'm going to school." She'd been so tired, so very tired. Whenever she closed her eyes, she heard her mother's scream — a new recurring nightmare where darkness overwhelmed her, followed by sharp, blinding light. She sat on the kitchen floor with her mother above her, screaming. She couldn't seem to get up, couldn't speak, and the screaming went on and on. And the feelings that she felt — that sense of

power and anger and betrayal. It felt so real.

There was a hard edge in her mom's gaze now—almost as if she loathed her.

LeAnn crossed her arms and shrugged. "The lady in the front office hates me. She keeps saying I'm disrespectful when I'm not doing anything other than looking at her."

"I'm not even sure I should let them test you for drugs if it comes to that." She laughed, but it was an ugly sound, devoid of humor. "Heaven knows what might show up on tests."

What the hell was she talking about?

"I'm just not...sleeping well."

Her mother looked through the window up at the stars and then shook her head. "That bastard. I wish I'd never met your father." She turned her accusing eyes back on LeAnn. "And you! You're a thankless brat—a waste of my time."

Nothing she did was ever enough. It was hard to believe her mom's words could still sting, even though she'd heard them over and over. They were the chorus to her mom's rant. She was just like her father. She should never have been born. The rage built inside LeAnn, gnawing at her. It was like a beast with a life of its own. Her heartbeat picked up and her breath came in ragged gasps. Her bones hurt—how they ached as she clenched her fists at her side.

Her mom's eyes widened as she watched LeAnn fight to control her temper.

"I don't need you," LeAnn ground out.

She caught it then—that smell—she recognized it—it was the sharp odor of fear. It had lingered in the house for days. A week ago, her mother would have slapped her for disrespecting her like that, for mouthing off. Or grabbed her hair and dragged her to her room. Her mother's control on her own temper had become nonexistent lately. But now she looked wary.

"What are you afraid of?" she asked her mom in a whisper.

Her mother stood up straight and folded her arms in front of her. "I'm not afraid of anything." Then she visibly swallowed—her throat jerking as she did.

LeAnn's gaze locked on her mom's throat. She could almost see and hear her mom's pulse. Maybe she could. Everything was so loud these days. Her head was pounding from the pressure of blocking out the world while maintaining her temper, which was fraying.

"Don't look at me like that." Her mother's hand went to her throat. "Stop it. Just stop it. Keep your damn eyes off me."

LeAnn blinked. The scent of fear was stronger. "You're afraid of me." There was a note of wonder in her voice.

"I'm not," her mom said, too fast, too breathlessly.

Hell, her own mother acted like she was some sort of monster. Her mother wouldn't even meet her eyes today. She was afraid—of her own daughter. Why?

I'm not a monster.

Though the building rage that lashed out at times made her feel like one. She was almost as tall as her mother. And at times, she was more mature—like now when her mother was whining about having a child. Being born was not her fault. And she was trying to control her temper, even if no one appreciated it. And no one did. In her mind, the beast growled and thrashed around. A flash of fur and fangs appeared and disappeared in her head.

Her mother backed up a step.

The scent of fear was making her want to hurl.

And it wasn't from her. She was no longer the little girl hoping to please her mother. She was strong. She was fearless. LeAnn spun away and walked toward her room.

"Where are you going?" her mother called after her.

She turned back, her own heart pounding. Something had just happened. That connection to this woman who shared her genes had broken. She was free. The beast inside her was right; she didn't need to be here, trying to make peace when it wasn't possible. Her mother would never understand her… not now, not when the beast was visible in her eyes and held her mind.

"What are you afraid of, Mom, that I'll leave…or that I'll stay?"

Ten minutes later, a backpack on her shoulder, she climbed out her window—though she didn't know why. She could have left by the front door for all her mother cared.

Maybe after the weekend, she'd come back. After the weekend, they could go back to their usual pissed-off avoidance. As long as she went to school and pretended to be normal, the stuck-up witch in the front office wouldn't call and remind her mother LeAnn existed. It was more of a holding pattern—no way could they make it until she graduated, but it was enough. And her mom was the only family she had. Family stuck together, right?

The air smelled fresh and clean outside. She inhaled. Her rage cooled, even if her pulse kept pounding. Outside, the two parts of her didn't feel so at odds. Leaning down, she ran her hand along the grass.

"Honey, can you grab me my pearls from my jewelry box on the dresser?" Mrs. Spade from next door asked her husband.

In the last week, she'd learned far too much about the Spades. At first, she thought they'd left the window open, but it wasn't open now. Something had happened with her hearing. Something was happening with her.

"Are you sure you want the pearls?" her husband asked. "You've never worn this necklace I gave you last month. Or these matching earrings from last week."

Mr. Spade was trying to buy his way out of his guilt that he came home every night smelling like another woman and sex. Not that Mrs. Spade recognized it. It was subtle. He was even wearing more cologne to cover it. Eventually his wife would start wondering about all the late nights at the office. In the meantime, his unworn gifts would accumulate. Sitting there. Unnoticed. Uncared for.

"No, the pearls. And we're late." A few minutes later, they were gone in a haze of mixed scents: fabric detergent, cologne and perfume, breath spray, deodorant, and the exhaust from their car.

They'd never even noticed she was here.

In the darkness.

And they'd left their house empty, and they'd forgotten to set the alarm. She'd have heard the beeping if they'd bothered.

Idiots.

She straightened up. Maybe she could stay with Nell tonight and then go from there.

The bright moon came out from behind the clouds. It was a beautiful night. She wanted to run. LeAnn wanted to revel in finally being free. And she could spend the night outside. It was a cool night, but her skin was hot and feverish.

Her fingertips tingled.

She looked over at the Spades' house.

Would it be so wrong to see what this buy-off necklace looked like?

A few birds startled and took flight to the left of her, and LeAnn twitched, blinking.

Did she fall asleep, or was that yet another blackout where flashes of her life broke through? So many of her days existed only in that hazy world of almost remembering, but trying to forget.

Hell, I'm so messed up.

Hopefully it was a flashback, because if she'd fallen asleep with an unknown quantity around... You never turned your back on an enemy, and you never called anyone a friend. And she'd just spaced out with a wolf female staring her down. Great.

Shaking her head, LeAnn sniffed the air.

Her wolf watcher was gone.

She went back inside, rubbing her arms, which felt suddenly cold. Okay, time to do a more thorough search of Ross's house. True, Travis and his pack had gone through this place, but they didn't know all the crazy spots people hid things. She did. She made a living finding things people had hidden.

Getting down on all fours, she crawled across his living room while looking up. Most law-abiding people only looked down while searching. While that might be slightly different for Lycans, she suspected they hadn't gone through here in wolf form. Bingo! She found an envelope taped to one of the lower shelves in his bookcase.

Sitting cross-legged, she opened it up. Empty. But it had held something. She held it up to her nose. Ross. Ross had removed whatever had been in here. She could still smell his scent on it. He might have done it recently even. With a sigh, she dropped onto her back.

He's family. And family sticks together, right?

"What the hell have you done, Ross?"

• • •

Unlike the usual boisterous, flirtatious crowd that looked like a singles meet-and-greet, his pack was more subdued as they met in the cabin's great room. Yesterday, they'd been anxious to fight, and the road trip to Glacier Peak had been high-spirited.

Going to a fight—hell yeah.

Taking down poachers—booyah.

Immediately afterward, they'd still been feeling the adrenaline rush and been exchanging stories. Today, things had changed. Tom and Eli were dead, and everybody liked them. The whole group was feeling their mortality more.

Other than Alanna, the females had been left to protect Jordan's house during the poacher takedown in case the other location was a trap. They were hearing everything second-hand yesterday and today. And he'd be surprised if some of the males hadn't been exaggerating their parts in the battle. Suddenly this pack of Lycans led by an Alpha felt like they were all Alphas—in their minds.

And right before the females in the group one by one went into heat. The next couple months should be pure hell. Lycan females only went into heat once a year, and it made the unattached males in the area get a little nuts competing for attention.

Last year, he'd been one of them—though he'd done his best to ignore his urges, because he hadn't wanted to pick an alpha female back then. Now he'd finally decided to pick Alanna, and look where that had gotten him.

Scent-matched.

To a crazy woman.

Who looked great naked.

It was so peculiar to be in front of them and not be attracted to any of the females in the room, even against his will. Merilee was in heat, but that was just…information. He wasn't drawn to her. Not that he would have acted on it with Merilee anyway. He might've been the only one in the room not to. Though Troy had been staking his claim more and more with her.

He could feel Alanna's eyes on him. Jordan had said he'd indulged her too much, and Alanna's perception of him was that he was weak. So he'd started ignoring her and treating her like a male pack member. It had seemed to work immediately. Thankfully, he hadn't made it beyond that.

From the moment he stepped up on the podium, the room hushed, and they all bowed their heads in deference—though Troy and Liam had fought the instinct longer than the others. Alanna stood apart with her arms folded rather than clasped in front of her like many of the others.

"As Tom's and Eli's families were near Glacier Peak, their memorials will most likely occur north, but I'll email out details as I hear them. Both of them died in form, so I'm waiting to hear whether their families wish them reported as missing or not."

Most of the time, Lycans had things put in place so that their deaths weren't complicated by the lack of a two-legged body, but sometimes they still had to go through the motions of the human world.

He felt like he was stalling.

He was.

There were definitely times he didn't feel up to being an Alpha of any group, let alone one as complex as this.

He cleared his throat. "I actually called you together for a different reason, though. Ross's sister flew in yesterday and is concerned about the whereabouts of her brother. I've tried to explain his death and the circumstances surrounding it, but she and her brother weren't…close, so she had no part of his plans, and she can't believe he'd do this."

Troy looked up at him with narrowed eyes.

There were going to be questions. He might as well deal with them directly.

"Yes, Troy?"

"How do we know she had nothing to do with this?"

"Because I've spoken with her, and *as your Alpha*, I'm convinced of it. She intends to find out what really happened, according to her, and if she needs to find out in her own way that her brother was a murderer…" He shrugged with a nonchalance he didn't feel. It was irrational, but he wanted her to believe him—because she was his mate—because he was Alpha—because he was telling the truth. Basically, because he said so. He was Alpha, and he said so.

Troy didn't bow his head in acceptance. He continued to stare at Travis.

Travis stared back. It took longer than it should have, but Troy eventually bowed his head. He could feel the others' eyes on him, even if they were trying to keep their heads bowed.

"LeAnn, Ross's sister, is pack, and no harm is to befall her while she is here."

Troy's head snapped up again. "Just because her brother was pack that doesn't mean she has a right to our protection. He lost that right, and so did his family."

Travis leveled him with a stare again. He was holding back the ocean with this one. He had a month tops before Troy challenged him. Probably less. Thanks to his own intervention, Troy hadn't been injured as badly yesterday as he might've been. And that was going to come back to bite him.

Several of the others had raised their heads slightly. To an outsider, this wouldn't appear to be spiraling out of his control as it really was.

He gritted his teeth. It was going to have to come out if he was going to keep LeAnn safe. "She's pack because she's my mate." A pin could have dropped and sounded like glass shattering in the stillness left behind. "I scent-matched to her."

Several of his pack looked up at this. All but Alanna looked down again. Eventually he gave up and nodded at Alanna.

"If she's Alpha, why isn't she here?" Alanna's eyes were narrowed, and her face was taut. She'd have a difficult time accepting another female as Alpha. She'd barely accepted *him* as Alpha.

"She's not…thrilled to be scent-matched to the person who also told her Ross is a traitor and dead."

I'm going to be dragging LeAnn kicking and screaming into being my mate. That almost made him smile.

"So she hasn't accepted the scent-match?" Alanna asked, raising her eyebrows and folding her arms.

Damn, he should have seen that coming. Technically, until LeAnn accepted him as a mate, she was more competition to the females in the pack than a member. In a nonvolatile pack, this would be nothing. In Rainier pack, she was another contender for Alpha…a favored contender. He'd never favored any of them. Not even Alanna. Well, not obviously, anyway. Many may have guessed Alanna was the most likely candidate, but he hadn't chosen her openly. It shouldn't be a problem. None of them had appeared interested in him. He was reading far too much into Alanna's question.

"No, she hasn't," he said, "but I have, and *as your Alpha*, I say she is pack, and you will treat her with respect."

The more he'd thought about that morning's confrontation, the more he'd wanted LeAnn. It wasn't only the scent-match. She intrigued him. She was a puzzle he looked forward to figuring out. It made him question his own sanity, but he was going with Mother Nature on this call and accepting her as his mate—whether she liked it or not.

At the very least, she was attracted to him. She hadn't been able to cover that up as well as she'd probably thought. Her scent sold her out.

Liam looked up.

He nodded.

"Is she Lycan?"

He closed his eyes for an extra-long blink. Yeah, this was going really well. "She says she's not, but her abilities say she is."

It was quiet again.

Might as well slam the lid on this coffin and end the

meeting. "She also says that she's caught the scent of Ross in our area. I tried to confirm this was wishful thinking on her part, but there is a very slim chance that Ross was not killed yesterday. If you catch his scent on any of your patrols, contact me immediately. LeAnn shares a resemblance to his scent, but she's different enough that you should be able to distinguish. I believe Ross is dead, but I'd rather not find out he is alive through another murder."

Half of his pack lifted their heads to stare at him. Great.

"We'll run normal patrols, but I know some of you sustained injuries yesterday. Contact me if you don't think you'll be able to patrol this week, and we'll accommodate."

Merilee was staring at him with wide eyes.

He nodded at her. She was harmless, at least. She was sexually aggressive, but she had no desire to be alpha female.

"Even if she didn't help Ross, is there any chance she's dangerous?"

He tightened his jaw. He should have expected this. Ross's murder of Colby had been ugly—even if no one here really had cared for Colby. "No. She's not." Well, she had pulled a knife on him. But still… Well, and she was insane. But she most likely wasn't dangerous. "I wouldn't antagonize her, but I'll keep an eye on her." He looked around the room. "In fact, I intend to watch her *very* closely."

Hopefully that would be enough of a threat to keep her safe…while he was still Alpha.

"You're dismissed." And he walked out of there. Immediately.

• • •

This time, it was him. She could feel his gaze from the same bushes. She'd found one of Ross's hidden weapons, and she took the shotgun and her dinner out with her.

"I'm going to hate Cup-a-Soup by the time I'm done here…oh, and I'm not your mate," she said, setting the shotgun down on the porch and sitting on the lowest step.

He stayed in the bushes.

She rolled her eyes and leveled her stare on where she knew he was. "Travis, I know it's you, and *you* shouldn't be here." Something strange was definitely going on, and she wanted to find Ross, get an explanation, and then get out of here before she did something she'd regret—something they'd both regret.

The wolf stepped out of the bushes, but then lay down and watched her from the perimeter of the yard.

"Wow, you're big. I bet you've scared the crap out of the locals," she said, eating a spoonful of soup. She held up the cup. "I'd offer you some, but I suspect you wouldn't eat this as a human, let alone as a wolf."

The wolf tilted his head.

"Your kitchen. I checked out your house before I woke you up. You eat real food apparently. Not a single Cup-a-Soup in all your cupboards. I like your gun safe. I've noticed that people in law enforcement always have decent gun safes."

He kept staring at her.

"I did wonder why the guy visiting you left behind his clothes. That was weird. There weren't any women's clothes anywhere, so I'm wondering if you're starved for attention and anyone will do." That thought stung as it went through her head. Nothing he'd said had suggested she had more significance than that. He acted like he was choosing her against his will, against his best judgment. It'd be nice if he changed back into a human to dispute that.

He didn't.

Of course he didn't. You'd think after all this time I'd quit believing in love, and hope, and someone actually wanting me for me. The cruelest thing he could do is to make me believe again.

"Seriously, you shouldn't be here…and you don't want anything to do with me." None of them did. People like her didn't belong. And a human in a pack of wolves? That would be as ridiculous as it sounded. No way would she fit. "Your pack won't want anything to do with me either. Especially if…" No, she wasn't ready to say it. If Ross was everything Travis said, she needed more proof—something tangible. And she needed to talk to her brother.

The tan wolf kept on staring. He was taking this watch-dog routine a bit far.

"You're really going to stay here and stay furry no matter what I say, huh?" She gestured behind her. "I could go grab you some of Ross's clothes if you've decided getting naked again in front of me is no good."

He growled—a quiet rumble of dissent. Apparently he didn't much care for Ross's clothing. That made sense. It all smelled like her brother, and he thought her brother kept body parts in his freezer.

"You could wear some of my clothes." There was no way, but maybe it'd insult him enough he'd leave.

Nope.

Oh, to hell with this. She set her cup to the side and pushed to her feet. Stalking over there, she dropped to the ground in front of the huge wolf—who'd gotten to his feet as she approached.

"Look…I know you don't believe me, and I'm not even sure why you're here, but I know my brother is alive."

It sounded like the wolf snorted at that.

"Fine," she said, standing up and brushing off her pants. "Don't believe me." She walked back to the house. "Don't come crying to me when your guts end up in his fridge."

Chapter Three

He woke up to someone watching him. Blearily, he focused on the woman curled up at the foot of the bed, staring. His body had recognized her even before he'd opened his eyes, because while his pulse picked up, it wasn't out of anxiety. Inhaling, he smelled her scent mixed with his on the cotton T-shirt she'd pulled from his drawers.

"I heard something. So I went out to my brother's front porch and then I was here." She held out her arms. "Apparently, I felt like going for a run. In the middle of the night. Here."

She sounded so bewildered, and his shirt hung on her, giving her a little-girl-lost look.

He rubbed both hands down his face. "It's near a full moon and you're surrounded by pack. Plus, I'm your scent-matched mate. It's instinct." He knew. Heaven help him, but he knew. It'd been difficult to leave her. He was always in control, but his wolf couldn't stay away from her.

She snorted and looked away. "I just need more sleep." Getting up out of his bed, she stood with her arms crossed. "And to get out of here."

The wolf inside him roared. He clenched his teeth and didn't comment.

She started pacing.

At least she didn't have a knife this time. He'd taken preventive measures to ensure that.

"Why were you stalking me earlier?"

Travis looked at the clock. He'd only left her place an hour ago. Inwardly, he groaned—he needed more sleep than he'd gotten the last few weeks. "I was keeping you safe."

"I don't need you to keep me safe. According to you, the scariest thing out there is my brother, and he won't hurt me." She stopped pacing and faced him.

He turned on his side to face her.

Inhaling, she widened her eyes and breathed out a soft pant. "You smell crazy good."

He leaned out and grabbed her hands, pulling her toward the bed as he sat up. "Sit down. We can talk."

He knew what would happen. He'd counted on it happening. That taut connection between them reeled her in. No sooner had she sat down than she leaned forward, burying herself in his arms. Her tongue touched the skin on his neck. Screw sleeping. He didn't need sleep.

"Ohh, you taste good, too," she murmured against his throat.

He ducked his chin and caught her mouth with his. Screw talking. They didn't need to talk. Talking only complicated things. Grabbing her by the waist, he turned onto his back, dragging her with him.

She cradled his head in her hands, her nails scraping his scalp lightly. He wanted her more than he'd ever wanted anyone. This was madness. He wanted her more than he wanted to breathe—and that was probably accounting for the slightly light-headed feeling he was getting from the quick breaths between deep kisses. Holy hell, LeAnn's tongue was downright illegal in the way she used it.

She dropped her legs down to either side of his hips, straddling him.

He slid his hands up her thighs.

This was irrational.

"This doesn't mean anything," she said between kisses.

Yeah, this was how talking complicated things. He turned his head, breathing like a marathon runner. "It does." Wow, his heart was pounding.

She went still. The only sound was their rapid, ragged breathing, and he could hear his pulse beating in his head. She swallowed. "Not to me," she said slowly as she lifted up off his chest.

He shook his head. "If we have sex, it'll be considered acceptance of the scent-match."

"Not by me." She slid off him.

"No, by the pack. And if you accept the scent-match, you're mine, LeAnn, and no one else's, and the pack will enforce that. It's our way."

He grabbed her waist before she got out of the bed.

"I wasn't planning on bragging that I bagged their Alpha." She tried tugging his hands off her before sighing and shaking her head.

"No, they'll be able to tell unless we're both going to hazmat levels to cover it up." And he didn't want to do that.

He wanted the pack to know she was his.

She kept shaking her head as she looked up at the ceiling. "You guys are psychos. You're insane. I should get out of here before I start spouting nonsense, too."

It felt like a sharp stick through his heart. He didn't want her to leave. Talk about insane.

She blinked rapidly and then swallowed. "Trust me. The last thing you want is me. In fact, you should really stop following me, let me get to the bottom of what my brother is up to, and then I'll get the hell out of here."

"LeAnn, I'm still fairly certain your brother is dead."

She shook her head, and her gaze dropped to his. "He's not. I thought that was a good thing, but I can't figure out why he'd come to your place last night and risk getting caught." She licked her lips, and despite the seriousness of their discussion, he wanted to drag her mouth down to his and make them both forget all of this. "I should go. I don't even know why or how I came here. It feels like a dream—like sleepwalking. I couldn't stop myself." She put both hands up to the sides of her head and winced. "It feels crazy." Laughing shortly, she added, "And believe me, I know crazy."

He smiled. He'd seen her tough and ornery, crazy and homicidal, and now she looked lost and confused…and sweet. "Stay."

Sighing again, she shook her head. "I'm not going to mess up your life. This thing between us will go away eventually—especially if I'm not here."

It wouldn't. She might think so, but it wouldn't. Not unless one of them died. Not according to all he'd heard about scent-matches. "Just stay tonight, then. We'll both get some sleep, and we'll figure things out tomorrow."

"Sleep?" She raised both her eyebrows.

Travis shrugged, trying to smother a grin. "We can try. If I didn't need sleep so badly, I'd have slept outside your house, but it's freaking cold tonight, so I'd rather not."

She groaned. "You don't need to guard me. I'm fine on my own. In fact, I should be protecting you."

He pulled her down. "Fine then. Come protect me. I'll watch over you while you're watching over me."

She settled into his arms with her head on his chest. "You know, it's damn creepy they'd have known we had sex from our scent."

"Also, the smirk on my face."

"Yeah?" He could hear the smile in her voice.

"Yup. I've been so busy with the pack and moving here that I haven't had time to think about women…and I didn't want to deal with picking an Alpha."

"Oh, so that's all it'd be. I'm *a* woman." She sounded disappointed.

"As opposed to…?"

"Nothing." She cleared her throat. "So, that chick at my brother's house earlier wasn't a jealous ex looking to slit my throat?" She yawned and draped her arm across his waist.

He'd smelled a few different scents at Ross's place, but so many of the pack had come and gone in the last few days that he hadn't ruled out that he was wrong. Damn, if only he was as good at tracking as Jordan. Plus, the scent-match was making concentrating on any scent outside of LeAnn's very difficult. He could now find her if she was within a ten-mile radius, but he might not catch someone in his own pack a hundred feet away. "What did she look like?"

"Furry. Four-legged. Female. She was in the same bushes

you were."

Hell, he was losing it. This is what came of two weeks with no sleep and then massive sexual frustration. His body was still screaming "screw talking" and not settling down without a fight. It didn't help that LeAnn's voice was sexy as hell. *Concentrate, Travis. You're a grown male, not an eighteen-year-old boy.* He cleared his throat. "As far as I know, none of the females in the pack were more interested in me than in any of the other males. You're sure it wasn't a male?"

"Yes."

That was probably a good thing. Not that he could see any of his pack attacking LeAnn, but the males could be idiots and unpredictable. Besides, he flat-out didn't want any other men watching LeAnn. It was a primitive reaction, but he'd have to rip their throats out.

He licked his lips and tried to go for calm and dispassionate as he said, "I told them you're pack and that no harm was to come to you." He'd basically staked his claim. She wouldn't understand how serious it was that he'd claimed her as pack.

She sniffed. "I can take care of myself." Then she lifted her head. "Wait, you told *them*…you told your pack about me?"

"Yes. I didn't want any of them attacking you thinking you'd had something to do with what Ross had done."

She scowled at him.

"What?"

"Why do you have to be like this?"

"Like what? Protective?" He was protecting his mate. It was instinctual. He was overwhelmed with instinct when it came to her. Half of his thoughts didn't make any sense.

Being scent-matched and sleep-deprived had dropped his IQ significantly.

"No. Well, yes, I mean good and decent and…" She put her head back down with a sigh. "I *have* to get out of here."

Yeah, she was getting out of this as easy as that. "What's your last name?"

"None of your business."

"It's fine. I'll take you in for trespassing tomorrow and fingerprint you."

"Smith."

"Or I can call up the place that rented you that car and find out that way."

"Jones."

"I'll handcuff you to the bed and go hunt down your license at your brother's place." She had to have a license if she'd flown here and rented a car. He should have done that yesterday rather than trying to hunt down a half sister through Ross's father. Ross's dad had been an ass of a man who'd basically considered himself done with fatherhood when Ross had shifted the first time. It shouldn't surprise him that he hadn't acknowledged a daughter.

"Taylor." Her breath fanned out across his chest. She was killing him.

"In fact, I can do that right now." He reached toward his nightstand. He waited for her to stop him. She didn't. He opened the drawer. She didn't move. He reached in and felt around. "LeAnn, where's my gun?" The handcuffs were still there, but his gun was gone.

She lifted her head and smiled. "I put it next to the knives you hid."

Great. He shut the drawer without getting his handcuffs

out. He was too tired to even make empty threats. "I can't believe you found those."

"Mm, Travis, there isn't anything you can hide from me that I won't find."

Actually, he was planning on hiding a helluva lot from her…including that he was not letting her run away from this scent-match. "I can't believe I don't even know your last name."

"It's Stewart."

"Really?"

"No. Now go to sleep."

"Brat."

"Jerk." She rubbed her hand across his stomach. "They'd really be able to tell?"

"Want to find out?"

She groaned. "Yes. So much yes. But leash your dog, it ain't happening."

"Damn."

• • •

It wasn't the most restful sleep she'd ever gotten, but she did wake up feeling…alive. Pulling away from him was one of the hardest things she'd ever done. She'd known him all of a day and a half. This was ridiculous.

Then she did something stupidly sentimental that she was taking to her grave. She watched him sleep for a couple minutes. Crap, in a few days, she'd be carving their initials into a tree.

He looked so peaceful and so incredibly sexy. Okay, she had to get out of here. Slipping through the house, she gathered a few things—things she shouldn't be stealing from him, but she was taking precautions this time. It was funny that she'd arrived here naked but she was taking stuff with her. Actually, that wasn't funny. Twice in two days? She hadn't come out of a blacked-out phase naked that frequently since they started happening when she was a teenager. She'd gotten it down to a few times a year.

Her old therapist said people did crazy things while sleepwalking and recommended she lock her doors and maybe put a chair underneath the knob. Then he'd seemed far too interested in the "naked" aspect of her condition. Thus ended her brief brush with therapy.

Not that she needed therapy.

The first thing she did as she left was inhale deeply while circling his house. Others had been by, but not close. Ross had once told her that the Alpha's space was respected and that encroaching on his land could have…repercussions. She should have listened to him about that. Because, whoa, had there been repercussions.

He also said most humans would show respect and deference to an Alpha whether they realized it or not. She respected Travis, especially after he'd had a knife up to his neck and hadn't panicked. That was a rare thing. Who knew what deference looked like, though? She'd yet to punch him or kick him in the nads, so that was something. Any other guy saying crap about her brother might have gotten both. Even if what he was saying turned out to be true. She would have beaten the hell out of the messenger.

If she hadn't already kissed him…and licked him.

And now she'd slept in his arms.

She was getting in deep with Travis Flynn. That had

to end. These days, she always left them before they had a chance to leave her.

As she worked out in a larger circle, she caught *his* scent again. What the hell did her brother want with Travis? She wanted to believe that Ross only wanted to explain his side of things, but it was hard to hold on to that in light of the evidence that her brother had been hiding a lot. She'd found and opened his safe…which the pack hadn't gotten into. Either her brother was a real weirdo or he had a bunch of clothing from other people for another reason. One of the scents was the scent of the wolf that'd stopped by his house, on a lab coat drenched in the smell of dogs and cats.

She walked back to Ross's place—her arms full of the stuff she'd swiped—as a precaution. It's not like she was planning on seeing Travis again. If she did, she did. When she reached the outskirts of her brother's property, she stopped and inhaled. Okay, that was weird. It smelled like Ross and someone else, but Ross's scent was stronger.

A tingling awareness made the hair on the back of her neck stand up. LeAnn turned to look around her. She was being watched. She pulled the knife out that she'd swiped before rehiding all of Travis's cutlery. Well, she'd also tucked one in between the mattresses last night. She'd left that where it was. Not that she was planning on going there again tonight, but she might.

There was another scent…her own mixed with someone else's. She clenched her jaw. What the hell?

She ran toward the house. So many scents. What the crap was going on? Whoever had been by had some brass ones. They'd left the door unlocked to let her know they'd been in her stuff.

She slapped her armload down on the counter before going back outside with the knife. "Whoever the hell you are, you come in here again, and you'll find this buried in you! And then I'll stick you in the fridge because that's what we do in my family!" Slamming the door on her way back in was deeply satisfying.

It took an hour and a long shower for her anger to dissipate, and even then, she still wanted to go scream outside a little more. Nobody broke into her place. Even if she was in Ross's house—it was her place while she was here. And they'd taken her favorite green sweater. Those bastards. Who did that? They better *hope* she never caught them.

She was grumbling under her breath while eating oatmeal when his truck pulled up. *Hm.*

This time, she went and stood out on the porch and waited for him.

He stalked toward her with more of the wolf in his eyes than the human. She couldn't read his mood. Was he pissed? He might be pissed. Maybe he'd noticed she'd taken some of his stuff.

When he reached her, he took the bowl out of her hand and set it on the porch railing. Okay. Interesting. A moment later, he'd spun her around and had her hands handcuffed behind her. And she stood there...blinking.

"Uhh." Normally, she thought faster on her feet, but she just plain wasn't expecting that.

Travis tugged her up against him and dropped his head to her neck, where he pressed a kiss.

"What are you doing?" It came out breathy and intrigued...so intrigued.

"Preparing to take you in for questioning."

"On what charge?"

"I don't know. I'll make something up." He bit her neck, making her squirm. "Tell me your last name," he murmured against her sensitive skin.

"Wilcox." She'd seen him note the license plate on her rental, and she knew he'd double-check her. He wouldn't find much. LeAnn Wilcox hadn't existed for very long. She had a fairly good credit history, though.

He ran his lips across her skin. "Where are you from?" His voice sent shivers down her spine.

"Baltimore."

"Hm." He pressed a kiss to her shoulder, then bit and sucked the skin.

She pressed her lips shut to stop the moan that wanted out. Then it was over, and she felt the cool metal of the key drop into her hand as he went around her and picked up her oatmeal while leaning back against the railing.

He spooned the oatmeal into his mouth as he watched her unlock the handcuffs.

"That's my breakfast," she said, standing in front of him.

"You owe me for this morning's treasure hunt. I didn't have time to eat."

"Treasure hunt?" Hopefully, he hadn't noticed all that she'd taken.

"My knives. I used to have a set."

"Oh, I think you still have a set." She held up the handcuffs and shook them.

He took the handcuffs and key from her while smothering a smile. "Now I seem to be missing two."

"You found them?" She smiled. This was fun. It was like being in a couple. She shouldn't get used to it.

"Other than the two you swiped—yup."

"Did you rehide them?"

"Of course I did. Some crazy woman threatened me at knifepoint two days ago. I hear she's still at large."

"Yeah, well, the local sheriff is an idiot. Can't seem to keep her in his custody."

He set the empty bowl beside him and stared at her.

She fought this crazy urge to lower her gaze. Instead she tipped her chin up and stared right back.

He narrowed his eyes. "You know, I don't think I've ever met a girl as mouthy as you." He pushed off the railing and leaned forward, dropping a kiss on her lips. "I think I'll have to come up with a way to shut you up occasionally." He wrapped his arms around her and kissed her again. Mm. She'd be okay with that way—for however long she was here. He tipped back and frowned while looking around. "Was someone else here?"

"No," she said quickly, nearly instinctually. He might be Alpha to the pack, but she could fight her own battles. She did that now. Once she'd let other people call the shots— first her mother and then her ex, but that was then.

He inhaled and narrowed his eyes.

She shrugged.

"If you saw anyone, I need to know." His jaw tightened. "It's my pack and my place to make sure they're following my edict."

"Saw anyone? No."

"Did you catch anyone's scent?"

"You mean other than my brother's, who you believe is dead...and thus my judgment is suspect?"

He went back to staring her down.

"Did you want to get naked again? I can call your work and let them know you'll be late."

Shaking his head, he turned to go to his truck. Ten feet away, he stopped abruptly and came back toward her. Whoa. Her heart started pounding, and she caught her breath. The intensity in his eyes had her backing up. Suddenly, she was flat up against the house, and he was right there. The fire in his gaze said he was as much a slave to this as she was. It overwhelmed her—this heat. It was as animalistic as the rage that sometimes built in her. This was her temper's twin, but no less passionate.

What would happen if I just gave in? If I stopped fighting the wildness in me?

Travis pressed up against her, cradling her head as he kissed her. Tender but insistent, his mouth mated with hers, his tongue sliding and caressing hers. The sharp tug of his hands in her hair and his belt pushing against her stomach kept her rooted in reality, but her brain was melting. No one but no one kissed like Travis. The females in the pack were fools. When he pulled back, she felt dazed and out of breath—and entirely out of control.

"Hey," she said shakily. She saw something in his eyes this morning that hadn't been there before she'd sneaked into his house this second time. Possession. She'd gone to him. She'd gone back. His eyes said "mine" as clearly as if he'd said it out loud. And right now, she couldn't disagree with that. They could go at it on this porch, and she'd be fully supportive. She might not even call his work to tell them she'd had their sheriff naked on her porch again—and that he'd be late.

"Be careful today," he said, "and I'll see you tonight."

If she didn't leave…

She should get out of here while she still had any de-sire to. No. No, there was no way she could stay here. In the middle of nowhere. With a guy who was way too good for her. She didn't exactly have a history of staying on the right side of the law—how on earth would she manage to sleep right beside it?

Still, she asked, "Your place or mine?"

He stepped back and scowled at the house. "Mine. I don't plan on eating in a place where a man dragged guts all over."

LeAnn narrowed her eyes. "And I was going to make myself some more oatmeal." Did he really have to remind her of that every chance he got? She'd finally opened the freezer yesterday, and it only had a few frozen pizzas and ice cream. But there was a strange scent in there that even the cold temperature couldn't disguise. If Ross kept remains next to his frozen food, he was as sick a bastard as they were saying. And it was getting harder and harder to see him as innocent.

"Definitely mine," he said, looking at her.

She got the feeling they weren't talking about residences anymore.

With a nod, Travis turned and was gone.

• • •

It might take him some time to get used to the fact that he was dating a criminal. There was nothing overt in her history of course. LeAnn's caginess extended to her life, and running her license had yielded no red flags for LeAnn Wilcox. As long as LeAnn Wilcox had dropped out of the sky not so long ago.

It probably wasn't classy to run a background check on your mate, but it was better to walk into this knowing full well whom he was with. If he knew what to expect, he was in control. And Travis would scrape for every bit of control he could manage with LeAnn. So far, she had a habit of leaving him feeling like a gibbering fool. He cashed in a favor with a friend to take the search to the next level…with discretion.

But now it was time to do something really stupid.

Because he wanted Ross out of his relationship with LeAnn. He needed to settle this once and for all. She needed to accept the scent-match. Once she was really and truly pack, he'd hunt down who'd been at her house last night because someone had. And Ross's scent was there, too. Though he suspected whoever had been by was using Ross's clothing to throw them off. Someone had been by, and LeAnn knew it.

So it was time to get to the bottom of this, even if contacting another Alpha two days after he'd married his scent-match was imprudent.

Going on their land without a warning was even more unwise.

Jordan answered the phone with a snarl.

He heard Christa laugh in the background before she said tiredly, "Stop it, you moron."

"I'm calling to let you know I'll be on your land in about three hours," Travis said.

That got Jordan's attention. "Where?"

"Up near the cabin." He didn't need to say which cabin. They both knew.

"It's cleaned up. I had a few of my pack verify it yesterday."

"I'm looking at something else." He didn't care about the actual battle site where they'd taken down the poachers. Ross had run off somewhere nearby with most of Black Tusk chasing him.

"What?"

He sighed, but his business was going to be spread soon enough. With how much family they had in common with Glacier Peak, it was probably only Jordan's "honeymoon" keeping him out of the loop.

"Ross's half sister is here and claims she's picked up the scent of her brother around. She says he's still alive."

"A half sister?"

"They weren't close, but she seems to care what happened to him, even if I can't seem to convince her he's a murderer."

"I don't think Black Tusk left you a body to find for her to bury." He could hear Jordan getting out of bed.

"I know, but…" Travis took a deep breath. "Miller said they never saw a tattoo, and there was that other wolf out running around."

"You think Black Tusk killed an actual wolf, and Ross escaped."

"No, but it's a possibility that I want to rule out so we can all get on with our lives."

"Have you caught Ross's scent?"

He wanted to bang his head against something. "I'm nowhere near the tracker you are, and I still haven't caught up on sleep. Plus, someone in my pack is playing tricks on LeAnn now. They've swiped clothes from her and from

Ross." She might think he hadn't realized it, but her scent was becoming the most recognizable to him, and the one leaving her house was a mixture of other scents and hers.

"LeAnn is…?"

"His half sister…and my mate."

Stunned silence.

"What is it, Jordan?" Christa asked. He must've looked as astounded as his silence implied.

"You scent-matched?"

"Yup."

More silence. "Okay, I'll meet you there in three hours."

"You don't have to."

"Actually, I do. I'm better at tracking, and Ross kidnapped Christa last time. If there's any chance he's alive…"

"Kidnapped!" Christa said. "Why did you say that instead of abducted?"

"Christa," Jordan said on a groan.

Travis grinned. It was sorta good to hear his former Alpha whipped like this. It made his last two days of desperate distraction thanks to LeAnn seem less pitiful.

"I bet if it'd been Vanessa, you'd have said abducted," Christa grumbled.

Jordan sighed. "I'll see you there in three hours after I treat my mate like an adult."

"Adult situations?" Christa asked on a laugh. "You know, Jordan Hill, sex isn't going to get you out of every argument."

"We'll see," Jordan said as he hung up.

• • •

Three hours later, Jordan's Bronco parked beside his truck.

"You smell more like Christa than you do yourself." Travis couldn't help the smirk on his face.

Jordan had a good three inches on him and a helluva lot more arrogance, so he raised his eyebrows and then sniffed the air and shook his head. "No wonder you're feeling pissy. I take it she's not happy as hell to be matched to you?"

No, she wasn't. And he probably smelled like a man who needed sex in a bad, bad way.

Then Jordan wrinkled up his nose. "You smell enough like Ross that I want to kick your ass…fair warning."

"Being scent-matched to Ross's sister…" Travis shook his head.

"That's about how I felt when I scent-matched to Dane's sister. Like the universe has a sense of humor."

"Still feel that way?"

"Somewhat. But also like maybe I deserved something good after all." He nodded at the cabin. "Shall we do this thing so I can get back to my wife before she moves on to a younger man?"

Travis grinned. "I heard she likes old men." Christa did work with veterans.

Jordan laughed, shaking his head. "You're lucky I'm in a good mood or I'd shoot you over that."

Travis looked around and inhaled. "Well, I hope you stay in a good mood, because I feel like this might be more of a wild-goose chase than Ross led us on last time. He better hope to hell he's dead, because I feel like killing him much more violently just for having to come back here. This place smells like death." And so many other scents. There was no way he even knew where to begin. "Where do we start? I can smell a hundred different Lycans and then two dozen men."

Jordan pointed at the cabin. "We go for the scent that there should be only one of."

"Ross?"

Jordan shook his head. "No, the wolf. It came out the back of the cabin. If the wolf got away, then we know they got Ross. We don't have to follow Ross's scent—just the only thing that could have kept him alive."

"That's brilliant."

"And you thought you were smarter than me." Jordan cast him a look as he walked around to the back of the cabin. There was a broken window there that they stopped beside. They both inhaled.

Frowning, Travis asked, "I'm not wrong—that smells a lot like Ross, doesn't it?"

Jordan scowled. "Ross is a bastard. I should've guessed he'd bathed that wolf in his scent so we'd follow it." He glanced over at Travis. "And you're hot for his sister?"

"Half sister."

Jordan raised his eyebrows.

"Semantics matter when you want to bang a traitor's relative."

"Okay then, well, let's follow the trail." Jordan nodded at the forest. "It went that way. It smells like some Lycans followed it initially, but they probably turned back when they heard Ross was still in the cabin."

He and Jordan were lucky the wolf bolted away from the battle, where the stench of dead Lycans and men made tracking more difficult.

About five minutes later, Jordan nodded. "Yep, we lose the other Lycans here, but the wolf's scent continues on.

They turned back."

"Is that good?" He wasn't sure how to feel about that. It was good that the wolf had gotten away. If the packs had killed a wolf thinking it was Ross—it'd be another reason to hate Ross.

"It makes it easier to follow."

They went another half a mile into the forest before either of them spoke.

"How does your pack feel about their new Alpha?" Jordan asked as he stopped and inhaled.

"LeAnn hasn't accepted the scent-match, so I doubt they consider her Alpha." If Colby had been more liked, they'd probably despise her brother for killing him, and she'd be roped into their disdain. He'd never been more glad that Colby was a bit of a prick who liked to stir the pot.

Jordan froze and turned to him. "That's not good."

He didn't like the look on Jordan's face. Jordan had been Alpha far longer and had more experience with other Lycan packs. "Why? I told them she was pack, and that I've chosen her as a mate."

"So you want her?"

"Yes." There was no pause there. He wanted her more than he wanted his next breath. Whether they could be mates without strangling each other was more debatable. And it was likely that adherence to the law was a gray area with LeAnn. Plus, he still had that nick on his throat to remind him his mate was crazy and…volatile. But he wanted her as his mate.

Jordan shook his head. "It's still only Merilee in heat, right?"

"Yes, why?" Hell, Jordan was starting to make him

uneasy. Every time he thought he had a handle on things, the ground shifted beneath him.

"Until your mate takes her place as Alpha, the spot is still open to challenge. A female in heat would be considered justified in challenging LeAnn and taking her place. Since it's a scent-match, it's a respected kill."

That sent a nasty chill straight down his spine and made his jaw tense up. Holy mother of…this had to be a freaking joke. "But it'd have to take place in front of the pack. I'd have to know about it. I'd step down as Alpha rather than have LeAnn go into a challenge." She might act fierce, and she'd already gone after him with a knife, but challenge fights could be ugly—especially if his crazy mate didn't change form.

Jordan shook his head. "Not under these circumstances. You'd be instinctually bound to stop the fight, so it's acceptable for it to be…spontaneous. It's different when it's an alpha fight among females. Among males, the fight is part of the process to gain acceptance. It's part of our honor. Among females, their honor is to perpetuate our species. If your LeAnn doesn't want to be Alpha, then it's acceptable for a breeding female to take her place…permanently. Archaic and primitive, but it's our way."

There was a sour feeling in his stomach developing and what felt like a vise clenching around his heart. He dragged both his hands through his hair. This couldn't be happening. "Jordan, that's insane. My whole pack is going into heat in the next two months. Even without this added complication, I know I'm going to be challenged myself. None of my pack is feeling bulletproof anymore, but they all feel like Alphas suddenly due to this." He threw a gesture back at where the battle had been.

"Tell your mate to take her place or get her out of there. And she should steer clear of Merilee—especially if you've ever had anything with her."

"With Merilee? No. I haven't."

Jordan nodded. "Because it could really go wrong for Merilee if your alpha female feels challenged. I wouldn't bet on Merilee in a fight—she seems weak."

Well, that explained why Merilee had asked if LeAnn was dangerous. "Does this sort of thing happen in other packs?"

Jordan shrugged. "It has. Pack law follows instinctual patterns, and with the well-being of the pack coming first—you know how vicious women can be. And a lot is forgiven of a female in heat. So tell your scent-match to step up or step out…fast."

"It's a scent-match. So wouldn't we…?"

"Go crazy? Probably. Have you been able to stay apart for very long?"

He was fighting the urge to hurry Jordan so he could get back to her. And she'd come to him last night. Then he'd gone to see her this morning. Hell.

His silence must have said enough. "You saw how I was when I was at Rainier last week instead of with Christa. I had Vanessa at my house for a bit after she'd scent-matched to Dane and she was mental. Both of you will never get over it while you're both alive. But she'll actually *be* alive. When your more aggressive females go into heat, that could change."

"I could step down as Alpha." He didn't want to. Being Alpha felt as natural as being in law enforcement. It fit him.

It made sense. Plus he liked being in control. There weren't many like Jordan whom he'd accept as an Alpha. And he'd only accepted that because he respected Jordan too much to challenge him. Still, if it meant being with his mate and her being alive…

"Sure, except it'd be considered losing a challenge, and whoever takes over as Alpha has the right to take your life so you're not a threat to the pack's hierarchy again. And even if they don't, it's your word against the new Alpha's that Ross's sister isn't a threat to them." He shook his head. "Besides, like hell will I put up with Liam or Troy. I swear, if you let Troy take over the pack, I'll find some obscure pack law to justify killing him."

"You would not."

"I would. He'd be a lousy Alpha and you know it. Stubborn jackass only thinks of himself."

"Which is nothing like all the other Alphas."

Jordan grinned.

He swallowed the unease he'd felt at Jordan's words. Merilee wasn't a threat to LeAnn. It'd be fine.

"You said Alanna goes into heat in March, right?"

"Yeah. She's the last."

Jordan nodded. "Good. That's good."

He shook it off. "Let's get back to…" He pointed the direction they'd been going.

A half a mile later, Jordan stopped and looked around, inhaling.

"What?" He'd been struggling to follow the scent. Jordan was much better at this than him. It was good the other Alpha considered Ross enough of a threat to come help him.

Jordan sighed. "I'm starting to get other scents. Hell.

They're coming from the east, but there was no reason any of us would have come up here unless they were chasing something." He closed his eyes for a long blink. "Okay, let's just keep going. Even if Ross headed this way, he had a whole pack behind him, watching him. He'd had to have gotten stupidly lucky to have caught up to the wolf."

"I heard you punched him in the face," Travis said, walking beside Jordan. A lot of crazy stories had circulated during the aftermath of the fight when they'd been cleaning up, but he tended to believe that one. Some of Jordan's pack claimed Jordan had shifted and punched a wolf in the face in a previous run-in with Ross and the poachers.

"Ross? Yeah. A little trick I learned from Dane. Lycans aren't expecting you to punch them in the face while they're transformed."

"I remember you had a black eye after our first time up here. I'm getting a suspicion on how you learned it." He tried to smother his grin. He'd come up as a deputy then to deal with a situation where a poacher had gotten his throat ripped out by a wolf. Jordan had looked like he'd lost the fight, rather than won.

"Yes, but I'm sleeping with his sister now, so I'm sure Dane's glad he got that in while he could." He swore and shook his head as he pointed east. "Ross couldn't be this lucky."

They went east, following the scent.

"Outside of your parents, you don't have any Lycan family alive, right?" Travis asked as they walked through the trees.

"Yep. I have some distant relatives I've never met, but my parents were only children, and I'm the only Lycan they had. I'm hoping when Christa and I have kids the ratio isn't so far off. You've seen what it's done to my brothers and me. My parents act like they're not Lycan when we're all gathered, to keep the peace." Travis had heard as much. Jordan had moved from a different pack to alpha Glacier Peak just so his siblings wouldn't take it wrong. "Christa's hoping to change that. Garret seems to like her…as a brother-in-law does. So we'll see. He left here the other day with Carly from the Olympics pack." He snorted. "It'd be funny if he ends up with a Lycan after all the crap he's given me."

"None of your brothers has the abilities of a Lycan, even though they're not?"

Jordan stopped and looked over his shoulder at him.

It was a stupid question. LeAnn was a Lycan. She was a crazy Lycan, but she was a Lycan.

"Like what?" Jordan asked as he went back to walking.

"This…the ability to track." She might have been wrong about everything else, but she'd recognized him when he was a wolf right away. Maybe that was the scent-match, maybe it wasn't, but he tended to think she had the ability to track scents.

"Not that I've noticed. Not to this extent, anyway."

"What about their hearing?"

"Normal. The two-footers we've got in our pack seem to have been skipped over, too. Either they're Lycan or they're not."

"So if someone has the abilities of a Lycan—they're definitely able to shift, right?"

Jordan snorted. "I don't think we've had a normal conversation yet today. I think you need more sleep and to get laid." He crouched down to the ground and narrowed his eyes.

Squatting down beside him, Travis said, "It's really strong here."

"Because they both were here. Ross, you stupid bastard, either you got really lucky or you're a lot better at tracking than I gave you credit for." He stood up. "You know, if I were in a panic, running for my life, no way in hell would I have been able to follow that wolf's trail."

"Do you think *that* runs in families?" he asked, standing up. If it did, maybe LeAnn wasn't quite as crazy as he'd been thinking. She was still crazy, but possibly not quite *as* crazy.

"Maybe. My father could track a scent blindfolded. We all knew better than to sneak out at night." He glanced at Travis and said, "It'd still just be among the Lycans, though." Peering out into the distance, he shaded his eyes. "If you're asking all this because LeAnn isn't a Lycan, you shouldn't even be here. Challenges don't take into consideration not being able to shift. A Lycan versus an unarmed human…"

"Yeah, well, I don't think LeAnn is ever unarmed, but… she's got to be Lycan."

"You mean you don't know?" And Jordan was back to being amused.

"Oh, I know, but she keeps telling me she's not."

"Why?"

"Hell if I know." That made even less sense than the rest of it. She had nothing to gain by claiming not to be Lycan. And she'd seemed genuinely amused when he'd mentioned it the first night. She had to be Lycan…which meant that she was delusional for not realizing it.

Her sanity was really highly questionable, which didn't bother him as much as it should. Even the fact that she'd held a knife to his neck didn't bother him as much as it should. Not even after running her license and discovering she likely had a criminal history.

She looked awfully comfortable holding that knife. That should cause him some concern.

Especially since she'd found and moved his gun.

And two of his knives were missing.

"I really need more sleep," he said.

"A scent-match doesn't really improve that." Jordan grinned. "I've barely been getting any sleep."

"Christa doesn't let you take naps? I should tell her, an old dog like you…you've probably only got a few more good years in you."

"I remember when you used to respect me."

"Oh, I still respect my elders."

Jordan ignored that. Their relationship had changed since Travis had become Alpha. A year and a half ago, he'd have felt the weight of deference. Now Jordan was his equal. In fact, he felt more like an older brother than a friend.

They hiked farther into the woods. The scent of other Lycans had joined in, and they had to move slower to make sure that they weren't missing Ross or the wolf escaping.

Five minutes later, they both stopped and stared. Blood. A lot of blood.

Jordan wiped both his hands down his face. "This was so not how I planned to spend today."

"Getting ripped to shreds by a pack of Lycans is not on my list of ways I want to go." He'd seen a lot of nasty and vile things as a cop. This took it. He wasn't sure if he wanted it to be Ross or not. Knowing this might be a Lycan activated his gag reflex. It was a good thing all he'd eaten today was

LeAnn's oatmeal. He inhaled and squinted. "I can smell something new, too."

"Mountain lion. A mountain lion came from the north and dragged off some of the kill. That's why we're not seeing bones or…a head…or…yeah."

Well, that was a mixed bag. Seeing a wolf's head would feel like a slasher film moment, but maybe they'd have been able to tell if it was Ross. There'd have to be money on the table for him to examine a severed head, though. He might have been able to goad Jordan into doing that. Ross had been in his pack at one point, too.

They circled the kill site going in opposite directions while staring down at the ground.

"Here," Travis said. There was a set of prints heading north. Something had sprinted away.

Jordan met up with him and inhaled. He shook his head. "It could be either. They smell too damn alike with all these other scents." Four hundred feet away they found where the survivor had hidden.

"Would an actual wolf hide?" Travis asked.

"No. Maybe. I don't know. It seems like it'd get the hell out of here." He inhaled. "It smells more like the wolf, but maybe that's me, hoping, because otherwise this is a nightmare, and I'm keeping Christa hidden in my bedroom until she's ninety or I've killed this bastard."

"I can't tell." Travis pounded a fist against a nearby tree. "Dammit. I feel worthless. I should be able to tell whether we're following a Lycan or a wolf. He's my pack. I should be able to tell."

Jordan pinched the bridge of his nose while shaking his head. "I should be able to tell. I've been tracking scents my whole life, but this place smells like it was sprayed with blood. It's got to be the wolf here. It smells like the wolf. Maybe it decided to wait it out until the threat had left." He circled the large bush, scowling. "I can't tell where to go next. So either the damn thing backtracked…or followed the mountain lion."

"Neither of those makes sense for a wolf to do." He glanced at Jordan. "Do they?"

Jordan shook his head, but then also shrugged. "It doesn't make sense for Ross to do it, either."

"Unless he was trying to hide his scent."

Jordan snarled.

That made sense. Obviously they both hated that it was a rational explanation. But it made sense. And made him want to snarl and punch something again. But he was in control. He was keeping his wolf in check.

He and Jordan walked back to the kill site and stood staring at the gore left from the pack.

"We've got a problem," Jordan said, looking up.

"It's going to rain, isn't it?" The air felt heavy and damp. Could nothing go right for them? Seriously?

"Yep. I can feel it. We're a couple hours from a decent rain that'll wash out any hope of tracking this bastard." He shook his head and then dropped his gaze back to the bloody grass. "We've got to have somehow missed something. Did Miller say they lost sight of him?"

"Miller said there was no way he'd gotten away. He just didn't see the tattoo."

"It was light enough that a phosphorous tattoo might not be visible."

"Yup." Travis closed his eyes and leaned back against

the trunk of a tree. "Up until we'd gotten here, I was ninety-nine percent certain he'd gotten Ross. I felt stupid even mentioning it to you and dragging you away from Christa."

"Now?"

"Now I'm wondering what Ross might want with me that he'd have stopped by my place two nights ago."

"Maybe he blames you and… Wait, what the hell am I saying? There's no way!"

Travis opened his eyes and stared at Jordan.

Jordan pointed at the gory earth. "Look at that…there's no way a whole pack of Lycans lost him long enough that he pulled this switch. We've got to be wrong. You're wrong. I'm wrong. We're both wrong."

This was a nightmare. He'd really hoped LeAnn was imagining things. She was clearly crazy in every other way—why did this have to be the one point she was rational on?

"Ross is dead."

"He's got to be."

Jordan snarled again.

"So, should we follow the mountain lion?"

"Until it starts raining and this whole thing is useless? Sure." He pulled a satellite phone out of his backpack.

"If I get tossed out of my pack for hooking up with a murderer's sister, can I come back to Glacier?"

Jordan was already dialing, but he said, "Sure thing, and maybe I can find some of Christa's clothes for you to wear, you big baby."

Chapter Four

She dragged Ross's map out to the kitchen table and spread it out. Ross was with the park service here, and they had the best maps ever—not to mention she suspected Lycans had a thing with knowing their territory.

Things were not looking good for her brother.

She'd called his work, and Ross had up and quit all of a sudden.

That might speak to his claim that someone was out to get him, but her instincts were sour on this. And she had good instincts. The same gut feeling that had told her to stay the hell away from Clayton two years ago was telling her that Ross wasn't acting defensively. Ross hadn't acted scared on the phone. Something wasn't right.

She should cut out of here—right now—right away. She wasn't going to find anything that was going to help her sleep better at night.

On the other hand, Ross was all the family she had left.

And she didn't like that he'd been by Travis's place.

She was protective of Travis—like he was hers.

And she'd never been territorial about a guy before.

She had a sudden driving urge to find out who that she-wolf had been in the bushes yesterday and to know more about *all* the females in the pack. Along with that, she wanted them to know that Travis was off-limits. They'd had their chance.

Okay, take a deep breath. He's not yours. You're not staying. This is a weird blip in your life.

She'd spend a couple more days here and then she'd leave…and leave this whole thing behind. She could even pretend Lycans didn't exist. Ross had said there weren't many—that they were a dying breed. She might not ever meet another one in her lifetime. Which was fine. Because they were insane. Especially the Alphas.

If only every cell in her body weren't screaming "mine" whenever she got within ten feet of Travis. If only his kisses didn't make her senses blaze like she was on fire. He was bad for her.

Well, maybe not.

But she was bad for him. She'd always been the one who didn't belong, but her with a cop? No way in hell could that ever work. She'd broken the law enough times that her resistance to doing it again was tissue-thin. She'd fall back on old habits. This was simply a hot case of lust. It would burn out, and they'd be staring at each other with nothing to say one day.

She did not belong with Travis Flynn. End of story. No happily ever after here.

"Concentrate on the plan," she muttered to herself as

she rolled up the map. Time to find her brother and leave werewolves to their place in fiction—where they belonged. After this, she might not even believe in them anymore.

So, hah!

She drove slowly with her window down. LeAnn had nixed the first rental car they'd offered after turning it on. The exhaust was too strong, and she knew there was a good chance she'd be doing some scouting around when she couldn't get a hold of Ross. The exhaust was still a freaking pain to ignore, but at least she could manage it.

Of course in the area around Rainier there were a million other scents to pick through, too. It was a nice change from all the places she'd bounced around lately, even if it was more interference when looking for the scent you wanted. Maybe if she stayed here longer, it'd become second nature to ignore the scent of pine trees and ferns and upcoming rain.

"Stop it. You're not staying around. Even if you want to." She blinked. "Not that you want to." Dammit. It was that last kiss from Travis. He'd practically branded her with that heat. She couldn't shake it.

Lycan packs tended to live near each other. She knew that from her runs to Travis's place. She'd passed a dozen other cabins that smelled…furry. It was time to meet the neighbors.

When she pulled up to the far-too-cute cabin, she almost had second thoughts. The female Lycan here was putting off enough hormones that they were activating a primitive instinct in her she didn't quite trust. But Ross had a bra of hers, back in the safe, and you didn't usually collect a bra from someone you didn't know well.

If she reminded herself around every twenty seconds that Travis wasn't interested in this female, maybe this conversation would go okay.

The twentysomething woman opened the door in a silk robe and nothing else, and her overly-done-up eyes widened when she saw LeAnn. When the scent of her fear hit the air, too, LeAnn relaxed, even before the woman dipped her head and looked down.

That was weird.

"Hi. My name is LeAnn."

The thin blonde in her twenties nodded, still not looking up. "You're with Travis."

Huh. Apparently she wouldn't have to remind herself of that—this chick would. "He seems to think so. I'm only interested in figuring out what happened to my brother."

"I didn't even go to Glacier Peak."

"Okay," she said, drawing out the syllables. Odd response. "What's your name?"

"Merilee."

"Merilee, I'm not accusing you of anything. I want to find out if Ross did what Travis said he did and figure out if my brother is still alive." She might've guessed it'd feel good to intimidate someone else, but this didn't really feel all that great. "I, uhh…" And she felt it—that tingling on the back of her neck…someone was watching. LeAnn looked over her shoulder while inhaling shallowly. They were staying downwind of them, and the air was heavy with moisture so their scent wasn't carrying.

"I didn't even like Colby," Merilee said.

LeAnn turned back to her. "Who's Colby?"

Merilee actually looked up at her before shifting her gaze down again to their feet. "The person your brother killed."

"Oh." Her shoulders sank. It seemed like Merilee wouldn't have much of a reason to lie. She also seemed quite certain that Ross had killed someone.

"Not that I blame him," Merilee rushed to add.

"You don't?" How could you not blame someone for murdering someone? LeAnn rolled her shoulders. Okay. This was just plain weird. She'd long ago accepted that Lycans existed. And she'd had enough brushes with evil and death that murder wasn't as creepy as it should have been. But Ross murdering someone? And someone being okay with that? Especially this slight-framed, nearly naked chick who looked like she'd scream if she broke a nail... Surreal.

"Well, Colby wasn't really pack, and he was always looking for a fight, and he pissed off everyone."

"Yeah, but I wouldn't kill someone for pissing me off." Fisting her hands, LeAnn fought the urge to shake this crazy woman. She wouldn't kill someone period, but for being an obnoxious bastard? No. No way. No one would survive a bus ride with her if she did that.

"That's good. Unless you have a reason to. In which case it'd totally be your right."

This conversation was getting psycho. Especially since Merilee wasn't meeting her eyes. And it still felt like someone was watching them. "Can I come in?"

Merilee nodded and stood back for her to enter. She gestured her back through the cabin to a couch where it looked like she had a studio setup of lights and then a high-end video camera. "They're all turned off," she said, waving a hand at the couch surrounded by recording equipment.

Alrighty then.

"I just finished."

"That's…uhh, good." What was she supposed to say here? She should just stand. They could stand. The couch looked…dubious. The whole place smelled a bit funky—like too many sweaty bodies sort of funky. If this couch hadn't seen some miles, she'd be very surprised. "How well did you know Ross?" Hopefully she wouldn't go into details. Especially not details including the couch.

"Ross? Not Travis?"

"Not Travis." If she mentioned Travis and the couch, LeAnn might have to kick someone for pissing her off after saying she didn't resort to violence. It was up in the air whether that person would be Travis or Merilee, though. Seriously, how many people had gone to Funkytown in this room? LeAnn started breathing through her mouth. It was better not to speculate.

"Because Travis and I aren't anything to each other."

LeAnn cleared her throat and pretended it wasn't good to hear that. Even though her heart felt lighter. "I'm really not here about Travis…at all. I found something of yours at my brother's place, and it seemed like you might have known him. And I'm trying to figure if he really did—all that I've heard he did."

"Oh." She visibly relaxed, but she still wouldn't make eye contact.

Okay, enough was enough.

"Why are you looking down instead of looking at me?"

Merilee froze. "Well, you're Alpha. Travis said you were. And it feels like you are."

She should correct her. She wasn't Alpha of anything. But maybe Merilee might answer her questions if she acted like she had some authority. "How well did you know my brother?"

"Ross? Ross was nice, but he wasn't ever interested in me if that's what you're asking. He was a little…intense."

"Like a good intense or a 'twist the heads off birds' sort of intense?" LeAnn held her breath. Please let him not be the latter. He was the only family she had.

Her eyes widened again. "I don't know. I didn't know him so well."

LeAnn huffed out a breath. So, the second one. If it'd been the first one, she would have said as much.

"Look," Merilee said, almost making eye contact. "I swear, I'm not a threat to you. I've been thinking of pairing off with someone, but it was never going to be Travis. He doesn't like me…like that. So even if I smell like I might be a threat—I swear I'm not."

Inhaling and exhaling slowly, LeAnn was forced to admit, "Merilee, I have no idea what the hell you're talking about." This woman had to be one of the least threatening females on the planet. She seemed terrified that LeAnn was going to go all psycho and kill her—which maybe, considering she was related to Ross, was a fair concern. "I gotta say, I've never lived with Lycans, and Ross said you've got a bunch of hierarchy rules that were too complex to explain, but I'm not getting why you're scared of me."

"I'm not scared. I'm showing respect."

Sure looked and smelled a lot like fear.

"Okay, so you weren't…a special friend of my brother's then."

Merilee shook her head. "Or of Travis's."

She clenched her teeth. It looked like Travis had branded her among the pack as his and as Alpha—which inspired terror in this nearly naked small chick. For some reason. It was a real family environment. So this was what running with the pack felt like. There'd been times when Ross had talked about pack and she'd been jealous that he had a place in something, and he knew what it was. But if it was based on fear and intimidation and murdering those who pissed you off…maybe it was "thanks, but no thanks" time. "So you didn't give Ross one of your bras?" It was a last-ditch question.

Merilee wrinkled up her nose. "Not that I can remember. There were a few parties that…got out of hand, but I don't think Ross was at those."

Great. Ross was a killer perv. He probably had her bra for its scent and not because of fond memories. It made sense in light of the other less-intimate articles of clothing he had—including the lab coat in her purse—but LeAnn had still hoped. And that hope had taken a nasty hit. Merilee had no reason to lie.

So that was it. Ross was probably a murderer. Maybe he had a reason. Maybe he didn't. It still wasn't right. Thou shalt not kill and all that. *Dammit, Ross. You better have had a reason.* He was all she had left. Her only family. It made her eyes sting with tears she wouldn't actually cry. "Thanks, Merilee."

She nodded—in this submissive, cowed way that made the bile rise a bit in the back of her throat. Okay, she didn't want anything to do with being pack. This reminded her too much of herself two years ago.

"Have a good day." And she left before the other woman had even replied. She'd planned on going and talking to the other people whose clothing she'd found—including the woman who'd visited in her furry form yesterday—but no…never mind. She got in her car and drove…and drove… down forestry roads that were edged with snow and back again. Finally, she parked at a closed trailhead and got out.

Standing in front of her car, despite the cold, she snarled and picked up a pinecone and threw it out into the forest… and then the tears came so she dropped to the ground and cried until she felt like the tears would freeze on her face and a light misting rain started falling.

It'd be dark soon.

She should probably head back to Ross's.

Or maybe go to Travis's.

Or she could even get the hell out of here. She could drive straight to the airport and get an enormously expensive ticket to somewhere…anywhere. Because she had no family anymore. A sob shook her. Alone. She was alone. Finding out she had a brother from her dying mother had felt like a reprieve. She wasn't meant to be separate and misunderstood by everyone. But that hope had been a lie.

If he'd killed someone, even someone who pissed him off—because that was still wrong no matter what—Ross was dead to her.

And if Travis was right, he was dead either way, even in the unlikely scenario that he was innocent.

Ross was dead.

Her only remaining family—dead.

The genes ended here…and maybe it was just as well.

It's not even as if she could pretend she was that much better than Ross. She'd killed someone, too. Someone she didn't even know. A wave of blackness threatened to swallow her, and for a second, she was back in that day. Her body shivered with numbing shock and she saw the spreading blood and knew she'd taken a life. Cold. So cold. And dark. Blinking and sucking in a deep breath, she forced the memory back. This wasn't the time or the place for another blackout and memory loss. After a few more slow, steady breaths, the beast inside her settled down.

Maybe Merilee had good reason to be scared.

She should leave. Travis had been wrong and right at the same time. He'd said following this would only lead to death, but he'd acted like acceptance was so much better of an idea. She could walk away from here and pretend that Ross hadn't done this—that Ross was still alive—that nothing had changed. She could add this to her box of things she repressed and pretended didn't happen.

Getting to her feet, she brushed the dirt off her butt. That's what she'd do. She'd go pack and leave it all behind her. Lock it up in her memory box along with Clayton and all the hateful words between her mother and her. Some people were just meant to be alone. It was better that way.

Her sixth sense for direction got her back to Ross's cabin as it was getting dark. She'd grab a few things—maybe that photo album she'd found. She'd burn the things she'd borrowed from Travis so no one could use them against him. Then she'd be gone. Florida was probably nice in late January.

Ross's scent hit her again as she got out of the car,

and she closed her eyes. No. No, it wasn't him. It was those clothes someone had stolen. Ross was dead. He was dead. She inhaled. Male this time. Not Travis. Not Ross. She'd found a sock from this guy in her brother's treasure trove of borrowed clothing. And the smell of ammonia was strong. Eww.

Opening her eyes, she stalked to the front door to his cabin and yanked it open…without using her key. Someone had broken in again—and peed on the front porch. Bastards.

She spun around. "I am feeling the love! You stupid, furry fangheads, I don't want anything to do with you and your sick, twisted 'let's kill everyone' world!" She was going to be hoarse from all this screaming, but she didn't care. They should know that they were a bunch of freaks. They were all freaks. Maybe her brother would have been fine if they hadn't warped his mind with this pack psychosis. He'd been drinking the Kool-Aid. "And it is not okay to pee on other people's property! You sicko! Bad doggy!"

She slammed the front door behind her.

• • •

It was dark when he got back to his place, and he'd been hoping she'd be there, even if he hadn't planned on sharing what they'd found at Glacier Peak. Travis wanted to hold her so he could be sure she was okay, and to remind himself that this was worth it.

This scent-match wasn't high on his list of favorite things right now. It could get both of them killed. Definitely not part of the life plan.

Instead of going to find her, he did what he should have

done when he'd realized that someone had been at her house. He pulled up the pack's tracking tags. He'd conned them into the high-tech and not-approved-for-human-use tags by having a few of the more popular Lycans go for it. The tattoos had been the same way. It felt a bit police state to tag and tattoo his pack, but that Glacier Peak experience of a couple years back had spooked him. There'd been a poacher among them. Even now, with the poacher threat gone, it still felt like they were being hunted.

It had to have been Ross that Black Tusk had killed. Even if they'd lost the trail of the mountain lion to the rain, it made more sense that Black Tusk had caught him rather than lost him. Ross was dead.

The tracking tags had been found to have a few serious flaws, though…ones that could be exploited. Ross had used a jammer to kill the signal—in addition to digging his own out, which must have been painful as hell. Then, there were these dead zones where the satellite dropped out. As he looked at the movement of his pack, he shook his head. Someone else was playing games. Several members of the pack had been there when they'd found Ross's methods of getting around tracking. He wasn't even entirely sure he knew where the jammer had gotten to.

Travis clenched his fists before loosening them on a deep exhale. This feeling that everything was spiraling out of control wasn't entirely accurate. Partly. But not entirely.

He was Alpha. He was a genius. He could handle this.

No one had gone anywhere near Ross's house, other than him…and then Troy today. Troy had been there a couple hours ago. That bastard. Other Lycans had been there—but they weren't showing up. He knew they had been. Troy, on

the other hand, hadn't bothered covering his tracks at all...
because that was the whole damn point. If he'd so much as
touched LeAnn, screw pack law and challenges—he'd go rip
out Troy's throat right now.

He sprinted back to his truck. It was tempting to switch
into form, but his truck was faster and he'd rather not be
naked for a confrontation until it was necessary.

When he drove up to Ross's, there was an eerie stillness
about the place that made his throat go dry and his pulse
speed up. Troy was a moron, but he wouldn't be dumb
enough to hurt LeAnn.

LeAnn's engine was still warm. Good; she hadn't been
here when Troy had been.

He circled the cabin sniffing the air. Troy...LeAnn...and
the residual scent of Ross—though it seemed oddly stronger
than previous times he'd been here. Hell, when this was all
over, he wanted to burn this cabin down to the studs and
never smell Ross's scent ever again. Wait...not just Troy.
He snorted. Troy had pissed all over the front porch. Travis
pinched the bridge of his nose. Please let LeAnn not recognize that scent. Nothing said "we're all friends here" like a
stranger peeing on your property.

The whole place was dark, and LeAnn wasn't moving
around. That didn't seem good. Why wasn't she moving
around? Had she already gone to bed?

"LeAnn?" he asked, knocking on the back door. She'd
have seen him drive up if she'd been anywhere near the
front door. There was a whole slew of windows.

"Go away!" she yelled, sounding like she'd been doing
a lot of yelling. Her voice was deep and scratchy, and she
sounded upset.

He grabbed the doorknob and twisted…unlocked. Why hadn't she locked the door? "I'm coming in to check on you." He was taking a real chance on catching a knife to his liver, but he was worried enough he was going in anyway.

Well, it wasn't a knife.

He opened the door to find her sitting at the kitchen table on the other side of the cabin with a shotgun pointed at his head and a scowl on her face.

"Is that loaded?" he asked calmly.

"Of course it's not, dumb-ass, do I look insane?" she asked, lowering it and setting it on the table.

It was definitely not a question he should answer, but he'd had a hellish day chasing her dead homicidal brother, and tomorrow he'd have to challenge Troy. He could probably take Troy just fine, but things were known to get ugly in challenges, and whether by right or by accident, fatalities weren't so unusual.

"Yeah, a little. You've already had a knife to my throat, so what's a loaded gun?" he said, striding across the cabin. He pulled off his gun holster and set it on the table, then sat in the chair beside her. It was probably best if they were both disarmed.

Her eyes narrowed.

He folded his arms. "I thought you were coming to my place." His concern after seeing Troy's tag here made his words sharper than they should've been.

She leaned toward him, not breaking eye contact. "You are *not* my Alpha. You are *not* my mate. You are *nothing* to me." He could see the tears shining in her eyes as she said it. So, she'd had a hell of a day too.

With a sigh, he got to his feet and went to the cupboard

where he could smell the faint scent of dehydrated vegetables and MSG. Opening it up, he grabbed out two Cup-a-Soups.

"What are you doing?" she asked in a completely different tone, but still in that scratchy voice of hers, which now sounded as if she was fighting crying.

"Making dinner. I've never actually made these, but it's probably difficult to really screw them up." He read the directions in the dark while noticing that she didn't seem bothered by the dark, either. Another check mark in the "she's a Lycan" category.

Why was he still tallying these things up? He knew she was. It was one of the few things he really knew about her. She had to be a Lycan. Anything else was illogical.

"Why?"

He turned on the faucet and tried to pretend that the sink and microwave had never even shared space with the fridge in the corner. Oh, yeah, he was brave. He ought to do fine in tomorrow's challenge. "Because you had a bad day and I had a bad day—and maybe if we're filled with...*hydrolyzed soy protein*, we'll be in a better mood to discuss it."

"How did you know I'd had a bad day?"

He put the first container in the microwave and started it. "Because..." He stopped and inhaled. "Why does it smell like I've been in here before now?" It was strange. The scent was strong and fresh and had a hint of...plastic. What the hell?

"Oh, I stole some of your stuff. So, how did you know I'd had a bad day?"

He turned around in the kitchen. Yup. Spiraling out of control. Why was he denying that? He was trying to mate with someone who only made sense about one-third of the times she opened her mouth. "What do you mean you stole some of my stuff?"

She got to her feet with a sigh and walked toward him. Reaching past him, she opened up a cupboard where there was a Tupperware container with his clothing in it. "You seemed creeped out by the thought of wearing my brother's clothes, but I figured you'd stubbornly come over here as a wolf again and refuse to get un-furry, so I swiped some of your clothes this morning. No one ever looks for things like that in a kitchen cabinet, especially if it's in a container to keep the scent in."

"There are two shirts in there."

"Well, I wore one of your shirts back here."

"I thought you ran naked."

"Not always. Not if I'm…paying attention. Not if there are people around and a risk of indecent exposure charges. Well, mostly not then. There was this one time…" She paused and cleared her throat. "Besides, I *wasn't* running." She gave him this duh look.

Unfortunately for her, she'd strayed too close, and even with that peeved look on her face, he still wanted to hold her. He grabbed her hand and tugged her into a hug. She stiffened at first before relenting.

He squinted. "Is that one of my knives on top?"

"Yeah. I like your knives better. Plus I didn't want to walk home unarmed." She wrapped her arms around his waist and sighed, sinking deeper into his clasp. Turning her head, she laid it on his chest. And she relaxed. He'd never comforted a woman like this before. He'd never sought the warmth of another body for compassion rather than passion. The wolf inside him was soothed. All the questions and concerns could wait. The constant dialogue in his head and the cataloging of sensory input from his environment faded to a dull hum.

He could just be. There was a harmony here.

LeAnn breathed in and out, her body rubbing against his, reminding him that she was female—and his. Biology had proclaimed her his mate—his alpha female.

He tightened his arms. Hell, she felt good—like she belonged.

Maybe his day hadn't been that bad.

No, it had. It really had. But at least he had this to look forward to at the end of a hellish day.

Travis watched the time on the microwave count down, feeling far too content for a man who might die the next day and who was about to eat crap. "You weren't here when one of the males from my pack stopped by, were you?"

Her back went ramrod straight, and she pulled out of his arms. "No. And that's disgusting. That's quite a way to welcome someone. I can't believe I even stayed here. I've broken a few laws in my day, but public urination was *never* one of them." She stepped back.

"Don't take it personally. It was aimed at me, not you."

"I'm not sure much aiming happened there. The whole front porch seemed fair game."

"No, I told them all, including Troy, to stay away from you."

"And you're Alpha, and none of them have any free will anymore so you expected them to obey you, even if my brother murdered their little buddy." She took a few more steps back.

He clenched his teeth and shook his head. So much for

that peace he'd felt. The accusation in her tone made his wolf side want to snarl. "Troy violated my order on purpose so I'd be forced to challenge him for my spot as Alpha." The microwave beeped, and he turned to pull his crappy dinner out and replaced it with hers.

"What does that mean?" she asked slowly.

He closed his eyes and forced himself to calm down. She didn't know about their ways. Her ass of a brother had never mentioned them. She didn't even think she was what it was patently obvious she was. "It means that tomorrow Troy and I will fight to see who is Alpha over the pack. If I lose, you can't stay here. I can only protect you if I win." Not to mention he might be dead. Not every victor accepted the forfeit of the loser's life, but Troy would. Troy liked to kill the local livestock. He'd really enjoy the sanctioned kill of his opponent.

"I can protect myself," she said in a somewhat shaky voice. Standing up taller, she cleared her throat. "Does this happen often? These challenge fights?"

"First time for me—though I've been expecting it since I became Alpha a little over a year ago. I picked up two members in my pack—well, inherited them from Glacier Peak. Two members who've seen themselves as Alphas since their first cut tooth."

"And one of them decided now was a good time?"

"No, I showed weakness in their eyes by scent-matching to you and trying to protect you. Also, this is the time of year when female Lycans go into heat for three or four weeks, and the unattached males in the pack try to prove themselves. This time, he's taking it a step further." The microwave beeped behind him, and he took the cup out and set it on the counter beside his untouched one. Letting them sit probably wouldn't drastically affect the flavor.

"What if I left…tonight? So it's not like I'm a problem for you anymore?"

It caused a stabbing sensation in his stomach, and the wolf in him rose up and wanted to snarl. *Mine. Mate.* He shook his head. "This was coming. It'll still happen, and it was bound to happen. But if you want to leave…I won't have to worry about protecting you if I'm not successful."

"Do you want me to leave tonight?"

"I should." His brain refused to process it—to plan it. At any given time, he had a dozen plans for each scenario playing out in his mind. None of them involved her leaving. The first thing he should consider was the last thing he wanted.

"What if I stayed tonight?" She took a step closer.

He clenched his fists at his sides and fought the change.

Her eyes widened for a moment, so he knew she could tell…then her pupils dilated and she smiled.

"Are you accepting the scent-match?" he asked. Heat flashed through him, and a fierce desire to possess her, to own her. If she said yes, they'd be making love in this kitchen in seconds. His eyes strayed to the freezer. Not this kitchen. Somewhere else. Hell, the way he wanted her, the woods would do just fine.

She shook her head.

No. Of course not. That'd be too easy…and good…very good. His jaw tightened, and a long blink later, he'd put away the wolf.

Not.

Yet.

He picked her cup off the counter and stuck it in her hand, then gave her a spoon before picking up his. "Mm," he said. Nothing cooled lust like rehydrated vegetables…or whatever was in this.

She watched him take a bite, struggling not to grin.

"This is terrible," he said around the mouthful. It was like eating mushy salt. The soggy texture implied that there was something other than salt in this, but it was hard to distinguish what.

She laughed before eating it herself. "I knew you'd hate it."

"What is this supposed to be?" he asked, showing her a floating speck of yellow.

It was dark. Too dark for a non-Lycan to see anything, and yet they were conversing as if it were light. She leaned forward and said, "That, Travis, is a piece of corn."

"Allegedly. I'm not sure any of this is what it says it is. As if anyone knows what hydrolyzed soy protein is." He tipped his spoon sideways and let the yellow thing fall back into the mix.

"I suppose you planned on having that leftover ravioli for dinner…with…what was that? A pesto sauce of some kind?"

He shook his head. "You went through my fridge, too?" Why was he surprised? She'd made herself at home and gone through his stuff. She'd even swiped some of his clothes. Though admittedly, the image of her wearing one of his shirts and nothing else didn't bother him. Or it did. It bothered him a whole lot. It was a shame she wasn't ready to accept the scent-match.

"Yep. That was before I realized people might put freaky,

creepy things in their fridges."

"Did you look in the freezer here?"

She pointedly didn't answer him.

He dug through his soup with his spoon, looking for something recognizable. He might die tomorrow. He should tell her about his search today. And he *wanted* to tell her. It was probably an asinine idea, but he wanted to. Most mates discussed their days with each other…that was all it was. It was the scent-match. And…well, she'd pulled a gun on him. He had to respect that. He was beginning to think there might be more between them than the scent-match.

"I went back to Glacier Peak today," he said, staring into his cup. He could feel her eyes on him.

"Why?"

"To look for your brother?" He looked up, meeting her gaze.

She licked her lips. "His body or…?"

He shrugged. "Well, I won't lie—I was hoping for that. I don't like to think what your brother might be capable of now that we've really pissed him off."

"So you believed me?"

He set his cup of muck aside and crossed his arms. "I believe that you believe what you're saying, but it was hard for me to imagine—having been there."

"You trust…uhh believed me enough to go look?" He wasn't so inept with female speak that he didn't recognize that there was more to her question than face value.

He shrugged again. It was hard to believe her when she didn't recognize she turned into a wolf, but he knew she legitimately thought she'd caught her brother's scent. And she'd seemed to recognize that Travis was right—that her brother wasn't who she thought he was. That was progress.

He held her gaze. He'd watched the staring contests between Christa and Jordan, and it'd seemed to be a sign they were meant to be together that she didn't break first to show deference. She saw them as equals.

"And?" LeAnn asked, setting her soup to the side, too. She didn't look away.

It made him smile—which was totally inappropriate for the subject matter and made her eyes narrow.

"If you make me guess, I'll go get my knife."

"It's my knife, and our search proved…inconclusive."

"What does that mean?"

"Your brother let loose a wolf he'd managed to coat in his scent…though I can't even imagine how he achieved that. He did it to trick Jordan into following the wolf rather than rescuing his mate. He thought that Jordan would put the pack's well-being over his mate's. He thought her brother, Dane, would come for her—whom Ross also hated and planned to kill, and then he could sneak out and kill Jordan."

"But Jordan didn't chase the wolf? I thought the pack was all-important to you people…that it justified everything?" The fact that she'd chosen to focus on this and not on his search for her brother was telling. The way she said "pack" nearly had an accompanying growl.

He grabbed her hand and tugged her closer. "No. I won't say that the pull of instinct and the pack aren't strong, but there's still a wild, stubborn streak inside us when it comes to our mating. I've heard others say that in our mind's hierarchy the welfare of our breeding partner and thus the continuation of our pack supersedes almost everything else. That it all goes back to the pack being our top priority."

"But you don't think that's what it is?" She was still meeting his gaze. If this wasn't her brother's place, he'd clear the counter with one mad swipe and to hell with everything—they'd be making love on the counter. But he *had* looked in the freezer...so that was no good.

"Well, I'm much smarter than the others I've heard that from, and I can't discount the fact that both man and wolf have primitive sides—and there's much better odds of having wild crazy sex if your mate is alive."

She picked up her cup of soup and handed him his. "Let's hope, anyway...or you're really freaky."

He glanced over at the fridge.

She huffed out a breath and said, "You're ruining food for me," as she put her cup to the side.

"This is not food." He set his cup down again and pulled her into his arms. "Pack up your stuff so no one else can swipe things, come to my place, and I'll feed you some real food."

She bit her lip, pretending to look indecisive. "I've never been to your place clothed."

"Well, I vote we don't ruin your streak then."

Rolling her eyes, she punched his shoulder and pulled out of his arms.

"Do I get extra points for using the word 'streak' there?" he called after her as she went to go pack.

She flipped him off over her shoulder.

• • •

Two hours later, he'd talked her into an early bedtime so they could both catch up on sleep.

From where she lay on his chest, she asked him drowsily, "So, Jordan didn't follow the wolf?"

"Not that day. He went in to rescue his mate and confronted your brother before tossing him out for another pack to deal with."

"And they caught him?"

He sighed; the action made her brown hair stir slightly. He brushed the wisps down while tangling his fingers in it. He might not actually sleep tonight, but he wouldn't regret that—especially not if he died tomorrow. He'd rather spend the night doing things other than sleeping, but holding her was good, too. "Today, we followed the trail of the wolf because there were too many scents surrounding your brother."

"He caught up with the wolf, didn't he?"

His hand stilled and he frowned down at her. "Yup. How did you know?"

"When he was teaching me how to track, he tried to mess with my head by following the trail of a pack of wolves. He stopped me just shy of cornering them in a den. He thought he was so clever. The next time he tried that, I had an air horn with me, and I snuck up on him and blew it right in his ear."

There was so much there that astounded him and made him want to kill her brother all over again. Talk about throwing her to the wolves. "Your brother taught you to track him as a Lycan?" That would explain why she seemed even more attuned to his scent.

"Yeah. He said it would be more fun."

Her brother was an ass. "But you didn't turn into a Lycan yourself to track him? You're sure?"

She lifted her head and stared at him. "You need more sleep. Trust me, I'd know if I could turn into a wolf."

He wasn't so sure. "Have you actually tried?"

"To turn into a wolf?"

"Yes."

She laughed. "Sure I did. Isn't that like a rite of passage for every girl…and their dog?"

"I'm serious, LeAnn."

"So am I. Did you have to concentrate to turn yourself into a wolf the first time?"

No. It'd felt instinctual and it'd just occurred…and been somewhat surreal. It would be a million times more surreal if you didn't know it might be in store for you—if you didn't know your father and brother were Lycans. It might have scared the hell out of her so she liked to pretend it wasn't happening. Or maybe she really didn't want to be part of a pack the more she learned about them. But she was a Lycan.

"See," she said, even though he hadn't responded. "Wouldn't it be funny if everyone was a Lycan but they never really tried so they didn't know?" She yawned and it made her lips brush his bare chest.

"Is there anything I could do to convince you to accept the scent-match if I win tomorrow's challenge?" He should tell her that she might be challenged herself, but she already wasn't keen on the pack—and that wouldn't help, knowing that there was the possibility some of them might want to kill her. And besides, only Merilee was in heat, and she was harmless, and LeAnne had no reason to be around her.

"Why? So we can have sex?"

"That's one of the reasons." A minor one, but he wasn't ready to admit to the others or explain some of the complicated mind-set of pack animals. "Is there anything that would convince you that it's a good thing—that we could make it work?"

"You don't know me well enough to know that."

He'd made her laugh over dinner. She'd caught him staring at her ass a dozen times. They *were* compatible. He wouldn't have believed it, but he liked her…a lot, and the insanity was almost endearing at this point. "I know you."

She turned away from him. "You don't, Travis. I've got a lot of stuff going on in my life that you couldn't understand and you wouldn't want a part of."

He wanted to shake her. *Then tell me already.* Did she not get that he wasn't going to judge her? If she'd just let him in, he could help her. Hell, he wanted to be a part of her life.

Her turning away from him wasn't as effective a deterrent as she might have thought. He pulled her tight against him, spooning his body around hers. She inhaled sharply and then sighed when his arm slipped around her waist.

Travis forced his arms to stay loose. LeAnn was like a spooked, trapped animal, biting mad and ready to bolt. She needed patience and understanding.

But he wasn't an idiot, even if sleep deprivation seemed to be affecting him fairly drastically. He knew she was hiding something, even before he'd run her license through the system. Admitting he'd run checks on her background probably wouldn't forward his cause, though. Telling her he'd passed all her information off to his computer hacker friend in Seattle definitely wasn't something he'd consider. But this was like a game with them. It was like her finding his knives after he'd hidden them. Eventually he'd find out her big secret, and it would be nothing, and they wouldn't even have to talk about it.

"Maybe I'm exactly what you need," he whispered, kissing her neck.

"Maybe you are—but maybe I don't deserve nice things."

Go slow. Go easy. Or something like that.

He bit her neck, making her jump. "Maybe I don't have to be nice."

"Mm." She arched against him, and her breathing sped up.

Yes.

Then she took a deep breath and said, "Go to sleep, Travis. We'll talk about it tomorrow."

Damn.

Chapter Five

LeAnn went to get up, but his arm tightened reflexively around her waist, and she paused, hoping he'd go back to sleep. Waking up with him…implied things. Eating breakfast with him as good as branded them as a couple in her mind, and it'd be really hard to walk away from a relationship that wasn't broken and unhealthy. Everything about Travis felt right and instinctual.

"Don't," he whispered, pulling her back against him.

Damn. But at the same time, some part of her had wanted him to notice she was leaving. No one ever cared that she left. He made her feel warm and safe. Her insides felt jittery with happy butterflies. This was dangerous. She couldn't get used to this. It'd only make things harder in the long run. "I should go."

"Where?"

She started to answer, but snapped her mouth closed. Okay, so she had nowhere to go. Finally, she sighed. "When you said your search was inconclusive does that mean my brother might still be alive and gunning for you?" That was the whole reason she hadn't packed and left before he'd arrived. It didn't make a lot of sense that she was trying to keep the huge muscular sheriff in town safe, but that was her excuse for staying another day. She couldn't get on with her "repress my brother" plan until she knew he'd be okay.

"We found where something was killed and something escaped—and they both smelled like your brother. But that would mean about a dozen or more Lycans lost sight of your brother long enough that he swapped places with the wolf he'd released. It's enough to make Jordan and Dane from Glacier Peak cautious, and they're planning on going back there today to see if Ross had a vehicle stashed somewhere. There were a bunch of vehicles from the poachers, but Jordan didn't remember any of them belonging to your brother, and it seems to me like they'd have contacted me to deal with it—since Ross was my pack. That doesn't mean anything. Ross could have been on foot for a while or caught a ride at some point, but it's a loose end that we're both going to be figuring out today."

"Would he come after you because you were his Alpha?"

"Up until he killed someone, I had no problem with Ross. He and I got along fine. He might feel betrayed, but his betrayal of our kind was far worse."

It made her sick to think about it, and this wasn't helping with her plan to pretend this was all some crazy nightmare. "But if he's…insane…he might think that?"

"If I agree with you, will it be enough to keep you here?" He brushed his lips back and forth across her neck, and that ache inside her increased a thousand times.

"You probably don't need my protection." It was silly to even think he did. There were a dozen reasons he didn't, in fact.

He moved to the side of her neck, where he kissed a path up to her ear. "Maybe I do."

She started to roll her eyes, but he nipped the sensitive skin below her ear, and she moaned and closed them instead.

"LeAnn." He flattened his palm against her stomach, pressing her against him. "I really want you." He lit a fire inside her—her bones felt like melting wax, and yet her pulse was pounding like she'd run for hours. She couldn't move. She didn't move.

She bit her lower lip. They had passion and heat. They had that in spades. Whether it was this thing he called a scent-match or whether it was out-and-out attraction, she wanted him just as much. Slow and deep. Fast and hard. She wanted him. "And then what?"

"Hm?"

"You don't even know me, Travis. And you belong to this pack that'll turn on you as soon as stand beside you… and I've had enough of that in my life. No one stays. No one sticks around when it gets difficult. It's better I leave before you want me to. I'm this complication in your life that you're hot for." She swallowed. "Less than forty-eight hours ago, you said I was the last person you'd want to be with. And I haven't changed in that time." It still stung that he'd said that—even if it'd been the truth. She blinked her eyes. Already he had the power to make her cry. This was dangerous. Travis Flynn was a dangerous man.

"I shouldn't have said that."

"Not if you were hoping for sex this morning," she

agreed. Was that a catch in her throat? So much for casual bravado.

"No, not because of that…because it was a jackass thing to say to someone, but I wasn't thinking when I said it." He sighed. "I'm a control freak, LeAnn. And I'm manipulative. I learned a long time ago that if people thought I was stupid, they'd give me this edge—they'd trust me. I'd probably score high as a sociopath if I were ever tested. It's made me a natural Alpha, this way I have of controlling people—of controlling situations. I haven't felt like I was in control since I woke up to a naked woman with a knife at my throat. You knocked me on my ass, and I haven't recovered."

That shouldn't make her feel proud, but it did…a little.

"And you know what? Maybe that's what I needed… someone I'd have to drop the act for and who'd keep me guessing. I still wish we weren't dealing with all that we are, but I think that's a sign that I'm lazy…and I never claimed not to be that. And I don't take off when things get difficult. I stay and fight for what matters—you should recognize that about me by now." He went back to kissing her neck.

Maybe he did, but she didn't. Leaving was…easier.

Why did he have to be everything she'd ever wanted and smell like it, too? Her body was so not siding with her brain.

"Look, I can't be with a cop."

He bit where her shoulder and neck met and sucked lightly.

And all her synapses fried. She inhaled raggedly. Her darker side, the beast she fought back, seemed to have a sensual aspect. The heat rose. A growl sounded in her head. It wanted release. No. No one could see that side of her. Especially not Travis. She sounded slightly desperate when she said, "Travis! Did you hear me? I can't. I sorta believe laws are made to be broken."

"Mm." His thumb was rubbing back and forth across her stomach…across her naked skin…as his mouth pressed kisses around the straps of her tank top.

LeAnn moaned softly. She couldn't think. She could only feel. Her whole body felt licked by fire. No. Her brain snatched around for anything…anything to stop him from taking them both over the edge. "Wilcox isn't my real last name."

That should stop him. It didn't. Oh, it really didn't. Her skin felt so hot and sensitive, and she could still feel every kiss he'd left behind. LeAnn flipped onto her back and grabbed his face in her hands. Maybe he wasn't listening to her. He didn't seem to be doing a lot of thinking since he'd stopped talking. She was struggling to think of much of anything other than him and her making the most of a horizontal surface.

"Travis," she said, meeting his eyes. Her hands trembled. She needed to stop this while even a small part of her had the strength to. He had such gorgeous eyes, and when he stared at her, it felt like he was seeing her soul. "I'm not right for you. I don't want to stay here." Her brain screamed at the lie, but she continued. "Frankly, your pack sounds like a bunch of rabid dogs. Not a bit of this makes sense between us."

He lifted his hand up to prop his head on and kept staring at her. "Where do you want to be?"

She licked her lips. "What?"

"You said you don't want to stay here—where do you want to be? Baltimore? I know even LeAnn Wilcox hasn't lived there all that long. I don't know what your name was before that, but it doesn't seem like you have a home base."

So he had been listening, and he'd checked up on her—she figured he would. "I don't know, but not here. Your pack is crazy." She drew in a deep breath as she felt the heat from his touch recede. They could talk about this and be reasonable.

He smiled. "They are. But you haven't really gotten to know them, and all you've seen so far is the most extreme of pack behavior. We don't normally attack each other. My pack is still trying to find its feet. When couples start pairing off, it'll be…less unstable."

"What if you're not Alpha over it anymore? Can you leave or do you have to stay here?"

The smile dropped off his face. "I can leave. Even if I win today's challenge, I can still leave."

She wanted to ask if he would if she asked him to, but that'd be implying a commitment that she wasn't ready to make. And besides, he might say no, and she wanted to believe he would—that she was *that* important to him. She'd never been that important to anyone. She probably wouldn't be again. Maybe that's why he was so hard to walk away from. How many times did you have a guy tell you that you were meant to be with him—and want that, too? In her life, this never happened. This was a fairy tale in her life of shadowed streets and dark, run-down stopovers. This was her Cinderella. It was a little hard to walk away from.

"How does it work?" she asked. "Today's challenge? You'll head over to his house and you'll kick this guy Troy's ass?"

He slid his hand across her stomach and went back

to rubbing her skin with his thumb. "It's slightly more… organized than that. It'll happen in front of the pack so that they'll recognize who the stronger Lycan is."

There was something he wasn't telling her. She felt it. He was keeping something back. "So, I could be there?"

"No, you shouldn't be there."

"Why not? You said I was pack. You told them I was." Not that she was sure she wanted to be, but he *had* said that.

"Your first experience with the pack shouldn't be a fight. This is an exception to the way we are. It's a…violent but necessary aspect to trusting that the pack is being led by the strongest among us." He smiled. "I don't even want to be there, but they might notice if I'm not."

They stayed staring at each other. His hand even stopped moving. "What aren't you telling me?"

"A lot," he said, raising his eyebrows.

She blinked. She hadn't expected him to say that. "Well, like what?"

He looked over at the phone on his bedside table. "Would you trust someone else to help you figure out what was happening with your brother if I sent you to stay with him?"

She shook her head but still asked, "No, why would you do that?"

"Because if I lose, you won't be safe on my pack's land possibly." He frowned. "Troy's a total ass and I can see him being vindictive…and ornery."

"Well, we can leave together."

He inhaled and exhaled before smiling, a pathetic half smile. "Okay." Then he sat up. "C'mon. Let's go eat some breakfast. I'll make you something better than oatmeal…

especially since I don't have to waste time hunting down knives this morning." He glanced at the window. "And since it's early because you were trying to sneak out of here before dawn."

"You were much easier to sneak out on yesterday."

"Yup, but now I've had plenty of sleep, so you won't be able to slide things by me nearly as easily."

"And you'll be in better shape to win this fight, right?"

"Yup."

She narrowed her eyes. The way he said "yup" was in this slow, dense voice. It was freakishly convincing. He even dropped his eyelids slightly so he looked as lazy as he was claiming to be. He looked like a stereotypical small-town cop.

He looked up at her and winked.

She rolled her eyes. "You're going to win, right?" It seemed like even if he did want to walk away, that it'd be better if it was his choice, not because he'd lost a fight.

"Yup."

"Stop that." It made her skin crawl—he was that good. Little old ladies in Buicks probably enjoyed getting tickets from him when he did that.

He laughed. "It used to make Jordan's eye twitch, too." He pulled a shirt on. "How do you like your eggs, LeAnn?"

"Over easy."

"Well, that'd be the first time anything about you'd be easy."

"Don't make me get my knife. And you might want to grab a hose. Troy must have hydrated before hitting your porch last night."

"I'm going to kill him."

• • •

"Travis, I think I've talked to you more in the last two days than I've talked to my wife," Jordan said when he answered his phone.

"That's because you're not feeling much like talking and you're hiding things from me because you think I can't handle them," Christa said in the background.

"I like your wife," Travis said. "Platonically."

Jordan sighed. "What now? If any of the poachers are alive, too, I'll come kill you for this aggravation. It's not a logical response, but I'll do it."

"I have a challenge tonight." It was strange that in this day and age he could send out a notification of a challenge by email. Their progenitors would have found it disturbing. He found it slightly disturbing. One of them might die tonight. Come and watch. It was a good thing LeAnn wasn't going to be there. She'd never understand the necessity of a strong leader. "I need you to make sure LeAnn makes it out of town if I fail."

Another sigh from Jordan. "Troy?"

"Yup."

"Stop that. You know I hate that."

It reminded him of LeAnn and made him smile.

"You're sure he intended to challenge you and you're not just…on edge? Because a challenge when Ross might still be alive…"

"He pissed on Ross's porch…which is where LeAnn was staying."

"It could have been aimed at Ross."

"Then he came and did the same thing at my place in the middle of the night when I didn't challenge him right away."

"Subtle."

"Yeah, well, Troy tries to keep it classy."

"Okay, what time?"

"Seven."

"I'll be there," Jordan said, and Travis heard him leave a room, closing a door.

"You don't need to be as long as you can send someone to make sure LeAnn is okay."

"No, I'm coming because I don't trust Troy, first of all, and, secondly, if he becomes Alpha, I'm taking some of my pack back. If Troy has a problem with that he'll get his first challenge. I trust you with those I care about. Troy can't seem to stop killing the neighbor's chickens."

Travis clenched his teeth and rubbed his forehead with his palm. He felt the same way about Troy. He wouldn't trust him with a pet, let alone a pack. He'd been thinking of stepping in between him and Merilee, because Merilee wasn't strong enough to not get beaten. Troy had all the telltale signs of an abuser.

"But you're not going to lose," Jordan said. "There's no way. I'd bet my Bronco on that."

It felt good to hear someone else say that. "You don't think?"

"You had an older brother, didn't you?"

"Yeah, he was killed in active duty twelve years ago." He clenched his teeth. The sting of his brother's death had dulled, but it'd never go away. It was an icy blast of water on his psyche. Josh was a good reminder of what happened when you didn't control your emotions. And his life had never been more out of control.

"Lycan?"

"Yes."

"Okay then. Younger brothers are the scrappiest of the lot. And the few times you and I settled our differences of opinion before I became Alpha…were memorable. If I hadn't tired you out, you'd have won."

"I won twice." He and Jordan had gotten into several fights when Jordan had joined the pack — over stupid things. They'd both been venting. Travis's brother had died. He'd needed to fight off some of his frustration. It'd been a private thing between him and Jordan that had ended right when Jordan became Alpha. But he *had* won twice. And against a male as big as Jordan — that couldn't be discounted.

"You'd have won more if I hadn't tired you out. You don't hold anything back for the second half of a fight. I had to admire that even if I also exploited it." Jordan added, "Just don't expect Troy to fight fair."

"Nah. I expect he'll fight rabid and all instinct, though." Which sounded like it'd make for a short fight — and Jordan wasn't wrong about him not holding back. The control he had as a human seemed to desert him as a Lycan in a fight. He couldn't hold anything in reserve.

"He'll fight bat-ass crazy."

Travis grinned and leaned back in his chair. "Miller says the crazy ones are more fun." He'd been talking about women, but it might actually apply in a fight like this.

"Miller is crazy. You should have seen him running off stark naked carrying those semiautomatics at the cabin. Christa's dad said he'd take that image to his grave."

It made him laugh. He could almost picture it, but he

didn't want to.

"Ahhh…I can't believe that was only a few days ago and already Troy is pulling this crap," Jordan said.

"The timing of this scent-match…was poor." He couldn't bring himself to regret it today. He felt more for LeAnn than he had for anyone before her. The scent-match might have forced them to spend time together, but the rest of this was hot-as-hell attraction and…something else. They matched in ways that didn't make any sense because they seemed so opposite. He wanted to cook her breakfast for the rest of their lives. It was insane, but he was going with it.

"Yeah, but we both knew it was a matter of time before Troy challenged you. I should have killed him before this. That's on me. I got soft after that whole thing with Sammy. But he's been a danger to the pack for a good long time. I'd have guessed he'd have beaten Ross to the line on going psycho and killing someone. Anything else you need if this goes south tonight besides me grabbing LeAnn and getting out of there?"

"You'll tell my folks?"

"Sure." He cleared his throat. "I might kill Troy for *his* timing, though. Married three days and this isn't exactly how I'd planned to spend my honeymoon. Chasing ghosts and attending a blood battle."

"I thought you weren't leaving until next week when Christa is fertile."

"Well, we're not, but…"

"What?"

"Christa told me I'm not supposed to talk about her cycle because it's weird, but I never got a real sense of that until after she said something. Maybe it's because she's once a month instead of it being once a year and a big deal. But her scent makes it obvious. Even if she doesn't go into heat."

"It's a little weird," he admitted. He couldn't tell when LeAnn would go into heat. He'd probably be able to tell when it got closer. "I guess that's one difference in having a human mate." And LeAnn was definitely Lycan. He had to keep telling himself that. Because nothing about her made sense otherwise.

"I suppose, but… Okay, Christa's coming. I gotta go."

"You're so whipped."

Jordan laughed. "No, I figure if she's walking around, she's rested up. I told you I was keeping her in our bedroom for the week." And he hung up.

He set his phone down. At least that was one less thing to worry about. Jordan wouldn't let anything happen to LeAnn—if he could help it. He turned back to his computer. Now it was time to track down what Ross might've been driving and see if it might have LoJack.

• • •

This might be a very bad idea, but the scent from the lab coat definitely came from here, and her brother owned no pets but had a vet's business card on his fridge.

LeAnn locked her car and walked toward the veterinary clinic. She'd never been one to skip around a problem when she could approach it head-on. She'd considered going back to Merilee for the information, but it didn't seem right. The poor girl was genuinely scared for whatever reason.

The front office was empty of clients, but there was a familiar scent here, one that matched the lab coat and that day from the bushes. It also had that earthy tone that she was starting to think was a Lycan thing. So this was her welcoming committee. She realized the receptionist was frowning at her. It was odd to walk into a vet's office sans a pet. Then again, it was funny that a Lycan was treating animals.

"I wanted to talk to Dr. Sampson about a non-pet matter."

"Oh, she'll know who you are?"

"Maybe." If she'd been present when Travis had explained she was pack, she would.

A tall, dark-haired woman walked into the reception area, gave her the once-over, and was *so* not impressed.

Huh. Something about this woman made the hairs on the back of her neck stand up and a growl form in her throat. LeAnn'd never hated anyone on sight, but maybe she could make an exception just this once. It was bone deep, instinctual. Sometimes, you just knew.

LeAnn stood a little taller…though not as tall as this freakstar. What was she? Six foot? And she was still wearing heels. Why? To tower over people to intimidate them into submission?

"Alanna, right?"

"Dr. Sampson," she said, slowly enunciating every syllable.

LeAnn narrowed her eyes. Definitely not feeling the love. The rage inside her bubbled up, but she clenched her teeth and forced it down. She could deal with this…woman without losing her temper.

"I'll see you in my office," the vet said.

"Great." LeAnn almost kept the sarcasm out of her voice, so she was calling it a win.

After shutting the door behind them, the woman made

pointed eye contact.

"I thought you were supposed to look down as a sign of respect," LeAnn said. Might as well throw it all out on the table.

"We are." Alanna didn't look down. She raised her eyebrows and folded her arms. "You're not Alpha. You don't even feel like pack."

She snorted while shaking her head. Unbelievable. Was it so wrong to claw another person's eyes out? Maybe LeAnn wasn't pack, but that was *her* decision to make. It was tempting to accept the scent-match just to put this witch in her place. Then again, accepting the scent-match meant being in the pack with her.

This was supposed to be a friendly question-and-answer session regarding the least awkward piece of clothing her brother had snagged. It wasn't going to be. LeAnn pulled the lab coat from her purse and tossed it on the doctor's desk. She'd grabbed it and the business card on the way out the door.

"My lab coat?" Alanna stared at it with a puzzled frown. "How the hell did you get that?"

"I didn't. My brother did. I want to know how and why."

Alanna wrapped her thick dark hair into a twist while considering it. "Well, it would have been easy to grab it from me here—though I'll certainly be more careful with my things. It's not smart to let anything with your scent go… missing." And she smirked.

LeAnn clenched her fist at her side. Oh, her things hadn't gone missing. They'd been taken…by this hag. "That was my favorite sweater," LeAnn said through gritted teeth.

"I have no idea what you're talking about," the liar said.

LeAnn was two seconds from tossing her purse to the side while yelling, "Oh, it is on!" and tackling this chick. "So, why did he have it?"

"I heard he'd stolen some clothing from various pack members to confuse Travis and Jordan into thinking that one of us had killed Colby. Though I'm sure Travis never even considered me a suspect."

LeAnn sucked in a hissed breath. Okay, she shouldn't even be allowed to say his name. LeAnn's fingers itched from the urge to scratch her eyes out. "Because you're not cunning enough?"

"No. Because if I'd killed Colby no one would have found the body."

Nice. Real nice. What a touching public image. *Alanna is so damn smart, we'd never know if she started putting down humans.* Why couldn't Ross have killed *her*?

Speaking of which…

"Was my brother a murderer?" She suspected Alanna might lie about a lot of things, but she'd relish telling the truth this time.

"And a traitor to his kind. He turned the names of all of Glacier Peak in to the poachers to kill."

So there it was. That was her answer. Not just a murderer, but a traitor. She'd just needed to hear it one more time before she could let it go. Damn. It was easier to hear it this time, at least. She'd been ready. LeAnn swallowed and shelved away her feelings for later. Since Alanna was such a font of knowledge, might as well get all of her questions out of the way. "Are you going to the challenge today?"

"Tonight? Of course. All of the *pack* is."

The truth again. Travis had called her pack, but she

wasn't allowed to go to the challenge. "Who is going to win?" Hopefully, her honesty wasn't too brutal on this. She had to say Travis…she had to.

"Well, physically, they're evenly matched, but Travis is a lot smarter than most outside and inside the pack give him credit for, so he'll be better at strategy. Troy wants to be Alpha more—and sometimes passion outweighs intelligence. I suspect Travis will win, but either way, it's probably good to have a doctor there to dispose of the body."

"Body?" LeAnn's stomach tightened, and her mouth went dry. If the good doctor had gut-punched her, it would have surprised her less. *The body?*

Alanna smiled. She'd shocked LeAnn, and it gave her an edge. "Never been to a challenge before? They're quite bloody, and the losing party forfeits his life."

Why hadn't Travis warned her? He was going to be risking his life tonight, but he didn't want her around. He'd even said that scent-matching to her had moved this challenge up. It was partly her fault—well, the scent-match's fault. She'd come here to find her brother, but found a murderer and got herself scent-matched. And that might cost Travis his life.

"So Travis will kill him?" It couldn't end the other way. She refused to even consider it.

The vet shrugged. And damn she looked beautiful and elegant while she did it. Seriously, if this woman ended up in a freezer, she'd deserve it.

"I can't see Travis going for the throat—though it'd be his right. There's also banishment, and if it weren't an honor challenge, but a hierarchy challenge, then the losing Lycan would most likely become Beta…or Omega in some packs. But it is an honor challenge, so it's either banishment or death. Troy will kill him if he wins. He's mentioned it before. If Travis does win, maybe he'll finally pick an Alpha."

"He picked me." He'd said as much, so that wasn't a lie.

"You haven't accepted the scent-match and, well, you don't see me bowing my head. Obviously the position of Alpha has not yet been filled. Perhaps for either gender, but I guess we'll know after tonight."

Perhaps for either gender, my ass. Travis is mine. The position has been filled.

Clicking her tongue, Alanna shook her head. "How is it you know so little about pack rules?"

"I'm not a Lycan. Hell, do you think everyone knows about your little cult rituals? Seriously…a battle to the death? Who does that?"

The other woman inhaled deeply and narrowed her eyes. "I don't know what game you're playing, but you're not going to trick me into believing something that stupid."

"Whatever." LeAnn went to the door and yanked it open. "Stay away from Travis or the claws come out." Travis could be with any other woman, except this one. Well, he could be with any other woman after she left. If she left. While she was here, Travis was hers.

"Watch your back, bitch," Alanna said.

Okay, that was it. She'd found one of her brother's hunting knives earlier. She pulled it out of her pocket and stared hard at Alanna. "That's funny…coming from you." If anyone was going to be tossing around the word "bitch," well… it shouldn't have been the Lycan. "Watch yours or you'll find this buried between your shoulder blades." And she walked out without looking back.

• • •

It was stupid, but Travis was going to have an empty in-box before he went to the challenge—in case the worst happened. He was industriously working his way through all the damn paperwork when her scent hit him, and he looked up to see LeAnn stalking through the small police station toward him after stopping briefly at Betty's desk. He smiled... he shouldn't have—she was in a fury.

Betty stared after her with wide eyes.

He tried to look reassuring, but the scent of LeAnn's arousal was hitting his Lycan side, and he wanted to meet her halfway and drag her onto one of the nearby desks. Instead, he shrugged as LeAnn passed and shut the door behind her.

"So..."

LeAnn narrowed her eyes and pointed an angry finger at him. "That...vet...Alanna Sampson. Did you sleep with her?"

He blinked stupidly. He never quite knew what to expect out of her mouth. Finally, he cleared his throat and said, "This office isn't soundproof, even if no one here is a Lycan." He'd been a professional up until she'd arrived in town. His people had respected him. Now they were avoiding his gaze or watching avidly. Great.

Her face fell, and she blinked furiously and turned away from him.

"Wait...what's wrong?"

"No wonder she was so damn catty. I'm surprised she didn't throw that in my face."

He grabbed her shoulders, but she shook him off. Of

all the times to have a window-enclosed office. The blinds were down on some of them, but he could still feel the eyes of everyone in the office staring at them. Luckily most of his people were out on business, even though January was generally a slow month. "LeAnn, I haven't slept with her. I haven't slept with anyone in the pack."

She didn't turn back around. She just wrapped her arms around herself.

He desperately wanted to hold her, and it felt like a losing battle to stop the inclination. "So, you went to see her?"

LeAnn shrugged, still facing away from him.

"Why?" Jordan's words about LeAnn facing a challenge fight were on replay in his head. Nothing could happen to LeAnn. She was his. *Mine*.

"My brother had her lab coat, and I wanted to know why. I also wanted to tell her to stay the hell away from… uhh…me…though I'm not sure she got that part of it."

"Your brother collected clothing from members of the pack to lay a false trail to…"

"Yeah, I know—to send you and someone else on a wild-goose chase so that he could try to wipe out all of Glacier pack due to some psychotic vendetta. Apparently you all think it's funny to steal people's clothes. That was my favorite sweater. My favorite one."

"I'm sorry someone did that to you. Do you know who it was?" She seemed better at tracking than him…which might be a blow to his ego if she realized she was, and if she recognized that she was a Lycan.

"It's none of your business."

"Actually, it is. They're my pack, and…"

"And I'm not," she said, swinging to face him. She wasn't crying, but her eyes were shiny like she was seconds away from it.

He took a deep breath, shoving down the Alpha inside him. He still should know who was harassing her, but it might need to keep for later—if there was a later. "LeAnn, you are. I've claimed you as my mate. I've told everyone you're pack."

"She said I wasn't…that I didn't feel like it…"

"Alanna?"

LeAnn shook her head, though he couldn't tell if she was answering his question or telling him it was none of his business.

Oh, screw everyone watching. He took a step forward and put his arms around her. He heard Betty gasp and one of his deputies snicker. "You won't feel like pack until you claim the scent-match and attend our meetings and…"

She pulled back to look at him. "Meetings like this challenge?"

"You're not coming to the challenge." The words were sharp and barked like a command, but dammit, she had no idea. She'd never want anything to do with the pack if she saw that, and it wasn't safe for her to attend. This was one thing he could control—one thing he could determine and plan for. If it took his last dying breath, he was going to keep her safe.

"Why don't you want me coming?" She raised her chin and continued to make eye contact.

What the hell had Alanna told her? His first act after the challenge might be to have a serious talk with Alanna about her treatment of LeAnn. He'd said not to antagonize her, and if this wasn't an antagonized LeAnn... Though he couldn't rule out that LeAnn had started it. Alanna seemed too cold and collected to start up a no-holds-barred girl fight.

"You're not coming. I don't want you there, and that's final." He couldn't tell her they might go after her if he lost. She already thought they were all insane. Even if he did win, she'd never accept the scent-match after she saw a challenge fight.

She hissed out a breath.

Oh, right, he'd forgotten he was talking to the only person less likely than Troy to recognize his authority.

She pulled out of his arms and glared at him. It was unfortunate that passion was passion when it came to her scent, and he wanted to sweep everything off his desk and give everyone in the place something to remember. And hell, he might be dead later, so why the hell not?

Then she started blinking faster. When the first tear fell, his heart clenched tightly, and he felt short of breath. Feisty, tough LeAnn and he'd reduced her to this. He'd never felt less like having sex in his life. He tugged her back into his arms, and she didn't resist. "LeAnn, I need to be able to concentrate and…"

"That's not why you don't want me there." She sniffed. "I don't even know why I'm still here. My brother is a homicidal bastard, and I've now threatened two people with knives since I've been here…"

His eyes widened, and he huffed out a breath. "Wait, did you pull a knife on Alanna?"

"Oh, she deserved it more than you did."

That wasn't a huge leap…he'd been sleeping when she'd done it to him. It'd be difficult to be sheriff if she did that all the time. It was unfortunate that hiding knives from her had proven to be so ineffective. "You can't run around threatening people with knives."

"Now you're defending her?" Her voice implied her knife was about to make a third appearance.

"No." There was only one right answer there.

She sniffed again and wiped her face against his shirt.

He winced and tried to be okay with that—though he did glance at the tissues on his desk.

"I should just leave."

It would be safer for her if he let her. Instead, he whispered, "Stay," and kissed her temple.

"Do you like tall women?"

Alanna was six feet tall. "No, hate them."

"I'm a normal height. Five five is normal."

He held her tighter. She felt so good in his arms. So perfect. "You're the perfect height. I can put my chin right on top of your head." It was a ludicrous thing to say, but half their conversations hadn't made any sense in retrospect. Maybe he'd end up telling everyone he wasn't a Lycan either.

She turned her head and pressed her face into his neck while wrapping her arms around his waist. His shirt felt wet where her face had been pressed. It was okay—only because it was her.

"You need a better safe. That one was too easy to get into."

He blinked. Wait. What? Why did he always feel like he was two steps behind LeAnn? He couldn't seem to predict her. She was like chaos theory in action. "You got into my safe? At my house?" He'd left before her, but he'd assumed the worst she'd do was rehide all the knives again. She probably had. Other than whatever knife she had on her.

She nodded.

"Okay." There wasn't much of interest in his safe. Mostly legal documents. Maybe some petty cash. Nothing that she couldn't see. She was his mate, after all. She was a part of his life. Hopefully.

"Your middle name is Dex?"

"Yes. It's tradition to name male children after an Alpha. Not everyone does, but my parents did…so I got the middle name Dex."

"Oh."

"You closed my safe after you were done with it, right?" He couldn't get around the fact that she'd managed to get into his safe.

"Of course I did."

Of course she did. He should really find out what Seamus had dug up about her past. At the very least, he'd likely found a few B&Es. Hopefully she wasn't a wanted felon. If she was, he'd be aiding and abetting a felon…and hopefully eventually having children with her and lots of sex.

"LeAnn, tonight, when I get home, we'll talk about all this."

"You mean after the challenge?"

"Yes."

"The challenge I'm not allowed to go to?"

He took a deep breath and exhaled slowly. "You can't be there. Trust me on this." It was as good as over between them if she saw that side of the pack.

Chapter Six

Oh, she'd be at that challenge.

It would be horrible to be waiting somewhere for him while he was fighting for his life. Nobody might even think to tell her if he did die. Hours would pass, and she'd just be waiting. Or maybe he would win, and she'd still have to wait to hear he wasn't bleeding out somewhere. No. She was going.

After they'd gotten back from lunch, he'd kissed her at her car and asked, "You'll be at my place tonight?"

She'd grabbed him by the neck and kissed him again rather than answer him. How was she supposed to respond to that?

That nice lady who picked up the phones had been leaving for her lunch at the time.

Which was why she'd upped the rating and slammed him against her car while pushing herself against him.

It was worth it to hear the woman say, "Oh my."

Actually, it was flat-out worth it. As far as good-bye kisses went, hopefully it wasn't their last for whatever reason, but they both broke away, out of breath and nearly cross-eyed. Travis clenched one of his fists before shaking it out and she saw that predatory look in his eye—that scalding-hot look that was part wolf. She might have gone too far, because he leaned forward, still meeting her gaze, and said, "If you're not at my place, I'll come find you and drag you back there."

"Kicking and screaming?"

He almost smiled, but he was still trying to tame that wolf look from his eyes. "Maybe some screaming."

She narrowed her eyes. "Tease."

"Stubborn fool."

"Jackass."

"Gorgeous." He dropped one last kiss on her mouth before going back in.

Alanna had said the challenge was "tonight" so she had some hours to kill, and the nervous energy was going to eat her alive if she didn't find something to do. Well, first she needed to find out what time "tonight" was, but that was easy enough, and anyone who'd broken into her brother's place deserved to have her do the same. She drew the line at peeing on his porch, though. Because normal human beings didn't do that.

Troy hadn't even bothered covering his tracks back to his place, and he wasn't home. He also didn't have any of her clothing or Travis's. So that left an unknown person who'd somehow masked their scent…or Alanna. At the very least, Alanna knew something about it. Not that LeAnn was going to tell Travis. She could fight her own battles—especially with that skanky troll Alanna.

Troy was a real freak. His internet search history would make a less jaded person want to impale themselves.

Preferably in the head.

In the eye region.

She did learn what was up with the couch and video equipment at Merilee's. Which was less disgusting than the rest of what he had on his computer.

Invitations to something as primitive as a battle to the death were issued by email? Damn, she could have hacked into Travis's computer.

Seven p.m.

Putting everything back the way she found it, well, most everything, she slipped out of his house. Troy'd be able to tell she'd been here, but she didn't care. Travis would probably freak out if he knew what she'd done.

But if he'd just told her the time…

Hell, he could have cc'd her on the pack-wide email.

When she left the house, it was there in the air. Not near-by, but definitely there. Her brother's scent made her chest hurt. So much for repression. She tracked him slowly and methodically, like Ross had taught her. Block out the other scents as if they were background noise. Focus on the scent as if it were a visible trail and follow it. It wove all over as if her brother had wandered around many of the properties of the pack. She found more of the owners of the clothes he'd taken. No Ross. Only his scent taunting her.

Maybe she was imagining it.

What were the odds?

Probably slim.

Her brother was dead to her either way.

Finally, as the sun started setting, she went back to

Travis's place. Her clothes were there. It made sense. Plus, she needed to check her email. Logging on to his computer was almost too easy. She ran a virus scan while she was on there and scanned his search history before deleting it… because you never knew who might access your computer.

She packed up everything in her car so she could leave if there was nothing here for her anymore when the challenge ended. That might be true regardless of how well Travis did.

Travis's search history had been downright boring. He spent so much time on science sites…no wonder he was sexually repressed. Then it looked like he also sometimes helped kids with their homework online. And this was what he did in his off-hours. When he wasn't out saving the world from criminals. Criminals like her. She'd been so far past three strikes even before she'd killed a man in cold blood.

The scents of the crime scene sometimes hit her in flash-backs. She avoided the meat section in the grocery store because the scent of blood there made everything hazy. It would be humiliating to have one of her naked running spells in the cereal aisle.

Then there was the scent of death. Even roadkill some-times ripped her insides up, and she had to pull over so she could hyperventilate safely.

What could she have done, though? What might she have done differently? He'd deserved to die for what he'd done to that family.

Maybe she'd inherited her dad's animal side, because she'd never felt remorse. Shouldn't you feel that when you take a life?

Travis probably would have felt guilty.

He'd probably feel guilty if, for some reason, he had

to kill Troy tonight, even if that porn-addicted creep had started this whole thing.

A long shower helped her relax…a little, other than all his soap and shampoo smelled like him. Now she smelled like him. It was like wearing his shirt all over again.

At six p.m. she drove over and waited outside Merilee's house. Of all people, she'd be the easiest one to track. The woman reeked of hormones, like she was oozing sex. And her whole house smelled like it, too. She could tell Troy made regular stop-bys. If she'd whiffed even the slightest hint of Travis there, she might have gone ballistic—even if that made no sense.

At fifteen minutes to seven, Merilee flew out of her garage, driving like a speed demon. Hopefully these things never started early. They arrived at a large lodge with five minutes to spare, but she parked farther from the place and walked toward it cautiously. There were a lot of cars. Thirty.

Whoa. How bad of an idea was it to show up uninvited? Three dozen angry Lycans might be ugly. It didn't matter. She deserved to know what happened tonight. If Travis really saw her as a mate and an equal, she would have been invited…it boiled down to that. Hell, if he even saw her as pack, she would have been invited. Her heart ached. It was just as well she'd loaded up her stuff and was ready to go.

She was quiet and kept to the shadows as she approached. Lights flickered on the other side of the lodge, and she circled to find there was a clearing the size of a baseball diamond with citronella torches circling it. Around forty people her age were gathered in a circle, talking.

The back door of the nearby lodge slammed, and Travis stalked out. The circle parted to let him through, and the group hushed and bowed their heads. He was shirtless, and his tattoo was glowing in the flickers from the torches.

She wrapped her arms around her waist and kept back. Her heart felt like it was stuttering and dying. What if he lost this? He couldn't, though.

Suddenly, Travis turned and looked at her, and she shrank back even farther. Of course he could see her. He was a Lycan. Ross had always told her how much better they could see in the dark. Travis looked behind him and nodded in her direction.

Okay, so maybe this was a bad idea. Hopefully the Lycan version of a bouncer didn't kill her.

A moment later, a deep voice whispered from behind her. "Hey...you must be LeAnn." He grabbed her upper arm firmly as he touched her back. "You're okay. Travis sent me."

She twisted to see a giant muscled guy—holy cow...how was this guy not Alpha? At least he wasn't Troy. That was good. He was tanned with dark hair and dark eyes, and she didn't want to be intimidated, but she still swallowed audibly before she whispered, "I'm staying."

He smiled. "Of course you are. And you get to stick near me so no one bothers you."

"Oh." She inhaled. "Oh, your clothes are in Travis's guest room."

He drew her closer to the group as he said, "I was here earlier this week, helping him track. I'm Jordan. I'm the Alpha over the Glacier Peak pack." He let go of her arm when they reached the edge of the circle. He leaned casually against a tree, but she noticed everyone was giving him a wide berth.

The hum of voices picked up again as Travis looked at the ground and seemed to be mentally preparing himself.

"He's going to win, isn't he?" she whispered to Jordan.

Another guy about Travis's size stepped forward on the other side of the circle. He was cocky and kept smiling and nodding at everyone in the circle. That was definitely Troy.

"Yes," Jordan said. "I once saw Travis take down a drunk-and-disorderly who was about twice his size and higher than a kite, too. And not like a sloppy drunk or a mellow high. This guy looked like he'd killed and eaten the last guy he'd faced off with. He attacked Travis the moment he saw him. Travis had his face to the pavement in under a minute. Guy never knew what hit him. And there Travis was reading him his rights while trying to wipe the guy's blood out of his eyes. The idiot got a second wind and tried to swing at him, nearly broke his own arm in the process. And Travis growls at this ass...and slams him back down. They'd drawn a crowd by then, and they all jumped back at that growl. I was afraid I was going to be explaining why their local cop had turned into a wolf, but no, he was fine. Calm as could be...he kept reading him his rights, and the idiot on the ground was as quiet as a kitten after that."

"You were there for all that?"

He nodded.

"And you didn't think to help at all?"

Jordan grinned. "Well, I clapped at the end."

She thought she saw Travis smile slightly, but it might have been a trick of the light.

Then everyone went still as Travis looked up.

Everyone besides the other guy in the circle and Jordan lowered their heads.

"Our hierarchy is pack, honor, Alpha, mate, self," Travis said, speaking firmly with his back ramrod straight. "As your Alpha, it is my honor to lead you when I am the strongest among us. That honor has been challenged. As the good of the pack is of a higher worth than my own life, I choose to answer this challenge. Who challenges me?"

"I challenge you," Troy said, stepping forward. Yeah, she didn't feel a bit bad about breaking into his place. Or kicking in his speakers.

Travis stared at him. "You will abide by our laws and accept the outcome of the challenge even if it costs your life?"

"I will."

Travis smiled…and it wasn't a good smile. If she'd been Troy, she'd have said, "Just kidding," about now. "Last chance, Troy," he said in a completely different voice, less formal, as he crouched into a fighter's stance.

Troy shook his head and dropped down, too. "You don't scare me. Merilee could take you on a bad day."

Across from them, Merilee's eyes widened and she shook her head slightly. Everyone had raised their head now—apparently you were allowed to watch the fight disrespectfully.

"So…trash talk?" she asked Jordan—with raised eyebrows. It'd sounded like there should be tribal drums beating up until then.

"We're still men," Jordan said, shrugging.

Then, quick as lightning striking, both men shifted and Travis snarled and, holy hell, she jumped.

Troy growled back, but it was nowhere as terrifying as Travis's. If her guy's bite was anywhere near as bad as his bark, there was no way Travis could lose.

The two wolves circled, growling under their breaths.

Her heart was pounding. This was insane. It was hard to believe she was even here—that this was even happening.

"He's going to win," she muttered under her breath.

"Of course he will. He's Alpha," Jordan said. He was standing there all relaxed and sure. She wanted to punch him for looking so calm.

Troy leaped forward with a snarl, but Travis darted to the side and turned in time to bite Troy's side. Troy twisted, snapping his jaws at empty air. Travis had already dodged out of the way and was circling again, fangs bared.

Travis's eyes were narrowed and hot. Up until then, she'd known that even if he won, Travis wouldn't kill Troy, but she had her doubts now. That was some serious loathing in his eyes.

Troy jumped forward again, going low, and sank his teeth into Travis's leg, but Travis slipped away while still managing to bite Troy's shoulder. When they went back to circling, she could see blood in both their mouths. Travis wasn't limping, though—that was something. Of course it might be because he was too proud, but she didn't think so.

Snarling and feinting forward, Troy approached, but then danced back. It looked like he was taunting Travis into making the first move this time.

Travis stopped and tilted his head.

"You can almost hear him thinking, 'Troy, you're a dumb-ass,'" Jordan said.

Troy charged forward, and the two rolled as they tried to get their jaws around each other's throats. Travis broke out and jumped at a nearby tree, kicking and twisting on the return so he landed nearly on Troy's back. He sank his teeth into Troy's neck, but Troy bucked him off a second later. Troy dived at him on the ground, but Travis scrambled out of the way.

"Bastard once used that move on me," Jordan muttered.

"Troy?"

"No, Travis. He's lighter weight—it's almost not fair. He moves faster."

"Travis challenged you?"

"No, it was before I was Alpha. He won that time, too. I've got a scar on my neck to show for it. Sneaky bastard. He started that fight if I remember right...it was over this girl named..." He glanced at her. "Uhh, never mind."

Narrowing her eyes, she stared down Jordan.

He smiled.

Troy growled and feinted forward again, drawing her attention back to the fight.

Travis planted his feet and snarled.

She jumped. Geez, Troy should run for it. He didn't. He bolted straight at Travis, and they went for each other's throats. They rolled and snapped, and she couldn't make out who was winning. It was a flash of Travis's tan fur and Troy's darker brown coat, and she held her breath when it slowed and Troy had his teeth sunk into Travis's shoulder. Travis tugged free and backed up.

She exhaled. Good. That was good. Travis was going to win. He had to.

"That's it...tire him out...tire him out," Jordan murmured.

There were large patches of blood on both wolves, and she couldn't tell how bad it was. Most of the blood might be Troy's—she hoped it was.

They went back to circling.

Another snarl from Travis, and this time she was proud that she stayed cool, even if it made her mouth go dry.

Troy couldn't seem to wait out Travis, and he dived forward, but Travis was near a tree again and jumped off it onto Troy's back. This time he didn't get thrown off as fast, and he tore a deep wound into Troy's shoulder that made him howl and buck frantically. When he finally tossed Travis, Troy was limping slightly.

Jordan stared at them with narrowed eyes, and he shook his head. "Idiot is going to make Travis rip him to shreds."

Her stomach clenched. Okay, she couldn't watch that. If that happened, she'd need to turn away. Hopefully everyone in the pack wouldn't think she was a weak baby, but she couldn't keep her lunch if she had to watch that.

Three more lunges and rolls later, Troy was staggering unevenly, even if he'd torn a deep gouge into Travis's side. And they were circling…and circling…and Jordan was right—Troy was going to fight until he was dead from blood loss.

She glanced around, and most of the other watchers were frowning. Alanna was watching with a slight smile and her head tilted. Merilee had her eyes covered and was crying, and a few of the other women had retreated back from the circle. Aside from Alanna, they didn't want this, but it was part of being a pack. They needed Travis to win, even if they didn't want to see Troy suffer. They needed this to trust Travis.

Troy lunged forward, and Travis jumped back. One moment, he was a wolf. The next, Travis'd shifted back and grabbed Troy by the upper body. Twisting, he slammed Troy's head against the ground. Troy's claws slashed his chest before he went limp.

Travis waited by the other Lycan's body, staring.

"I'll be damned. I've never seen that before," Jordan whispered. "There's no way I could keep my wolf's instincts reined in enough to think of that in a fight. Travis has an almost sick level of control."

Merilee looked up and sniffed. The clearing was quiet other than Travis's thick breaths as he stood watching Troy.

Troy drew in a breath, but didn't move.

"Knocked him unconscious," Jordan said, tilting his head. He nodded at the two. "He should kill him."

Travis reached out a hand and pressed it against the wolf's neck. Then he stood up, looking somber, and went back to where his pants were and pulled them on. "Liam, when he comes to, make sure he's gone by tomorrow." He twisted his arm to look at a gash on the back with a scowl.

"I would've killed him," Jordan said, still looking at Troy.

"Why?" she whispered.

"He's vindictive, and he enjoys seeing things suffer. He's got no place in a pack, because he's got a mean streak that he doesn't mind feeding." He clenched his teeth. "He's like a dog that's got a taste of blood so you have to put it down. That's Troy."

She shuddered. Her ex had been like that. Someone should have put him down. "I can understand that. I can't see Travis ever doing it, but it makes sense."

"You okay?" Jordan asked her.

She nodded. Her relaxing muscles felt shaky from how tightly wound she'd been. The adrenaline crash from this was going to be nasty. But he'd won. And that was all that mattered. "He did good." She was sorta proud of her man.

"Told you he'd win."

She smiled halfheartedly. It was over.

It felt good to see the pack so subdued, and she could almost feel them pulling together to get beyond this...to get over this. It did feel like family—it felt like when Ross had pummeled her ex to protect her. You did what you did to protect the people you cared about, and sometimes it was violent. This made sense.

"Do you need that stitched up?" Alanna called to Travis, who was wiping the blood from his mouth while examining the gash to his side.

LeAnn wanted to tear into the woman. Even if she was a doctor...no...just no...

Jordan chuckled softly, and Travis went still.

"What?" LeAnn muttered.

"You growled," Jordan said, clearly amused. "I take it you and Alanna aren't BFFs?"

"I'm fine," Travis called over his shoulder. He spit out blood from his mouth and shook his head, as if trying to clear it.

"That wasn't a bad growl," Jordan said. He inhaled. "Travis tells me you said you're not a Lycan."

"Of course I'm not," she said, still watching Travis. She saw Alanna look up and stare at her. What the hell was her problem?

"He said that, too," Jordan said.

"That I'm not?"

"No, that you're a lot of fun."

She turned and squinted at Jordan. Was that supposed to make sense?

Everyone went still as Travis tossed down the towel he'd

been wiping the blood from his mouth on. He turned toward the circle. Everyone lowered their heads, except her…and Jordan. She bit her lower lip. Maybe she should bow her head. If it was a sign of respect…

"My place as Alpha stands. My will is law," Travis said. "LeAnn is my mate and is pack, and she's not to be harmed."

Even if no one was looking at her, she felt their eyes on her.

Then Travis looked up and stared at her, and he was livid. He had not wanted her here. The force of his anger hit her hard—like a hurricane. It knocked the breath from her lungs and made her chest ache. LeAnn looked down—not from shame, or from respect, but because she'd seen that look before in a man's eyes, and she hadn't wanted to see it in Travis's. She'd disobeyed him, and he was furious. She wasn't his mate—mate implied they were partners, equals. She was his possession. And he'd told her to stay away. She wasn't in this damn pack. Actions were louder than words. So that was that.

"I take it you were told not to come?" Jordan said quietly.

She felt the moment Travis turned away, and she glanced up to see Alanna smirking at her from the other side of the circle. She'd been chastised in front of someone who was begging to have her eyes clawed out. Fan-freaking-tastic. The knife Travis had rammed into her heart twisted.

She had to get out of here. She had to leave. LeAnn spun away as Travis went to go into the lodge and the others began moving again, their supernatural stillness over.

Jordan caught her arm. "He'll want to talk to you."

LeAnn jerked her arm from his grasp. She had a few

seconds before she started crying, and she was not going to cry here in front of Alanna. "Oh, I really don't think he will." There was nothing left to say to each other. That look of his had said a whole helluva lot. Bastard. She'd thought he was different. She'd thought he was kind. Stupid. Stupid. Why did she always think this time it'd be different?

"LeAnn." Jordan tried to grab her again, but she stepped away.

"It's fine. Really," she said, walking quickly to her car. It wasn't fine, but if she could fake it until she was far away from here—she might actually believe it.

· · ·

He was in the bathroom washing the remainder of the blood from around his mouth and face when the door swung open and Jordan stepped in. He spit more of the blood from his mouth. He'd be tasting Troy's blood long after he'd washed it out. And LeAnn had seen him like this. There was no way she'd accept the scent-match after that. It was even uglier than the few challenges he'd seen. Troy was determined to see it out.

Jordan closed the door behind him and locked it.

Travis threw him a glance over his shoulder. "You probably still shouldn't have left LeAnn alone."

"Oh, I didn't."

He froze. "Somebody was with her?" There was a spike of jealousy through him. He wanted to shred whoever had approached her. He shook it off, blinking.

"No, she stormed off after your little death glare. You should have started off the challenge with that. I think even

Troy would have dropped dead." Jordan sounded pissed… well, he didn't understand how bad it was that LeAnn had come.

Maybe he'd gone a little far with that look he'd given her, but she might have distracted him at a time when he needed his control, and he'd had a good reason for insisting she stay away. "I told her not to come. In fact, I *ordered* her not to come." She should have trusted his judgment.

"Yeah, I think Christa would have shot me if I'd tried that. At the very least, I would have taken two shoes and a lamp to the head."

He tossed the wet rag into the sink and turned to face Jordan. "She shouldn't have been here. She's never been to a meeting with a pack ever…and that's her first experience?"

"So what? Instead she was supposed to sit around knitting and hope you came home alive?"

He shook his head. "She didn't know what was at stake. I didn't tell her."

"Oh, she knew. Someone told her."

Travis looked in the direction of the door and shook his head. "Alanna. Alanna must have told her." He grabbed the towel again and ran it across the gouge in his side. He should have it stitched up. Though he wouldn't have had Alanna do it even if LeAnn hadn't reacted to the other woman like she had. If he'd gone near LeAnn smelling like Alanna, she'd have challenged the other woman.

"That's deep," Jordan said, nodding at the cut.

It was still bleeding. "I'll live."

"You wouldn't have if you'd let your vet stitch it up. I thought you'd lived through the challenge only to have LeAnn take your head off there."

He gave a weak laugh. "That was fairly impressive."

"Especially for a non-Lycan."

He glanced up at Jordan and almost smiled. LeAnn. He'd have to catch up with her. Maybe he could downplay how bad that challenge was. Though not if he was still bleeding everywhere. "Are you gonna let me bleed to death or are you gonna help me?" he asked as he pulled a first aid kit from under the sink.

"So, she really doesn't think she's a Lycan?" Jordan asked as he sorted through the first aid kit. "We could try gluing it."

"That might make it stop bleeding, at least. No, she really doesn't."

"But she is. She could see in the dark as well as any of us—and she smells like a Lycan."

"Yeah, well, didn't you tell me the crazy ones are hot when I brought up Cheri earlier this week?" Jordan didn't really have a leg to stand on with this conversation. His alpha female prior to Christa had gone psycho and tried to kill people, too.

"I don't think I said hot. I might go with Miller on this, though. She does seem like a lot of fun." He opened the tube of glue they kept in the kit and frowned at it critically.

"Fun. Hot. The difference being?" He really needed to get out of here and go after LeAnn.

"You're going to hold still so I don't wind up glued to you, right?"

Travis gave him a bland look.

"Okay, but this might sting." He leaned in and applied the glue to the seam of the torn skin.

"Holy effing dammit to hell...hell...that's..." He hit a

fist on the countertop. That stung like hell.

"Well, the difference between hot and fun is that, though they're both three-letter words, they use different letters of the alphabet, and I'm not letting it get back to Christa that I said some other woman was hot."

"They're both three-letter words? Really?" He slammed his hand against the countertop again. "What the hell is in that? That can't just be glue. Is it like acid?" He said every profane word he knew. Twice.

"Those are four-letter words. Look. I can count even higher. *Sesame Street* would be proud."

"You're an ass—another three-letter word—and I can actually feel my IQ dropping." Travis took a deep breath. Okay, that was better. *Now* he might live.

Jordan tossed the capped glue back into the first aid kit. "At least you didn't take a blow to the head. That was clever. I'd never have thought of shifting to pound their head against the ground to knock them out. I've seen them go unconscious due to blood loss—and that's where Troy was headed. Shifting was smart if you weren't going to kill him."

"Yeah, well, punching a wolf like you and Dane sounded mean." Though he'd considered it. He hadn't partly because he didn't want Jordan claiming it as his suggestion—which Jordan would have.

Jordan grinned. "And you're all flowers and candy." He pointed at the cut on his arm. "You want to do that one, too."

"No, I think I'll opt to staple my tongue rather than go through that again."

"You *are* a big baby."

He sighed. "Was she upset?"

"LeAnn?"

Travis nodded. He'd been a bit high on adrenaline and worried it was over between them.

"Oh, she was crying before she'd even made it ten feet away. I think if you were going for cowed and brokenhearted, you nailed that one. She's sweet, too—even if she is crazy. I wanted to slam your head against the ground when she started crying."

He closed his eyes in one long blink. He'd made her cry. Again. He was an ass. He was such an ass. He wanted to punch something. Clenching his teeth, he hissed out a breath. He could fix this. He was smart enough to fix this. Maybe she was at his place…or Ross's.

"You've got another problem," Jordan said, rubbing the side of his face while frowning.

"What?" The last thing he needed was more problems.

"I've seen a pack handle a few extra alpha males for a good long time, but having two females who want to be Alpha—that gets ugly fast. LeAnn needs to accept the scent-match, and even then, you might need to get rid of Alanna."

"She's a vet here. She was even here first—with her practice. I can't toss her out because she and LeAnn aren't getting along."

"Then they're going to kill each other. And when you do find LeAnn, and you've fallen down on your knees and groveled your way back into her life, you should thank every higher power out there that she saved you from Alanna. The way Alanna looked during that fight—I'd call it vastly entertained. Alanna would have carved out your liver by the end of the year, and you can ask Cheri—that's not as fun as it sounds."

Travis snorted. Even if Jordan had a point…

"Well, this has been fun, but I'm heading home to my wife after I pick her up from Dane's. I didn't trust her alone just in case Ross really is out loose." He yawned. "And I have to show Lucifer who's Alpha again. He thinks all our time spent in the bedroom means he owns the rest of the house. Damn thing."

"Christa's cat?"

Jordan shook his head as he went to the door. "I think I'd have better luck with the actual Satan."

"Jordan, thanks."

"Don't mention it, and don't call me tomorrow." He opened the door and stopped. "And so help me if anyone challenges you again this week, I'll come kill them in the night."

Well, that was loud enough for his pack to hear, and almost made him smile.

"One more thing. Give me a hint." If he couldn't find her quickly, he might beg Jordan to come back and help—and that wouldn't be pretty.

He pointed south. "She was headed that way when I walked inside."

Chapter Seven

Why had she thought he could be different? He didn't even know the worst of it—of that other side of her and the things she'd done. If he didn't like her now… LeAnn jerked a hand across her eyes where hot tears steadily leaked. For once, it wasn't raining, and yet her vision was as wet and blurry as if it was. *Stop it! Stop it, he's not worth it!* LeAnn bit her lip and the pain stopped the tears. She wasn't like this. She couldn't afford to be weak. She hit the steering wheel with her fist. Dammit, why had she started hoping again?

Some people were meant to be alone.

And she started crying all over again.

She drove, trying to get lost. Something held her back from leaving. It was ridiculous. In the end, she followed the same path she had previously and ended up at the closed-for-the-season trailhead where she stopped and parked. It was cold outside, but she still got out. This time she didn't scream…she didn't feel like it. She just cried and cried.

"This is so stupid," she said, trying to stop as she leaned against the hood. She should leave. She should have driven straight to the airport and boarded a plane to somewhere…anywhere…someplace warm, maybe. She should have gotten out of this crazy, crazy town where things like a wolf fight made sense and where her brother had thrown it all away. For one brief and shining moment after the fight, she could see herself joining a pack where they banded together for strength and fought out their differences. She could see herself in a pack with Travis. And it'd blown up in her face.

That look from Travis…

She didn't belong in the pack. He didn't want her in it. The scent-match might be forcing his hand, but… It was the same old song all over again with a different verse. Life kept tying her to people who didn't actually want her. Her mother. Her brother. Now Travis. This was the worst of them all. Her mother and brother had seemed to know there was a side of her that should be kept hidden—a darkness she was born with. She'd even seen that side to Ross—though she'd never guess he'd be capable of murder and betrayal. Travis hadn't seen that side…that wasn't who he was rejecting.

A raw sob broke free, and she wrapped her arms around her waist.

Damn you, Travis. Why did you make me want things again? Why did you make me believe?

She'd done this before, too. Clayton had started off so nice. Then he'd sensed something in her that needed to be beaten out. He said she didn't respect him—he could see it in her eyes. She'd changed herself over and over again because being alone was so damn hard, but it was never enough. She was never enough.

Okay, so maybe she couldn't follow orders.

But sometimes orders were stupid.

And just the fact that Travis hadn't wanted her there, when it was partly her fault his life was on the line, meant that he didn't see her as anything more than a possession. And she'd had enough of that.

She'd been doing so well, too. She'd learned to wall up and repress that side of her that blazed through emotions, the side that ached and raged and craved. She'd buried it under sarcasm and detachment. And Travis Flynn had blown it all.

LeAnn scrubbed at the tears on her face, only to have new tears replace them. Ugh. She was not a crier, and yet here she was—bawling her eyes out.

One more day of looking for Ross. Maybe he was visiting the pack because he had regrets…maybe he wanted to make it right somehow. If she found him, she didn't know what she'd do, but she still wanted to find him.

One more day and one more day. Listen to her. She sounded like an addict. Travis Flynn was simply another addiction she couldn't seem to walk away from. He was that empty house in a rich neighborhood with a shoddy alarm— too beautiful to resist.

"I never should have come here," she whispered. Even as quiet as it was, it echoed. So she shouted it. "I never should have come here!"

Then she went back to her car and waited for the sun to rise on another *one more day.*

She slept in uncomfortable segments of time. An hour here

and there when she could stop her brain from thinking and obsessing and when she had the car warm enough to sleep in. Finally, she gave up on an actual sunrise, because a light mist had started falling in the early hours and it looked like the sky getting slightly brighter was all she'd get. It fit her dark mood.

LeAnn drove back to her brother's without a single wrong turn. It was a sad fact that she couldn't seem to get lost, no matter how hard she tried.

When she got there, she dragged his map out and spread it across the table. Today was definitely the last day. If Ross was around here, he had to be holing up somewhere during the night. It was cold as hell last night, even with the cloud cover trapping some heat in.

She felt eyes on her. With a sad feeling of resignation, she went to the cupboard and pulled out the Tupperware with the clothes in it and tossed it out on the front porch. They might as well have this out. She usually was gone before a confrontation. That was her MO, even if it wasn't Travis's. But if he was going to come yell at her for being there, he should at least be dressed. It'd help her concentrate.

There were limits, though. If he threw a punch, she was stabbing him…nonlethally. She couldn't imagine him doing that, but he'd been furious, and she hadn't known him long. He could yell all he wanted. Maybe that would help her quit this place and end this addiction. Finally. She had to get out of here.

The door opened almost silently, and he approached slowly from behind her as she bent over the map, trying to ignore him. If she focused on the map, she could maybe not cry over this ridiculous relationship they had where she'd fallen for him in a matter of days. Why him? Why now?

His hands touched her sides, and his body was only inches behind her. They both waited, tensed.

Then he wrapped his arms around her waist and put his face down against her neck as he pulled their bodies together.

She blinked. This wasn't at all what she'd expected. Where was the yelling? Where was the Travis of last night who'd glared at her and was furious?

A moment later, he pulled back, took the gun from the back of her waistband, set it on the table beside her hand, and went back to holding her with his face pressed against her skin.

It didn't make sense. He didn't make sense.

His ice-cold skin made her shiver.

Her pulse picked up. The only reason he'd be out in the cold was if he was looking for her. And maybe not to yell at her if his behavior was any indication. He'd had plenty of time to work up a whole lot of anger, and he didn't seem mad. Actions spoke louder than words, but she still wanted to hear him say it. "Have you been out all night?"

He nodded. Lifting his head, he whispered against her shoulder. "I think sometime around three a.m. I found religion…when it started to rain and I couldn't follow your trail any longer."

She swallowed. "I didn't think you'd look for me when I didn't come to your place."

"I've traced your steps for the last few days like twenty times over. Troy had recovered well enough to shout about what you'd done to his speakers, by the way. You were somewhere south of here, I think, but you backtracked and went down enough forestry roads that…" He shook his head, his lips brushing her skin with each movement. "I am not a tracker. I've never felt that inadequate." He sighed, a ragged sound. "And then the rain came."

"But you didn't want me." That look he had given her would stick with her for a long time. It said a lot of things, especially considering the reason behind it: he hadn't wanted her to be in the pack or that part of his life.

"Not want you?" He pulled her tighter against him and kissed her neck. "I want you. I need you. I'm a little crazy over you." He kissed her neck again. "I didn't want you there at the challenge because I didn't want you seeing that. And hell, if I'd failed, I didn't want Troy going after you to prove something. That would have ripped me to shreds more than he could."

Her mouth went dry, and she sucked in a shaky breath. He wanted her? But… That just didn't happen, not in her life. He needed her? None of this made sense. As much as she wanted it to be true, she couldn't ignore what had happened. At the very least, he hadn't wanted her to be involved with his pack and that was half his life…maybe more. "But you said that I'm pack and the pack was supposed to be there." Either she was pack or she wasn't.

He went still and murmured against her skin, "I thought there was no way you'd ever want to be pack if you saw that."

"But that made sense." His lips against her skin felt heavenly. It was frying her synapses, making it difficult to concentrate on all the reasons why she should walk out of here right now.

"Me not wanting you there?"

"No, why the pack would be there for a challenge and

why it was important to prove that Troy didn't belong but that we all belong to you." We. She'd said "we." Hopefully he hadn't noticed. His arms tightened around her, and his sigh gave her goose bumps.

"I was an ass. I forgot that you'd be instinctually drawn to pack behavior. It's been a long time since I've been outside a pack and joined one."

"I've never been in a pack."

"You are now."

She exhaled noisily. That was…impossible, wasn't it? His arms around her felt like the only thing holding her together. It was a crazy thought. Pack. She was pack.

He went back to kissing her neck. It didn't help with her goose bumps. His words made her heart burn in her chest. She shouldn't want to be pack. It wasn't like a family, even if it might have felt like it last night for a short amount of time.

Most of all, she wasn't pack. "I thought I had to accept the scent-match." He could say she was pack until he was blue in the face, but until the rest of them accepted it, she wasn't.

He went still. "Are you?"

She shrugged, and her shoulder bumped against his face. Wow, his nose was cold. Then she shook her head. At one point, the cold, harsh light of reality would have intruded into this beautiful fantasy—might as well be now. "Travis, you don't want me. You only think you want me because of this crazy thing between us and because you don't know enough about me." She couldn't tie him to her. He didn't *know* her.

"Then tell me about you."

Well, she'd opened herself up for that. She bit her

lower lip. He had a right to know what he was getting into. But where should she start? And then if he hated her…or wanted to arrest her…

He seemed to sense her indecision and reached out and tapped his gun on the table. "You got into my gun safe. I thought it was a good one."

"Well, it is, but it's not Fort Knox."

"I noticed there wasn't a knife with these clothes in that Tupperware. Should I disarm you just in case I say something wrong?"

"I traded you the knife for the gun."

"I appreciate that." He kissed her neck. "There was only one shirt in there, too."

The other was packed in her luggage. She was a sad, pathetic addict.

"What was the gun for?" he asked.

"In case Troy won. Though there was no way that was going to happen."

"You were going to shoot Troy?"

She shrugged. It was what it was. No one got away with attacking Travis. Well, except her, and she wouldn't do that again. Probably.

"The pack would have killed you."

She shrugged again. "But I would have shot Troy, and that would have felt damn good."

He shook his head. "I'm glad Jordan came."

"I would have shot him, too, if he'd tried to stop me."

He slid the gun farther away from her. He inhaled against her neck before kissing it again. "You smell so good. I'm not letting you out of my sight for the rest of my life. For so many reasons."

She smiled and blushed—both were stupid. "You don't even know me."

Pulling back, he tugged off his shirt and dropped it before wrapping his arms around her again. He slid his hands under her shirt to rub the hot skin on her stomach.

She felt all her synapses frying again. Swallowing, she said, "When I was almost fourteen, my mom said I was just like my dad—that I reminded her too much of him—and she didn't want anything to do with me. It was a change from the screaming fights and the accusations, but obviously not one for the better. She just…gave up on me. She quit—like I was too much for her to even tolerate. I wasn't even worth yelling at anymore."

"Did she say you were like him because you could see so much better in the dark and hear better, or because you looked like him?"

She frowned. "Probably everything about me. She hated my dad."

"Hm. Okay. Go ahead."

She cleared her throat. "And so we stopped speaking to each other, and I moved out when I was fifteen. I moved in with some friends. I went to school sometimes…sometimes not….and…" She paused and looked over her shoulder at him.

He took the opportunity to kiss her cheek and the corner of her mouth.

"You have a really unhealthy fascination with volcanoes…and algebra…but mostly volcanoes."

"Uhh. How do you…?"

"Oh, I logged in to your computer. I updated a few things. You had some adware running in the background that I killed. But volcanoes?"

She felt him smile against her neck before he said, "Rainier is an active volcano. So is Glacier Peak. They're both on par with Mount Saint Helens for danger of erupting."

"I know that now. I checked a few of the sites to see if they were some sort of veiled porn sites, but they really were about volcanoes."

"Did these friends you moved in with teach you your hacking skills?" He liked to do that…talk about only one thing until they were done with it.

"No, I'm not really much of a hacker, but it's easy to figure out passwords when you touch the same keys again and again, and you're not much for typing. Troy's was even easier. I'm not sure he uses his keyboard for anything other than putting in his password—and looking up creepy sites that make me want to boil my eyes. I should have shot him anyway."

Travis moved the gun farther away again. "Is that how you get into safes—scent?"

"And sound and finding keys that you keep in the bottom of drawers thinking no one actually looks in drawers, but keys smell different than clothes. Keys and I have an… affinity."

"Hell, you might be better than Jordan."

"At what?" Jordan was huge. There wasn't a whole lot she'd be better at.

"At finding things."

"Oh. Maybe." She sighed. "I started that when I moved out. Stealing things. Not things that would be missed right away. Just things that people tried to hide from other people. And things they could afford to lose. I tried to stop a bunch of times, but…I'd slip back into it."

"Have you ever been convicted?" He was still kissing her shoulder and neck, and he was acting like this wasn't a big deal.

"No. I've never been caught. I usually wear gloves, but I might have my fingerprints on some unsolved case somewhere."

That made him stop. She bit her lip. Now it came. Now he'd ask her to get out of his sight.

"Okay." Then he bit into her neck and sucked, and she arched her back and tipped her head against his shoulder. Oh. Whoa. When he moved on, she was pretty sure he'd left a mark and that was okay, because she was already branded as his on the inside for the most part.

She swallowed and tried to slow her racing heart. "Then, five years ago, my mom was dying, and she had a change of heart and told me about Ross. And after I met Ross, I wanted to be better, but I kept slipping back into stealing because the money was so good and it was so easy."

She inhaled and exhaled. She could do this. He deserved to know who she was and why this wouldn't work out.

"Three years back, I was out…at night…and I ran across a guy holding a family hostage in their house." Her hands clenched into tight fists, and she blinked. "I forget things. Sometimes on purpose. Sometimes not. But whenever I close my eyes—this is waiting." She swallowed. "And the time is all funny—like some of it seems as if it lasts forever but I barely remember getting into the house. And it was dark that night, but it's all so bright in what I see in my head. It's lit up—like Christmas." She huffed out a breath. "I mean like hell—like the worst sort of hell. And the smell…"

The kids' crying drew her from her run. She hated to hear kids crying. Kids should be happy and know they're loved.

She stared up at the mostly dark two-story. The hallway lights upstairs were on, as well as one dim light in one of the rooms. It was probably nothing. A nightmare. A nightmare that two kids shared?

LeAnn glanced up and down the street and pulled her hoodie up over her head. She'd check and be back to her run in a couple minutes. Nodding to herself, she took inventory of all her options. Most of the entry points on the front of the house were out if she wanted to leave no trace. Jogging silently, she hopped the waist-high fence and examined the back of the house, avoiding the kids' toys that littered the yard. See, they had toys—toys they were allowed to leave everywhere. Clearly, their parents loved them. It was good that she was checking things out. LeAnn sighed. So much for her latest resolution not to do this anymore.

The dining room window was open and the screen lay on the ground.

Worry soured her stomach and made her pulse pick up.

Hell, it wasn't just the kids crying. There was a woman... sobbing—trying to be quiet.

No. Something was very wrong. She slipped into the house a moment later. Adrenaline hit her system, making her hands shiver.

"Don't...just take the money...take it all...just..." The man sounded terrified.

"Shut up! I told you—just shut the hell up." A gun cocked.

She huffed out a breath. Of all the times to have nothing… She looked around. Think, LeAnn! Think! The sobbing upstairs was too much. She couldn't just stand here. There had to be something. She opened the closet beside her, hoping for a baseball bat, and found something far more deadly. Her hands shook as she loaded the handgun as quietly as she could.

Then she was walking up the stairs. It took forever. It was like there were five times as many stairs, and yet she still stumbled over the top, catching herself before she could be heard.

What was she doing? She fought for control. Her vision went hazy like when her rage took over, but she didn't feel angry—this was terror. What was she about to see?

Her pulse pounded as she slipped down the hallway, past empty rooms. They were in the bedroom at the end. A bedside light must be on.

The crying. The crying was making her ache and weak and… Then the smells hit her. Blood and sex and fear—so much fear. Her throat jerked as she gagged.

"Make her shut up!" And there was movement in the room. Bodies scrambled and the sobs broke and were choked back.

She gripped the gun in her hand as she put her back to the wall beside the door. LeAnn exhaled slowly. Her blood was coursing too fast for her to be as calm as she was at the gun range, but she couldn't wait for something that impossible.

Ducking her head around quickly, she counted heads and marked locations. The family was all against the outside wall with the bastard between her and them, and he had a gun hanging at this side.

"If you don't make them shut up…"

There was no time. They were crying again. Even the father was crying this time. There was no time. She spun and entered the room. She lined up his body with a blank spot of wall.

Pop. Pop. Pop. Her arm jerked in quick succession. He was dead with the first shot, but she couldn't stop. The window in front of him shattered with the third shot. Dropping the gun to her side, LeAnn sucked in a shuddering breath and wished she hadn't.

Death had a scent all its own.

She saw it in a bright strobe of horror—the bedside lamp seemed like a spotlight suddenly. The little girl looked down at the blood that had spattered across her and started shrieking, screaming.

LeAnn took it all in and then closed her eyes against it.

She'd been too late. Why hadn't she gone for a run earlier? The woman was so bloody and that smell of sex…was so recent. And the kids…wide-eyed and horrified. The father was trying to shield them all with his body. The hell of it… she could never open her eyes again. Her whole body was shaking.

And the screaming didn't stop.

She'd just killed a man in front of two little kids.

She'd shot him in the back.

And she ran—from the smell, from the screaming, from the part of her that had felt…powerful.

She jerked and blinked. The blackness of her vision receded, and she drew in a deep breath. It was gone—that fast—and all she remembered was the highlight reel of blood and bruises and the glass breaking…and the scents…oh, the scents. She swallowed a moan. For a year after it happened, the smell of sex activated her gag reflex.

Travis's arms were holding her snug against his warm body; his thumb was stroking the skin of her stomach soothingly. "Shh, LeAnn. It's okay. You can tell me," he murmured against her skin before he pressed a kiss on her shoulder.

She inhaled again and tried to even it out. She didn't know what happened during her blackouts. It made her feel vulnerable that he'd been here for one. Licking her lips, she cleared her throat. "Uhh. Sorry. I space out sometimes." Who knew how long she'd been gone that time. The fog cleared from her head. "So, yeah. I could hear the crying from outside. The wife was a mess. He'd beaten her, raped her, and the kids couldn't stop crying. I got into the house, found the father's gun…and shot the guy…when he had his back to me. I didn't give him a chance to do anything more or explain or anything, and I didn't call the police. I just shot him. His blood…it got on the little girl and freaked her out. I dream about that sometimes."

He kissed her neck. "It's not your fault."

She chewed on her lower lip. "And I got the hell out of there. I ran for an hour before I realized I still had the gun in my hand, and then I puked into someone's bushes for what seemed like days. They looked for me for a while—police and other people—so I moved, changed my last name… again. I did that every so often." She sighed. "The wife committed suicide a year later. I checked on them. I wish I'd gotten there sooner. Some things you can't live with, I guess."

"I'm sorry." His voice had a raw edge she hadn't heard before.

She shrugged. "It was a bad time. I'd been trying to hold down jobs and be...normal. I'd even been paying taxes with my new name. I started dating this guy. He thought I had... too many opinions. He used to shove me around—punch me."

Travis tightened his arms.

"I thought maybe I deserved it, so I let it happen. Then I ended it, and it still kept happening. Ross came to visit." She smiled. "He kicked my ex-boyfriend's ass—thoroughly— and he told me no one should treat a woman like that."

"Maybe Ross wasn't as bad a brother as I thought."

"No. He wasn't." She looked down. "He did good things, too. I think maybe our parents messed both of us up a bit. When your family doesn't want you, it makes you desperate to find that thing that'll fix that hole in your life. He felt it, too. He said there was this girl he liked two years ago, but she'd disappeared. I guess she died. He was different after that. He didn't want to talk to me anymore. I was surprised when he up and called out of the blue."

"That's what he has against Jordan and Dane from Glacier. The girl he liked killed two people, and either Dane or Jordan killed her when she was attacking Dane's mate."

She sighed. "It doesn't make it right, of course—what Ross did—but...we're so messed up. Anyway, I asked him to teach me how to track after that thing with the family being held hostage. I thought maybe I could do some good with my skills instead of stealing things. Every so often, I did. Stopped a few attacks out on the streets. I got stabbed once for it by the victim, who was all panicked and crazy. I thought that was unfair." She cleared her throat. "Anyway, so you and I don't fit. A cop and a thief…maybe a murderer?" She shook her head.

He shook her lightly. "You are not a murderer. And right now, it looks like LeAnn Wilcox is in data entry and gainfully employed."

She laughed—weakly. She was drained by all she'd said. Her bones felt like noodles. His arms were the only things holding her upright. "Yeah, but do you know how boring that is? I mean, I'm fast at typing—fast at a lot of things, but you can't get in trouble if they catch you typing and doing your job. They give you raises and eventually that gets boring, too. Besides, I gave notice before coming here. And I still steal things all the time."

She could feel his smile against her skin as he said, "I can't imagine that."

She waited. But that's all he said. "And?"

"And what?"

"I told you I'm doing the things you arrest people for all the time and you don't have anything to say about it?"

"Well, as I see it, I have two options."

She was certain her heart had stopped beating and sat there like a lead weight in her chest. She took a deep breath and held it. Here it came. Whatever happened, she should be ready for it. No more tears.

She'd never been in a relationship that actually felt like a relationship. And it was about to end. As it should. Because she didn't deserve good things.

"First, I can make sure you don't ever get caught… which it sounds like you're pretty damn good at avoiding. I imagine being able to see in the dark, hear well, and move quietly helps."

What? That didn't sound very letter-of-the-law for a guy who seemed to like control as much as Travis did. She exhaled in a huff. This made no sense.

"Second option…"

Her pulse pounded in her ears in the silence his words left. She swallowed thickly. Here it came…he hauled her in. It was over. He'd deserved to know, but it was over.

"Second option is that I find some way to keep you busy so that you're only stealing from me. There's gotta be a few jobs around that'd use your skill set that are legal. I know I could use a good tracker every so often, and it'll be nice to not have to drag Jordan over here ever again."

She blinked rapidly and she felt light-headed. Pressing her hands to her stomach, she tried to process his words. He wasn't taking her in. How could that be? He might actually let her use her…skills? This had to be a trick. "Travis?"

"Yes?"

"Neither of those involves you arresting me." Her whole life had been spent waiting for the other shoe to drop once she revealed her darker side. Now she was here and nothing was happening.

"No. In fact, I'm glad I never fingerprinted you to find out your name…besides the fact that it sounds like it would have been pointless."

"Do you not understand what I am? Who I am?" She was shaking from the release of finally telling someone, and he was acting like it was nothing. How could he be acting like it was nothing?

He kissed her temple. "Oh, I think I might understand you better than you do yourself."

"Maybe I didn't explain it well enough." There had to be words she could use so that he'd see what her mother saw—what others saw. It was suddenly imperative that he see her for who she was. She'd come this far. He knew more than anyone…and it felt like a relief. Her mind dragged her memory for something she could confess that would make him see the real her.

"LeAnn, I'm not judging you. It's enough." He hugged her tightly. "Let it go. You deserve some peace in your life."

It was too good to be true. So either the bottom was about to drop out, or she was asleep. She couldn't trust something that seemed this good and real. She didn't entirely trust Travis in fact, though she wanted to. That was a start, right? She wanted this. Maybe enough to stick around and see what was wrong with it.

He cleared his throat. "So, as I said, going forward, we'll deal with it together."

"And you won't arrest me?" This was madness…from the sanest, most logical man she knew.

"No, but I might bring out my handcuffs for other reasons." He sighed. "In fact, I'm tempted to handcuff you to me for the next month so I don't have to chase you down anytime soon." He tapped the map. "What were you looking for?"

"Well, I'd decided to stay one more day and look for my brother one last time."

"Yeah, I'm definitely handcuffing you to me. And we'll be taking a lot of showers."

Her cheeks heated up at that. The idea had its appeal. In fact, she could almost visualize it. Him. Naked. Rivulets of water coursing down his muscled chest, along his abs, and…

"Speaking of which, I should really drag you home with me and do that now."

"Handcuff me to you?" Her voice had sounded squeaky. *Control yourself, LeAnn.*

"No...well, yes...but also, shower." He stepped back. "I'm covered in layers of dirt."

He smelled good. His scent was stronger from exertion, and the dirt didn't detract from it very much. He smelled amazing. She turned around to tell him she didn't mind and got a good look at him. "Travis! Why didn't you tell me you were so scraped up?"

He had claw marks across his chest, deep gouges in his side and on his arm, and various scrapes here and there—along with streaks of mud and blood. He looked exhausted, too...even if he was smiling.

She tentatively touched his side. That looked really painful. She bit her lip and winced. "You should have gotten stitches."

"Nuh-uh. I heard your opinion on that. You growled loud enough that anyone in a mile radius heard it."

She blushed again and rolled her eyes. "Well, not from her...she's a skanky whore, but you should have gone into an ER."

He cupped her head in his hands and leaned down and kissed her lips softly. It was so tender it made her want to cry all over again—for a whole different reason.

"I told you I'd hunt you down and drag you back to my place yesterday. It just took me longer to find you than I'd expected."

She looped her arms around his neck and tugged his mouth back down. She should be soft and sweet, considering his lips might be the only uninjured part of him, but she stood on her toes and opened her mouth to his. Mm. As his tongue brushed hers, she was sure this really was a dream. He grabbed her butt and set her on the table before slipping in between her legs to grind their bodies together.

Heaven. This is heaven.

"LeAnn," he whispered against her mouth.

"Mm."

"We stop now or we don't stop at all. And you can't take off on me once you've said yes."

She pulled back reluctantly.

His sigh brushed across her wet lips, leaving tingles.

"Eventually, you're going to come to your senses," she said.

"No, you're going to come to yours. I've already decided." He tipped forward and pressed their foreheads together as he took deep breaths. "You're still coming back with me, though."

She tried to stop the giddy thrill she got that he wanted her. This wasn't real. Maybe it was that scent-match, and she'd won the lottery for weird magical love voodoo. "Fine."

"Hm. Yeah, I'm handcuffing us together. I feel like I could sleep for a week after last night." He stepped backward, pulling her along with him. "You can even bring your map," he said as she hopped off the table.

She turned to roll up the map. "You know, another thing I'd worried about with your research after reading that Rainier was a volcano…I thought maybe there was some Lycan virgin sacrifice ritual that Ross didn't tell me about."

He laughed.

"You laugh, but you'd be in trouble if that were the case.

Your whole pack smelled like they were all getting some fairly regularly."

"Not me," he said. No. He smelled turned on the whole time they were together, but they were both heading fairly deep into sexual frustration—especially now.

"Well, no, but I might be the closest thing to a virgin, and then there's Merilee on the other end of that."

He went still. "I could tell you'd stopped by Merilee's. You know I don't like her, right?"

She turned toward him with the rolled-up map to see him eyeing her with a frown. "Like you hate her?"

"Maybe," he said slowly, elongating the syllables while still watching her.

"That's weird. Sure, she's slutty, but she seems nice. Twitchy and freaked out, but nice."

He exhaled in a huff. "Well, why were you at her place, then?"

She squinted. His response was weird, but…whatever. "I had her bra. Well, my brother had her bra. I was hoping they'd hooked up."

He blinked and shook his head. "You were hoping that?"

"It was the less freaky reason he'd have her bra…which sounds weird now that I've said it out loud. Instead, I guess he was using it to cover his scent."

"It seemed like you stopped by again last night…in your car."

"Yeah, she's the easiest to track. She smells really strong. And I didn't know where the fight was."

"Ah, that makes sense." And he looked relieved and a bit surprised—though she didn't know why; she always made sense.

She stared at his chest and shook her head. "I should have shot Troy."

He picked up the gun from the table and tucked it in the back of his waistband. "I'll get cleaned up, and you can play doctor, and we can sleep."

"In handcuffs?"

"In handcuffs. You might as well get used to it."

"How do you know I'm not?"

. . .

She nuzzled his neck in her sleep, pressing her body tightly to his. He was about as aroused as he'd ever been in his life, and she was rubbing up against a few of the cuts he had on his chest…but this felt healing.

Holding his hand out for a second, Travis watched it shake before sniffing in disgust and dropping it back around her. He'd faced armed morons high on meth without so much as blinking, but he couldn't seem to recover from those ten hours of looking for her and finding empty road after empty road. When he'd caught sight of her car at her brother's, he'd thought he'd been hallucinating.

She's still here.

Mate.

Mine.

Her face screwed up in a frown, and she twitched in his arms.

"Shh, LeAnn."

Her taut muscles loosened, and she sighed in her sleep.

It didn't surprise him that she had nightmares. Anyone with her past would have demons. When she'd spaced out for a couple minutes, it'd scared the hell out of him initially, but she'd come back to him. They could get through this.

She'd shared her past with him, so he had a part in them, too. Hopefully, he'd be able to help her deal with them. She'd thought hearing about what she'd done would turn him off—instead, she astounded him. She was a survivor. And it was about time she had someone to help her find control in her life. Though he wasn't doing so great a job at finding it in his own these days.

The worst was behind them, though.

Last night's challenge would establish his role in the pack and give them some room for her to get comfortable and finally accept the scent-match. She'd see what a pack was like, and maybe she'd start to recognize the Lycan side to her. If she weren't so at odds with herself and in conflict, maybe she'd shift.

She has to be shifting. She is a Lycan.

"Mm, Travis," she murmured.

"What is it, honey?" Dipping his head, he kissed her temple. Honey…he'd slipped and called her that a few times. She smelled like honey. Sweet, sweet honey. Her skin tasted sweet, too.

"What?" she asked drowsily. She must have been asleep before when she said his name. It made him smile.

"What what?" he asked.

Tipping her head back, she wrinkled up her nose as she squinted at him. "I thought we were sleeping."

He'd called in sick to work. He should be sleeping. Or he should be making sure that Troy got the hell out of town. "We are."

"I thought so." She closed her eyes and huddled up

against him again.

He hadn't been kidding when he said he'd found religion early this morning. He had to remember to be kinder to widows and orphans and find a few charities to donate to. If she'd disappeared on a plane and reinvented herself… It made him want to puke. He'd watched the road leading out of town after the rain had started. Then he'd decided to make one last stop by her brother's before going back to his place to switch to a two-legged search for her.

He inhaled her scent. Hell, she smelled good. She smelled like she'd been drenched in honey.

"Do you know I'm crazy for you?" he whispered.

She startled and rubbed her mouth back and forth against his collarbone before settling down again. She was also an insanely light sleeper. With her being a flight risk, he wished he was. It was keeping his eyes pried open—if he went to sleep, he might wake up alone. He couldn't be without her. It'd happened so fast—too fast. This felt like more than want and need…this felt real and deep and a whole lot like love. He'd never felt anything like this for anyone.

Jordan had once said he was weak for Christa, and damn if he wasn't right about feeling that way for your mate. All his control, yet Travis had nearly lost his mind last night when he thought she'd taken off.

"Mm, Travis?"

"Yeah?"

She leaned back and stared at him. "I like your tattoo."

He grinned. "You want one?"

"Me?"

"Everyone in the pack has one."

"And I'm pack?"

"You're pack." She seemed more open to that after the challenge. It even seemed to appeal to her. He might never entirely understand the way her mind worked, but belonging to a pack called to her—as it did most pack animals.

She smiled. "I've never been in someone's pack before."

He brushed his finger down her nose softly before using it to tip her mouth up for a kiss. "We can get you inked as soon as you want."

"If I stay."

"You have to stay. Remember…handcuffs…lots of showers." She thought he was only kidding. The challenge had been nothing compared to what had followed.

"Would I have to get it on my arm?"

His grin widened. "Where were you thinking of getting it?" This had to be one of the sexiest conversations he'd ever had—especially since she sounded all drowsy, and he was surrounded by her honeyed scent.

She rolled her eyes. "Why do they glow?"

"Phosphorous in the ink. I wanted them visible in both forms."

And her smile dropped off, and she looked down at his chest. "Oh. Right."

"What?"

She sighed. "Are they only accepting me as pack because you keep telling them that?"

He could lie to her, but it sounded like Alanna had already planted the seed of doubt about it. "Yes. Until you accept the scent-match and take your place as Alpha, you don't feel like pack to most of them."

"Well, and the fact that I'm not a Lycan."

Oh hell. This would have to be worded carefully. "We

accept non-Lycans into the pack. While Jordan was helping me, he had a non-Lycan leading his pack—Dane. Besides, not all offspring born to us are Lycans. Even between a Lycan and a Lycan. Jordan's parents were both Lycan and he's the only one in his family."

Except that she was Lycan. But she somehow had some serious repression going on. It probably started with her mother when she started changing at puberty. It was so far beyond what he could imagine, though. She likely could use a good therapist. But the only Lycan he knew in the medical profession was Alanna…and he felt guilty even thinking about her with LeAnn here.

Maybe she never shifted or had only shifted a few times before she started pretending it wasn't happening.

It probably wasn't a good idea to keep hammering at it, especially when other people were around. He found her insanity charming, but it might look…okay, it *would* look crazy to the others, and Merilee had smelled downright frightened when she'd first seen LeAnn last night at the challenge. And with the other females going into heat…

"You know I'm only attracted to you, right?" he asked. Her hanging around Merilee's place had made him uneasy.

She looked up at him.

"I don't want anyone else in the pack or out of the pack—just you."

"Because of the scent-match?" she asked, tilting her head.

"It started with the scent-match, but also…it's just you. I only want you."

She grinned.

The phone rang. And he mentally argued with himself

over answering it, but the moment was already broken, so he leaned back and grabbed it.

"Hello."

"Merilee is gone," Liam said.

"She went with Troy?" He might have expected that. It was a bad call on her part, but he could only do so much.

"No. Troy sent me to ask her if she would, and she's not here. But I could smell blood. Her blood. I followed it and found that…uhh, someone had dug out her tracking tag—they left it in her bed."

Ice shot through him. "What?" This couldn't be happening again.

LeAnn had gone still and was looking up at him with a concerned frown.

"Can you smell the scent of anyone else?" Travis asked. Ross. This reminded him far too much of Ross. But saying that was admitting that he was still alive, and he wasn't ready to accept that as an established fact. It was still supposition, wild speculation. It had to be.

"I can." *Don't say Ross. Don't say Ross.* This couldn't be happening again. He'd expected drama in this pack, and they had it in spades, but death…like this? No.

Travis waited. Finally, he asked, "And?"

"I can hear your mate's breathing. Do you really want me to answer that?"

Liam was a hotheaded ass, and Travis had dealt with the problem head-on by making him help Troy leave so that he'd see which way he was headed. His thinking was less predictable, so the statement could mean anything.

"I'll be there in five minutes," Travis said finally.

"Okay." And he hung up.

"What did he mean?" LeAnn said, getting up when he did.

"I have no idea. It might mean that he didn't want to scare you." Though it was hard to imagine Liam actually being considerate of LeAnn's feelings if he didn't see her as pack. There'd even been a bite to his voice when he'd said the word "mate."

"I don't think that's it," LeAnn said. She was almost too perceptive. Not that he'd be attracted to someone he saw as inferior, but he'd always assumed his intelligence would make it difficult to find an equal partnership. LeAnn felt like an equal.

She was dressing quickly like he was…as if she were coming along. *Hell.*

"I don't think you should come with me." He added, "At first," when she scowled and narrowed her eyes. "I can call you…because I might need your help tracking, but I don't really trust Liam anyway, and I want to know what he's getting at."

"You don't trust him?"

"He'll be my next challenge as Alpha if things don't change."

Her eyes widened.

"It's fine. I'll have a gun, and he knows pack law for challenging an Alpha."

"Maybe you should have two guns."

He liked and disliked the way she thought. "Okay, I'll take two guns."

"And a knife."

"I have claws when I shift. A knife is just an extra thing to carry."

"Oh. Good point. I don't think of that because I don't have those."

He blinked at her. That was never going to be easy to let slip by. "Okay. You have to stay here, though."

She looked down. "Okay."

"You were planning on sneaking out after me."

She folded her arms.

"LeAnn, if someone is killing members of my pack, I need to know that you're here and safe, or I won't be able to concentrate."

He didn't want to tell her, but there was an instinctual aversion to harming someone in your pack. It made you hesitate. It made you even turn and defend them if you were in Lycan form. It was hard to fight the instinct. Once you were accepted as pack, you had that protection. He and Troy were both fighting it last night during the challenge—though he suspected it was more difficult for him than for Troy. No one had that instinct for LeAnn currently. He could say she was pack for the rest of her life, but until she took her spot in his life and the pack, they wouldn't feel it, not when they were Lycans, and certainly not the dimmer instinct when they were on two feet.

Hell, he wasn't even sure he could have killed Ross if it came right down to it. He was glad Black Tusk had taken it on.

"Please stay here," he said, grabbing her hand with one of his as he reached for his holster with the other. This was eating up his time, and the word "please" sounded and tasted strange on his tongue as an Alpha.

"Okay," she muttered, not meeting his eyes.

It'd have to do. He leaned forward and kissed her

cheek…which she didn't acknowledge because she was too busy sulking. He tried not to smile. "I'll call you *when* I need you." That lightened her scowl…slightly.

When he arrived at Merilee's house a few minutes later, he actually drew back as he got out of his truck. No. He shook his head. No, this couldn't be happening. Dammit. Couldn't anything go right for him? One day of peace. One day.

Liam was on the porch waiting for him and smiled grimly and snidely at his expression. He wasn't feeling the need to show deference apparently, and this wouldn't help stomp down that moron's issues with authority.

He dragged a hand through his hair and shook his head. *Hell.*

The whole property smelled like LeAnn.

Chapter Eight

She'd gone to the door to watch Travis leave, but stayed there as another scent hit her. It was distant, but it was there. Ross.

"Ross," she called softly. "Come in and we can talk." She had no idea what pack law said in this situation, but she'd handle it if he came in. She waited and sighed when she didn't hear any movement. Leaning against the doorframe, she said, just as quietly, "You probably don't know what to think about your sister shacking up with the local sheriff, huh? It's weird. But he's a nice guy." Also, they weren't really doing anything. "I guess you probably see him more as Alpha than a sheriff, though."

Nothing.

"I'm sorry if our dad messed you up and made you think revenge was worth all this, but it really isn't. I'm sorry you can't take it back." The Ross she'd known would have eventually regretted what he'd done. There were no take-backs with some mistakes, though. Especially killing someone.

Whether or not they deserved it…and sometimes they really did deserve it. And not just by being annoying.

The cold was seeping into her skin—her skin that was still warm from lying next to Travis. She belonged to him. Even if she didn't belong *with* him. Shivering, she rubbed her hands up and down her upper arms. Here she was, standing between two men—her brother and the man who'd be her mate if she let him. One she belonged with by virtue of her blood. The other had bonded with her soul.

If she did talk with Ross, Travis might see that as a betrayal of his trust—especially if she did it in his place. But maybe she could talk Ross into giving himself up. Travis might kill him anyway. If she talked Ross into showing himself and it cost his life, she'd have betrayed her own brother. There was no way to win here.

Why is it so cold?

Maybe because she'd been so warm.

Maybe the reason she was staying with Travis and considering staying with the pack was because she'd been alone for so long, and the last of her family was as good as dead. She'd learned the hard way that it was better to be alone for the right reasons than be with someone for the wrong ones.

LeAnn waited another couple minutes, just because, and then she went to go have breakfast and wait by the phone… as long as she could. She was going to try really, really hard to stay here this time. At least this time, Travis had a good reason for asking her not to come with him, and it's not like the whole rest of the pack was in on it.

• • •

"Did you tell anyone?" Travis asked as he approached.

Liam finally looked down.

Hell. "Who did you tell?"

"Melissa went into heat last night and Lara is due to. They deserved to know."

Travis shook his head. "LeAnn didn't do this. Someone stole her clothes and used her scent, but she didn't do this. She even said Merilee was nice." And this was not nice. There was too much blood in the air for a tracking tag being yanked out. It also ruled out Merilee getting scared and taking out the tag herself and running for it. He could assume that Melissa and Lara had panicked and called around. Travis stopped on the porch and inhaled. He hissed out a breath while clenching his teeth.

Well, that's only the second-worst scent to have here. I can't catch a break. What the hell? Who did I wrong in the universe?

"Ross," Liam said, stopping too. "I didn't notice that before." Probably because he wasn't looking for it. He'd condemned LeAnn in his mind already.

He ran a hand through his hair and fought the urge to punch something. He couldn't lose control in front of Liam. His movements were stiff as he tried to minimize his responses. *Keep it together. Act calm.*

This couldn't be happening. Every time he thought it couldn't get any worse, it did.

"Maybe Ross told her to do it," Liam said.

And there it was. That was definitely worse. He wanted to throttle him for saying what everyone else was going to assume. A brother-sister killing team.

There was no way. Even knowing her history, knowing

she'd killed a man... She wouldn't do this. Not in her right mind. He inhaled and exhaled slowly. Even if she wasn't in her right mind... The niggling worry surfaced in his head warning him that he'd underestimated her in the beginning. But that was before he knew her—before this morning.

No. He could trust his gut instinct on this. LeAnn was being framed.

Sitting on Merilee's porch swing, he opened his laptop. Merilee's tracking device might be here, but the movement of other tags might be useful, though he doubted it. If they'd gone to the trouble of pulling hers out, which must have hurt like hell if she was still alive, then they'd cover up their own. Angling it away from Liam, he looked up the tags. Holy hell. He'd thought that tagging them would help. His crazy need for control. Instead, it was fairly damning if anyone else saw it as he dragged through the check-ins. Someone must have placed those jamming devices all over. Nearly half the pack disappeared after the challenge when they left. The only person running like crazy everywhere including past Merilee's a couple times...was him.

He shut the laptop. If they went by that, it was either someone without a tag and a reason to hate Merilee...or him. Great. He pinched the bridge of his nose. A headache was building in the base of his skull and behind his eyes from the tension. He'd faced greater challenges than this and stayed cool. He was known for being easygoing. He should be able to handle this—to bring it back under his control. He was a damn genius. Why couldn't he pull it together?

LeAnn.

The stakes had never been this high before. And she had him off-balance and needy at the worst possible time for it.

He had to protect her from everyone, and hell, if someone killed Merilee, who was next? And why were they trying to frame LeAnn? If Ross was doing this, he might have to kill his own future brother-in-law. That ought to win points with LeAnn.

Okay, Travis, deal with one thing at a time. Control the closest things to the problem and widen your circle from there. You're a damn Alpha—act like it.

"Liam, go home and wait for me to contact you," he said.

Liam snarled under his breath, but turned and stalked away.

After Liam's SUV was out of earshot, he pulled out his phone and stared at it. He could do this on his own. He didn't need help. Setting his phone and laptop to the side, he walked the perimeter of the house, trying to catch any other scent besides LeAnn's and Ross's. There were faint traces of others, but… He wiped a hand down his face. He was not a tracker. Give him something more than a faint trace of scent to follow. Clues. Facts. Logic. But scent? Hell. It was either bringing in Jordan…or LeAnn. He picked up his phone.

"I hate you," Jordan said.

"I've got a missing pack member, but I think Merilee's dead." He set his laptop by the door as he walked through her place. Death and sex. The whole place smelled like too much blood, death, and sex.

"Who's your most likely suspect?"

"They've framed LeAnn."

"Are you sure she's being framed?"

Travis gritted his teeth but forced himself to answer the question reasonably. "Merilee's place smells like LeAnn… like she came here and didn't even bother covering it up.

Someone stole her clothes a couple days ago, and I spent the whole night chasing her. I swear she was *not* here last night. At the very least, I would have run across her in the time it took to do this. She was in her car, and her car was not anywhere near here. She was somewhere south of here because she was still pissed at me for last night." He realized how that sounded. "She wasn't pissed...she was upset."

Jordan sighed. "If she felt betrayed, you can't predict her behavior when instinct hit her."

"I can. She doesn't feel threatened by any of the females in the pack besides Alanna. I asked her about Merilee this morning because I was thinking about what you said, and I told her that I didn't like Merilee. She thought I was saying I hated her, and she thought that was weird because Merilee was, in her words, nice."

"Did she talk about her in the past tense?"

"No."

Jordan got up from bed after murmuring to Christa, "It's okay, baby, stay asleep." A moment later, Travis heard the door shut and a cat meow as Jordan walked. The place was huge, and the echo of feet sounded eerie as Travis waited for the other man's opinion.

"I've got other females going into heat," Travis said when Jordan's silence got to him. "And Liam was the one to find Merilee missing, so he called them to warn them."

Jordan swore under his breath. "So this is bad."

"Someone dug out her tracking tag and left it on the bed."

"Ross."

"His scent is around here."

"Hell. But he's dead."

Travis rubbed his tired eyes. He'd been exhausted, and he still was, but this was certainly jogging his adrenaline. "Ross did dig out his tracking tag." He was now more than willing to blame his mate's brother, even if it meant he'd returned from the dead. "That's another thing. LeAnn doesn't know we have tracking tags. I never mentioned it." She *was* being framed. He might question a lot about LeAnn, and hell, she needed that therapist, but she didn't do this.

"And you're sure Ross never mentioned his tracking tag?"

"Hell. No, I'm not sure." He could imagine Ross mentioning it. They'd all found it futuristic and funny when they'd done it. None of them had ever assumed it'd become this big a deal. This was insane.

"And she's never seen you on your computer?"

He closed his eyes. She'd broken into his computer, but he wasn't going to tell Jordan that. "She's never seen me. And I know she hasn't accessed the program itself—it keeps a record of when I log on." She might have seen the program on his computer and guessed. But it would take a cold and calculated person to then extrapolate that she'd need to remove her victim's tracking tag to hide the body, and a freaking psycho to actually do it. He shook his head as he stared at the bloody tag in the middle of Merilee's bed. LeAnn was framed good and strong. "It's got to be Ross. But why would he frame LeAnn?"

"I don't know, but Dane found tire tracks yesterday up at the cabin. Up beyond where we parked. There was another car there. They might have been older tracks and something other than whatever Ross was driving, but he said another car was up there beyond the cabin recently. I meant to tell you when I saw you last night but I forgot, because that still seems so implausible."

"Someone might've taken some of Ross's clothes, too."

"So you're saying someone is framing both of them?"

"Maybe."

"Wow, all the sickos ended up in Rainier pack."

"Yeah. That's helpful. Thanks."

"Well, what do your tracking tags tell you? You've looked, haven't you?"

"Someone put jammers all over, I think. Half the pack disappears after the challenge…except for me. So, yeah, it could also have been me who did this."

He heard the smile in Jordan's voice as he said, "I'm discounting you as a suspect."

"I make as much sense as LeAnn."

"You know that's not true. And as I told you, pack law allows for challenges with alpha females to be settled in private, so if LeAnn did this, she didn't break pack law as far as tradition goes."

"She didn't do this—and she doesn't even know tradition to know this is allowed."

"It sounds like it's your word against the evidence. And we're only talking about pack law. The actual law, on the other hand, that silly human law that you've sworn to uphold… if you find a body and don't deal with it, your pack may turn on you since you're a sheriff, and then you'll be circling getting charged with a crime yourself. You know how much we depend on the pack's secrecy. The fact that most Lycans die as wolves helps, but if Merilee turns up as a two-legged, you're screwed."

The ache in his brain grew sharper, and a muscle in his

eyelid twitched. He growled. This was hell. Pure hell.

"If it comes to that, LeAnn could make a real defense for insanity."

He growled louder.

"Actually, she'd be telling the court that she can't turn into a wolf, whereas we all know she can, so that might not work out."

"Jordan, quit being an ass. She didn't do this. I need real solutions."

"You're going to have to have a meeting with LeAnn present. She comes across as harmlessly crazy in person, so that might help." He sighed. "Actually, I like her. I won't say that she doesn't have me unsure of what she's capable of, but my gut instinct is that she's harmless...other than to Alanna. She'd gut Alanna. That's a cage match waiting to happen."

Travis rubbed his forehead with his palm. He could use a couple ibuprofen and a dark room—in a perfect world. Too little sleep. Too much stress. Too little time holding LeAnn. "You know it can't be LeAnn because of all the proof that it was LeAnn."

"I'm doubting your IQ is thirty points higher than mine again."

"Why would LeAnn bother with jammers all over if she was going to walk in here and leave her scent and when she doesn't even have a tracking tag?"

"To create reasonable doubt that it was her."

"Yet, she did this instinctually in a moment of passion after I upset her last night?"

There was a moment of silence before Jordan said, "No, you're right. That doesn't make sense. Also, digging out the tracking tag sounds more premeditated and vicious than I think she's capable of." It felt like success up until he added, "But if Ross was helping, I could see that."

"It's crazy to think that she suddenly found her brother and went along with a bizarre vendetta of his. Ross may have done it without her, but she wouldn't have done it. When I found her this morning, she was looking at a map planning on another day of looking for him, and she definitely didn't look like she'd spent the night overpowering and killing someone. She didn't smell anything like Merilee, either. It doesn't make sense that it's her."

"Your pack won't see it that way, though. Because the other option is that it's one of them, or Ross is stalking his own pack now."

"So what do I do? I want to chase down any possible trails, but I gotta admit, while LeAnn might give you a run for your money at tracking, I'm not doing so well. I can swear there's another scent here, but they must have scrubbed down and put on LeAnn's clothing."

"LeAnn is good?"

"She's really good, I think." He didn't want to tell Jordan that she'd been a successful thief for over a decade thanks to her skills. He still wasn't sure what he'd be doing about that. This sense of pride he felt that she was that good wasn't helping, though. It was hard not to be impressed that she was an amazing thief, but he'd have to try.

"I think meeting with your pack is your first order of business. You don't want anyone acting rashly, and the longer you let their thoughts fester, the harder it'll be to swing their opinion on LeAnn. But you can't have it until I get there, and this feels too much like Ross's trap last week for me to up and go without making sure Christa is safe somewhere."

"Why can't I have it before you get here?" He had a lot of respect for Jordan, but this was still his pack, and he wasn't sure that Jordan was far enough on LeAnn's side.

"Don't be an ass…think about it: you've got too much emotion invested in LeAnn and you've scent-matched to her. You're going to be overprotective. They need someone impartial to balance you out and to stop you from saying crazy things. And if anyone gets aggressive toward LeAnn, instinct will make you blind and stupid. I've been there. I nearly killed Dane once when I was like that. I couldn't think straight. You need an Alpha there who doesn't have a dog in this fight."

"That's what I don't like."

"I like LeAnn, and the more I think about it, the more I realize this doesn't make sense. But I *can* act rational and impartial. You've wanted to rip my throat out about half of this phone call. You keep freaking out my cat…uhh…Christa's cat." Then he said in a lower voice, "Lucifer, what the hell? Yeah, you better go find Christa. You better run."

"Are you threatening a cat?"

"This thing isn't just a cat. It's like an imprisoned minion of evil. I'll be there in three hours. That ought to be enough time to settle Christa over at her brother's. Everyone meets at the lodge and no one goes within five hundred feet of Merilee's." He paused and then asked, "You're sure she's dead? That you shouldn't be out looking for her?"

"It smells like death in here. It's got a cloying sweet smell even if it's faint. Someone died in here."

"Okay, so having everyone sit tight in the meantime won't matter."

"No. I don't imagine it will." It was a shame. Merilee

could be raunchy and foolish, but she didn't deserve to die. "Should I hunt down some of these jammers?"

"No, you should go home and keep LeAnn in your sight and watch out for angry mobs."

Travis sighed. Going home to LeAnn was the thing he wanted most and least. She'd have questions—questions he couldn't answer. She was starting to trust him, and keeping this from her would piss her off. She'd see it as a betrayal. "This sucks."

"You're telling me. I'm thinking of forwarding your calls to Miller—let him deal with some of this."

"No, you aren't. Half of them used to be your pack."

"Nah, you're right. I think that's the other reason why I should be there—they used to listen to me."

"We pretended to, anyway."

Jordan snorted and hung up.

• • •

He'd come back right when she was about to go after him, but then he'd spent most of the time on the computer and answering her with short, curt answers.

Yes, Merilee was definitely dead.

No, they couldn't find her body.

No, he didn't know who'd killed Merilee, but they'd be having a meeting.

No, she couldn't go to Merilee's place—no one could.

Jordan would be coming to the meeting so they were waiting on him.

She would be at the meeting—which made her freak out a little. It was her first meeting with the pack, and it was right after someone had died.

How could Merilee be dead? Who could have done it? Was this normal in a pack to just kill people if they bugged you? Maybe she should have paid more attention when Merilee was discussing that. She couldn't stop shivering. She'd just seen Merilee last night, and now she was dead. And she was about to be surrounded by this pack in a meeting. What if they all turned into wolves and attacked her?

"Are the meetings when you're human? Or are you all furry?" Was she going to be the only human there as they all stared at her? Holy hell. She hadn't even considered that.

Travis stared at her. "We're all in human form. Lycans can't talk when they're in form."

She nodded. "Right. That makes sense. I'm just…" She gestured around vaguely while shaking her head. She wasn't making any sense. She knew that. But Travis wasn't helping. Someone had died—and he wasn't telling her enough. "Maybe it wasn't murder. Maybe it was suicide and she wandered out into the woods as she was dying."

Travis just stared at her.

"I suppose you would have noticed if she'd done that." That would be easy enough to track. "I can't believe she's dead. I mean, I saw her last night."

"When?" he asked sharply.

"At the challenge." She snapped her fingers. "Troy. It was Troy. Troy did it. Did Liam stay with him the entire night?"

Groaning, Travis wiped both his hands down his face. "Look, LeAnn, I'm trying to make sense of everything, but I need to be able to concentrate, and I need more answers than I have…so I can't answer your questions when I don't have the answers."

She tried so hard not to be hurt. But he wasn't sharing information with her, and there *had* to be a reason for that. So she nodded and went to stare out the window with her arms folded. At least she wasn't dead. There was someone in the pack having a worse day than her.

Travis hadn't touched her since he got back, either. Not once. After that morning… These days were seeming longer than was possible. How she felt in the morning was nowhere near how she felt by that night. She was ricocheting between emotions.

He had been at a dead pack member's house. Maybe he didn't feel right touching her after being so close to death—even if it was just a scent.

Of all the people to kill, Merilee was a weird choice.

It was sad.

She'd actually met Merilee and spoken with her.

"You're *sure* she's dead?" she asked again, turning to him. "We shouldn't be out looking for her?"

"What makes you think she isn't dead?" he asked.

She squinted. That was a strange question. "Well, who would kill her, for starters? She doesn't seem the type to have enemies." She licked her lips. "What makes you think she's dead?"

"Her place smells like death. Decay has its own smell and…"

She nodded quickly. "No. I know. People put off a scent when they die." She shuddered. "That man I killed. I didn't even have to check for a pulse. He was dead. I guess I should have remembered that." She shook her head. "It's just I think someone would kill me before they'd kill Merilee." She turned back to the window to stare out, but she could feel Travis's eyes on her.

The time crept by. Finally, Travis said, "We can head there."

It'd given her time to think. "Maybe I shouldn't go." She wasn't really pack. She didn't belong at a pack meeting—especially one involving someone they cared about and she hadn't really known. Besides, they probably all hated her because she was related to Ross. It'd be like a slap in their faces if she were there.

"Jordan says you should be there." His words were all measured and clipped like a stranger's. He'd been different the last few hours. All the kindness and tenderness he'd shown this morning had disappeared. Men did that sometimes. They had their best faces on before they knew they had you. And he had her—he had to know that. She kept coming back to him like the stray he'd fed.

Time to buck up, buttercup, and cut your losses.

"I can just leave. I'll leave your pack alone. Leave you alone. It'd probably be better for everyone."

"No. I don't want you to leave."

He could have fooled her. To think, they'd been planning on sleeping in each other's arms all day.

He came to her and wrapped his arms around her, as if he'd somehow known what she needed.

"We need to figure out what happened to Merilee," he said, resting his chin on the top of her head.

LeAnn nodded, sniffing back the tears that wanted to fall. "Sure. Yeah. I guess I was being selfish. She deserves that."

Ten minutes later, they walked into the lodge. It was big and open with a raised platform on one end where there was a whole wall of windows. And it was full of Lycans who dropped their chins and quieted down when Travis walked in.

Jordan was already at the front on a podium, surveying the crowd with his dark eyes.

Travis had been holding her hand as they walked toward the building, but dropped it the moment they'd entered. And outside, it'd felt more like he was towing her and making sure she wouldn't run off than a cutesy couple thing to do. She followed him as far as the raised platform before she drifted toward a nearby wall, away from everyone.

Travis looked back over his shoulder at her, but she shook her head. No way was he getting her up there to stand in front of everyone. She'd spent her life hiding in shadows, and it felt like where she belonged. Until she found her footing in this Lycan world, she was sticking to the shadows.

"It's fine," Jordan murmured.

She sent him a grateful smile that he didn't return—he just stared hard at her as if he were trying to read her soul.

Him, too, huh? She couldn't seem to be on anyone's good side today. In fact, it felt like everyone in the room was giving her space like she was a leper. Screw it. She looked down. Not out of deference but because she was ready to be out of here and the meeting hadn't even started.

First, Travis was acting like he was barely tolerating her.

And she'd believed Jordan thought she was okay, but apparently not. He'd been nice enough last night, but today…well, today…was different.

She was surrounded by Lycans…who didn't really want

her as pack.

She was surrounded and alone…very alone.

LeAnn sent a surreptitious look toward the closest door. Maybe once the meeting started, they wouldn't notice if she left. And she'd really leave. She'd get in her car and not stop. There was more than enough money in her account to buy a fake ID and a new life.

"As you all probably know by now, Merilee has disappeared, and someone dug out her tracking tag and left it," Travis said.

Tracking tag. She'd forgotten to ask him about that. Liam had mentioned it on the phone. Travis probably wouldn't have explained it anyway. She'd found a program on his computer that'd needed a separate password so she didn't feel right checking it out…plus, it wasn't as easy to figure out.

"We haven't found her, but we'll be looking for her. I suspect she's dead. I…uhh…yes, Melissa?"

"I'm with Sean. I'm staying with Sean. I'm with Sean."

It was such a weird thing to say that she actually turned to look at the woman speaking, only to find her staring straight at her with a frightened look on her face.

Frowning, she turned back around. That was weird. Maybe it was because she was Ross's sister, and they all assumed she was on the verge of going psycho. When she looked up, she found that both Travis and Jordan were staring at her, too. Okay, this was creepy.

"What?" she mouthed at Travis. Seriously, if this was how the meeting was going to go, she was out of here.

He shook his head and looked back out at the group.

Alanna was directly across from her and making pointed

eye contact with Travis.

He clenched his teeth tightly, but nodded at Alanna.

"Why don't you just ask her?" And now Alanna was staring at her—and that was not okay.

"What?" LeAnn asked aloud.

"Nothing," Travis said before looking back at Jordan, who shrugged. Travis rubbed a hand against his forehead. "Okay, I'm going to go straight to it. LeAnn did not do this."

"Then why was she there at the time?" a voice she recognized as Liam asked.

"If she did, I'm sure it was fair," another female voice said, sounding timid.

"What didn't I do?" LeAnn asked, looking around. And it hit her suddenly. "Me? Kill her?" She even pointed at herself—it was that shocking. "Why on earth would I kill Merilee?"

"So she wouldn't take your place," Alanna said in a bored-sounding drawl. She was begging to be slapped. Hard.

"Take my place? How would she do that? I don't have a place. I'm just here for right now. And why would I care?" This made no sense. It was like she'd dropped into a play in the middle of the second act. She felt the tingles on her skin of everyone's attention. She hated this. So much for being in the shadows. And this was what being in a pack felt like? When they turned on you?

"You didn't want her taking Travis," Alanna said above the low hum of voices, drawing the attention her way again. She probably liked the attention. Total drama whore. "She was in heat. She was allowed to challenge your position because you haven't taken it. But I don't think it was a fair challenge, which is why you're trying to cover it up."

She blinked and blinked. No, she'd really said that. This wasn't just some bad dream. "I would *never* kill Merilee. Wait, she was in heat? Is that why she smelled like…oh, never mind." Well, that explained a lot. Though Merilee probably always smelled like sex.

And everyone was back to staring at her, and very few of them were trying to hide it.

"As I said, LeAnn didn't do this. Someone stole her clothes a couple days ago, and they tried to make this look like her." Travis cast her a concerned look, though…the same look he'd been giving her on and off when he said strange things.

Oh holy hell. She leaned back against the wall and took a deep breath before sending Travis a disgusted look. He'd been worried about her going nuts and killing Merilee, too—that was what was with all the strange questions about Merilee. She had almost earned that by telling him her past, but killing some woman she'd just met versus killing a man holding a family hostage was a whole different thing. Yeah, he didn't really know her at all. She was so outta here. After she proved she didn't kill Merilee.

"Why would I challenge her for Alpha when I haven't even said I wanted it?" LeAnn asked Alanna directly. "Or what comes with it?" And Travis got a look at that. Bastard. Like she would ever do this.

"Maybe you couldn't help yourself," Alanna said.

LeAnn narrowed her eyes before turning and addressing everyone. "Let me be perfectly clear. I came here to find my brother, and he turned out to be a murdering bastard, but I would never kill anyone here besides Alanna, and I think most of you can agree she is one grade-A bitch. No, wait, that's an insult to canines everywhere. So if you find Alanna dead, you can come right to me because not only will I be proud, you'll see me dancing, maybe even a touchdown dance."

"She's not serious," Travis said.

She was totally serious. Alanna had it coming and then some.

"And why would I kill Merilee? She was nice. A little odd maybe, but she seemed nice."

"So you could be Alpha," Alanna said again.

"Oh my hell, it's like your mouth and your brain have never met. Do I look like I'd be the first to throw down some sort of Lycan death match? You even had to tell me about a challenge—I didn't even know. I didn't even know enough about Lycans to know she was in heat. I just thought she smelled like sex. But you all do. And more power to you because I'm not getting any, and I'm approaching Alanna's levels of bitchiness."

"Uhh," Travis said, trying to break in.

"And if I wanted to be Alpha, I would have accepted the scent-match, but to be honest, I've been here less than a week, and it's been weird and I'm not one for staying in one place, let alone in a small town with a bunch of people who might hate me. Besides all that, Travis could do a lot better, but he's not the one holding this thing up. I am. Me. So I'm not exactly rushing to take my place when we might all regret it if I did. Travis deserves the right person. This pack deserves the right person…and I'm just me. I'm a hell of a lot better than you"—she pointed at Alanna—"but you're a horrible, horrible person."

Alanna narrowed her eyes. It was true. In fact, she was

95 percent convinced that hag had killed Merilee for some reason. Maybe just because she could.

"LeAnn," Travis tried.

"So why would I kill someone over being Alpha?"

"Because you're crazy," Alanna said as if it was obvious.

The pack was swinging their heads back and forth like this was a tennis match.

"*I'm* crazy?"

"Yeah. That's what I said." Alanna had been mimicking her pose of leaning against the wall, but she pushed forward and asked, "Are you a Lycan?"

"Aww hell," Jordan muttered quietly.

"What?" LeAnn asked.

"She doesn't shift," Travis broke in. "She hasn't shifted the whole time I've been with her."

"Yes, but is she a Lycan?"

Everyone around LeAnn looked confused. What had Travis been telling them? They should know that she wasn't a Lycan. He'd said they accepted non-Lycans.

"No. I'm not. My father and brother were, but apparently it skipped me. I'm not a Lycan. If that means I can't be in your pack, fine. If that means I can't be with Travis…" She shook her head. She wouldn't say it, but she was beginning to think there was a whole load of other reasons she shouldn't be with Travis. Starting with the fact that he thought she might have killed Merilee. "But no, I'm not a Lycan."

Alanna threw her hands up and said, "See! She's crazy. She killed Merilee because she's freaking insane."

"Whore!" LeAnn returned with a glare.

"Slut!"

"Hag!"

"Bitch!"

"Asshat!"

Then Travis pulled out his gun and shot the ceiling.

And that might have been it. They might have ended it. But then Alanna had to say one last thing…call her one last name…under her breath…and no woman in the world would let *that* one slide by. No one but no one called her *that*.

"Oh, it is on!" And she bolted toward Alanna.

Of course that whore shifted.

Travis grabbed LeAnn around the waist and hauled her backward, kicking and punching. Jordan shifted and pounced between them, facing Alanna. The other Alpha let out a snarl that had everyone backing off real fast.

"You just met her. How can you already hate her that much?" Travis asked, adjusting his grasp as she went for his gun.

"You heard what she called me! Anyone who uses that word deserves to be shot!"

Travis set her against the wall and held her shoulders while glaring into her eyes. "Behave!"

Behind him, she could see Jordan and Alanna both had shifted back and were tugging on clothes while hissing at each other. The rest of the pack looked simultaneously alarmed and entertained.

She'd broken eye contact with Travis, and he shook her shoulders and moved back into her eyeline. "Stop it. You're my mate and an adult and you need to start acting like it!"

Ouch. She held his gaze for one more second before dropping her eyes. Whatever. She was so out of here.

"We move to a vote," Alanna snarled. "When one member of the pack threatens the well-being of the rest, a majority can declare their life forfeit. It's our way."

It was like a punch to her stomach. She couldn't get in enough breath. A vote?

Travis's hands loosened on her shoulders, and she looked up to see him closing his eyes in a wince. "Damn," he whispered.

Over his shoulder, Alanna straightened up and smoothed down her clothes with a triumphant look on her face.

"LeAnn hasn't accepted the scent-match," Travis called over his shoulder, letting go of her entirely.

"You've said she's pack. Melissa and Lara are both in heat. Merilee is dead. As Alpha, you must uphold our laws. And our laws state that a majority can declare her life forfeit."

"She doesn't even know our laws!" Travis snarled.

"That *doesn't* matter. In fact, the law doesn't even stipulate they be Lycan, but we all know she is."

"Oh for the love of…" LeAnn muttered, rolling her eyes. "I'd *know* if I turned into a damn wolf!" What had she gotten herself into? This was all so crazy. They were going to vote whether or not to kill her?

"Alanna's right, Travis," Jordan said. He met LeAnn's gaze and narrowed his. "About the law, I mean. She didn't shift then, and I've never seen that—not in a fight."

"Not a Lycan!" *How many times do I have to say it?*

Travis was still looking at her, and he shook his head minutely and mouthed, "No."

If he didn't allow it, he'd lose his place as Alpha and possibly go through his own challenge. Her brain sorted through alternatives. Pack was everything to Travis—he'd been willing to die last night to keep his place and keep the pack strong. And she'd brought on some of this mess by coming here. Last night was Travis's challenge. It was only fitting if today was hers. She owed him. She owed them. This was part of being a pack. It felt right.

And it's not like she could turn into a wolf and have it out with Alanna instead.

If she could, she'd have thrashed her skinny ass.

She glanced around. Most of them had their heads bowed. The fact that some didn't was a bad sign—bad for the pack and their Alpha. Jordan was trying to communicate something with his stare, but she wasn't sure what. He was probably telling her to do the right thing. And she would.

LeAnn licked her lips. "Fine. I'll agree to my life on the line on one condition."

"You don't have a right to make stipulations," Alanna said.

"Oh, will you shut up!" She glared at Travis. "And you didn't let me slap her! Look, regardless of whether you vote to kill me or not, can we all go figure out what happened to Merilee? Because I sure as hell didn't kill her, and I want to know who did." She stood up straight. "Also, I'm sorry for what my brother did. If you do vote against me I can finally try to make that right. I didn't know him as well as I thought, I guess."

. . .

If someone had plunged a knife into his chest, it would have hurt less. Her words opened up a gaping wound inside him. Last night, he thought he'd grasped the depth of his feelings for LeAnn...when he thought she'd run away. Either her shared confidences or this fatal threat of losing her laid waste to what he'd believed. He was in over his head and drowning with her. He needed time to examine this…to get a handle on it.

Travis shook his head. "LeAnn." She couldn't do this. This was the height of unnecessary risk. He needed her. If anything happened to her…

"Travis, this is what a pack does, and this makes sense. They protect their own," she whispered. "I'd want my pack to protect me, too, if I was…in one."

He exhaled, clenching his teeth. How could he deny her this? Even if a sick sense of dread settled in his stomach. She wanted to be pack—she might deny it, but her stories of her past said she'd been searching for a place to belong her whole life. It was why she'd clung so tightly to Ross's innocence.

There was nothing else he could do. He couldn't undermine the stance she'd taken—she was behaving like an Alpha. He certainly couldn't condemn her desire to act like she was a member of the pack.

He also couldn't live without her.

Travis met Jordan's gaze. The other Alpha nodded minutely.

He shook his head again, but yelled, "Fine, but I don't want to be here for the vote, so Jordan can tally. I don't want to know how you vote. For what it's worth, LeAnn has no reason to feel threatened, and she knows that because I've only wanted her since we've met. So she's not a threat to anyone." He frowned. "Other than Alanna."

"Whom I've yet to kill," LeAnn added.

He nodded toward a door. "Come on. We'll wait outside."

The cool air felt good after the tense atmosphere inside. The vise around his chest eased up just from getting LeAnn out here, with him.

They walked to the edge of the porch where the voices inside were no more than murmurs and leaned against the rail side by side.

He stared off ahead. Things needed to be said between them. He hadn't handled the morning well. Actually, from what she'd said inside, he hadn't handled their relationship well.

"If I do die without slapping Alanna, I'll never forgive you." There was a stinging pain in his chest, and he drew in a sharp breath. He didn't even like her joking about it. If he lost her, he'd go mad. In a short amount of time, she'd become more important to him than anyone. She wasn't going to die. He wouldn't allow that to happen. He was going to make sure she got the chance to heal and be a part of something.

But this wasn't the time for that. He needed to be calm and collected. Who knew what the next ten minutes might bring. There'd be time to examine his feelings later—he had to believe that.

He cleared his throat. "Like you were only going to slap her." He shot her a wry look. "I nearly caught a kick to my privates for holding you back. If that was over a slap…"

She shrugged. "Yeah, it would have been ugly." She glanced at him. "But I would have won."

"You would have." He wasn't coddling her, either. She was stronger than she looked, and she backed up the verbal ferocity with quick, dangerous reflexes. LeAnn had the instincts and moves of a street fighter—which she'd probably earned, if her story was anything to go by.

"Even if she cheated and shifted."

"Totally cheated." LeAnn hadn't shifted. For a moment, he'd doubted she was Lycan, too. But she had to be.

LeAnn cleared her throat. "Earlier at your place…"

"I was an ass because I didn't know how to tell you or not tell you because I didn't want you to think I believed it. So I was trying not to say anything."

"Oh." Then she pointed in the direction of her brother's house. "But you kept telling me earlier today that you weren't interested in Merilee, like you thought I was capable of it and you were trying to prevent it."

"No. I thought you were capable of what I stopped between you and Alanna." He tipped his head in the direction of the cabin, even as he tried not to think about what might be going on in there, tried not to make out the mumble of voices. He clenched his fingers tighter around the railing. Nothing was going to happen to LeAnn. If he had to take on the entire pack, nothing was going to happen to her.

"Oh. I am. Just not against most people. Actually just against Alanna." It was amazing that she seemed almost calm about what was going on. As if their relationship was at the forefront of her mind and dying for a crime you didn't commit was no big deal.

"Jordan warned me that you two couldn't be in the same pack, but I thought he was exaggerating." He hadn't been. They were going to kill each other despite neither of them outwardly wanting to be alpha female.

"She started it."

Travis stood up and pulled her into his arms. "Yeah, but you were about to finish it." There was a hint of pride in his voice, and the spark in her eyes and half smile said she'd caught it. So much for being the enforcer.

"I can't believe you told me to behave like an adult."

He grinned. "I seem to remember someone shouting, 'Oh, it is on!' before hurtling toward the other side of the room. I was concerned about collateral damage. You two are lucky we don't have any kids in the pack yet."

"You heard what she called me."

He answered her by kissing her.

She pushed him backward until he slammed up against the side of the lodge, and then she wrapped her arms around his neck.

"Mm," he said against her lips as he tightened his arms around her.

She stood up on her tiptoes to deepen the kiss.

He pulled back and grabbed her face. "I don't think I can do any better than you. I don't even deserve you. You're *exactly* who I want. You *are* the right person—for me, for the pack. So never say that again—never think that again. I want you." He'd wanted to shake her when she said that. How could she not realize they'd gone way beyond that point?

Today was a semitruck careening out of control on hairpin curves. He'd been out all night searching for her...only to find her and connect with her. Then he'd stupidly pushed her away to compartmentalize things, and he was now facing losing her again. He needed her more than he needed his next breath, but he couldn't seem to find the right words to make her understand that...and showing her clearly wasn't working well for him.

She licked her lips, drawing his attention to them. "That's because you're crazier than me."

He smiled.

She tipped in and kissed his smile.

Opening his mouth, his tongue stroked hers as his hands slid down her back to grab her butt and lift her right off her feet. If only they didn't have all these clothes in the way. If only she'd accept the scent-match. She moaned softly into his mouth.

Footsteps sounded inside the lodge, and he tightened his arms around her.

"Okay, break it up, kids," Jordan said, opening the door.

They broke the kiss reluctantly, but she stayed leaning up against him.

"I told them no one travels alone, and that anyone able to go look for Merilee needs a group of three," Jordan said. "I also stipulated that the area immediately around her place was ours to check out."

She swallowed. "So they didn't vote to kill me?"

Jordan shook his head. "Only a handful, but I think they would have voted to kill Travis, too." He grinned at her then. "Are you kidding? I would pay to see that at meetings regularly. I think they're all hoping every meeting turns into Thunderdome." Then he shrugged. "Besides, as you pointed out, you've yet to kill Alanna, and that was a compelling argument. She's not even in heat and you still despise her—it spoke to your motives."

"I can't believe you shot the ceiling." LeAnn stared up at Travis with her head tilted. "That was over the top."

"Was it? It didn't feel like it."

"Well, shall we go see what's up at Merilee's?" Jordan gestured at their parked cars.

She glanced over at the lodge. "So that's what a meeting with the pack is like? I swear that ended nearly the same as a couple of the bachelorette parties I've been to. Well, not the voting to gang up and kill someone." Then she wrinkled up her nose. "Not *kill* them. Maim…yes, but they'd have deserved it, and you don't vote, not in so many words."

Travis and Jordan stared at her.

"What? Seriously. There are some really bratty maids of honor out there. I once threw one out a window." Then she looked at Travis and said, "Shooting the ceiling was still over the top."

It'd felt so right, though.

"I'm glad the pack didn't kill me," she continued as they walked.

"I wasn't going to let that happen regardless," Travis said. No way in hell. He'd die trying to save her first.

"I would have tried to hold them back while you guys took off," Jordan said.

"But it's a pack law." LeAnn's jaw dropped. She'd actually expected him to follow pack law when it came to her life? She'd even made peace with it.

Travis shot her an aggravated look as he held the door open for her. "Yes, but laws were meant to be broken." It was strange to hear the words leave his mouth.

"Who are you and what have you done with Travis Flynn?"

Part of his attempt to control everything had been a rigid adherence to laws. He'd do anything to keep her beside him, though. It was the new law of his life.

Chapter Nine

Considering how little sleep and how much duress he was working under, he really shouldn't be driving.

LeAnn pulled out a camouflage hunting knife and started studying it.

Was he seeing things?

"Wait, you have a knife? Where were you hiding that?"

She pulled up her shirt to reveal a sheath. He should really disarm her before taking her anywhere.

"So you could have started a knife fight in the lodge with Alanna?" He'd definitely have to disarm her before meetings.

"No, I would have *finished* a knife fight in the lodge with Alanna. I'm pretty certain we already established that. And she shifted, remember? And *I* never pulled it out."

"No, but you went for my gun."

"Which you'd already fired into the ceiling."

"What does that matter?" Considering the circumstances,

that'd seemed reasonable.

She shrugged and put the knife away as he pulled into Merilee's.

Jordan pulled up behind them as they stepped out.

LeAnn inhaled. "I'm starting to figure this out, I think. I've never had people try to cover their scent with other people's scents so it was harder at first, but I can smell the polyester of my sweater and the stale scent of me…it's not fresh. Bringing it to this area is fresh, but the source is older." She scowled. "Whoever has that sweater is going to die. Seriously. I loved that sweater."

Jordan walked up behind him and inhaled, too.

"Knowing it was that material, I think I can almost see what she's saying, but"—he shook his head—"it's far more subtle."

"Then there's the alcohol they used to cover up their own scent, but it's really changed it, not blocked it."

Jordan looked at her with raised eyebrows. "You might be better than me."

Travis grinned. His day had vastly improved. His mate had shown up Jordan—who was widely acknowledged to be the best at tracking anywhere around here. "Can you tell who did that?"

LeAnn wrinkled her nose and squinted. "Not for sure. And I'm not sure if I want it to be her so much that I'm thinking that."

"Alanna?" both men asked in surprise.

"Hell yeah, she's the one who framed me." Her accompanying look implied they were both gullible fools.

"Why?" Jordan asked.

"To get me killed."

"How can you already hate each other so much?" Travis asked again. He felt far less strong about Troy, and without a doubt, Troy would have killed him if he'd won.

LeAnn shrugged. "She even told me that if she killed someone we'd never find the body. I should have taken that more seriously. It was like she was telling me she was going to do this." She gestured at the house. "This is almost my fault. I should have killed her in her office yesterday." She started walking toward the house, but added, "That probably would have seemed excessive to you, though."

His jaw dropped and he turned to see a similar look on Jordan's face.

"Wait." He caught up with LeAnn as she stepped onto the porch. "Alanna said to you that we'd never find a body if she killed someone? What the hell was the context on that?"

She took a deep breath before saying, "She was talking about…" She stopped and looked around, and her shoulders dropped. "Damn. Ross was here."

Jordan stepped onto the porch. "He was." He pulled out his phone, shaking his head.

"Are you sure it was recently and not just his clothes?" Travis asked.

Jordan paused and looked up.

LeAnn folded her arms and wouldn't make eye contact. "Yeah, someone has been planting his scent, too, but not this time, and he's been visiting a lot of people in the pack. And it's recent—he probably came here before he was at our place this morning. It smells earlier—in fact, I think it was around the time it rained—which is why it's stronger on the porch."

He'd been to their place? Wait, she'd called it "our place."

His mouth went dry. That had to mean they were that much closer to her accepting the scent-match. But Ross had been at his house? Why? The bastard wasn't getting anywhere near his sister.

There were so many things in this conversation that they'd need to revisit. Hopefully he'd remember them all, because LeAnn only seemed to answer questions rather than volunteer information, and she was distracted at the drop of a hat.

LeAnn turned and went inside. "He was in here, too." She pointed to the right. "He went that way."

They followed her as she went down the hallway and ended in Merilee's room.

LeAnn winced. "Yeah, she's dead. They killed her and dug that thing out of her." She pointed at the tracking tag. "It doesn't smell like pain or even fear, so they must have injected her with something while she was sleeping, because I can't smell a gunshot, either. Ross was here around the same time. Polyester LeAnn smell is in here, too." She muttered "that whore" under her breath.

"You'd make a great detective," Jordan said, his hand still poised on his phone.

"I don't tend to work on that side of the law." LeAnn covered her mouth and nose with her hand and shifted back and forth on her feet.

"Ross used injection to kill Colby," Jordan pointed out, looking at him. "He killed him before he gutted him."

Ross *had* first killed Colby with an injection and then cut him open.

"He did?" LeAnn asked, dropping her hand. "Wait, don't answer that." And she gagged before bolting from the room.

They looked at each other before glancing after her. She was on the front porch gulping in deep breaths.

"I could have put that better," Jordan said.

"I'm not sure if that's what it was." She'd seemed less affected by her brother's crime the previous times they'd discussed it.

Travis followed her back out to the porch where she was leaning on the railing, biting her lip while blinking rapidly. He rubbed his hand down her back.

"That smell...you know? I thought I could handle it, but that smell. It suddenly took me back, and I could see that guy's wife, and he'd raped her, and so the place smelled like sex and then death and...Merilee's room..." She shook her head. "Sorry. That was stupid."

If he'd doubted her at all—which he didn't—it was obvious she hadn't killed Merilee. Her brother may have, but she hadn't. It was even unlikely she could kill Alanna despite what she kept saying.

"You are probably thinking I need some serious therapy." Her jaw clenched as she stared at the ground below the porch.

He decided to be honest. "I've been thinking that since I met you. I think it was the *naked with a knife to my throat* thing."

She smiled and turned her head to look at him. "And yet you want me?"

"That might even be part of why I want you. I'm not ruling it out, anyway." She needed him. She needed his logic and control. Travis felt uniquely appropriate for the role of her mate. He'd never anticipated how attractive that was.

Plus she looked great naked.

Inside the house, he heard Jordan call Dane to warn him Ross was still alive. From LeAnn's stillness, he could tell she'd heard it, too. "Has anyone else been here that you can tell?"

She stood up. "A lot of people have been here. I can smell my scent from when I came here last time and, oh, damn, I had Alanna's lab coat with me then. I left everything else in the safe because I didn't want to get caught carrying around a bra and a sock in my purse, but I *had* her lab coat with me." She grinned. "So I guess, technically, I tried to frame her first. It's a shame I didn't put on the coat and sashay all over Merilee's house in it while I was talking to her." She shook her head. "Anyway, I'm still sure that I can smell her *actual* scent faintly. Then, there's some other male—recently, so maybe Liam, you…" She inhaled. "Troy was here. So was one of the other guys I have a pair of boxers from, but that smells older and fainter."

"You have a pair of boxers from a male from my pack?" The jealousy was so fast and hot that it staggered him.

"They're my brother's."

"You have your brother's boxers?" That was both weirder and less weird. At least it dampened the jealousy.

Standing up, she leaned toward him and made eye contact. "You need sleep."

He shook his head, but sat down on the porch swing anyway. He was starting to feel bone tired. He'd been chasing ghosts for too long. If Ross was really leading them on another chase, he'd go nuts. *He'd* need therapy.

"My brother had a bunch of clothes in a safe. I guess he was using them to fake you guys out. He had Merilee's bra,

Alanna's lab coat, Troy's socks, and then a few other things."

"I hate your brother for that," Jordan said, walking out. "I had to smell a bunch of the pack's clothes to rule them all out and discover we were being screwed with. You found those?"

She nodded. "They're still in the safe—other than Alanna's lab coat. I figured it'd be a good excuse to talk to her so I grabbed that. Little did I know I'd want to strangle her with the sleeves within seconds of meeting her."

"He picked up all but the lab coat at an orgy they had at the lodge one night." Travis rubbed both his hands down his face. He was so tired of this. It was strange to love LeAnn while despising her brother so much.

Travis froze. He *loved* LeAnn. It skipped into his brain as naturally as if it belonged there, as if he had loved her for a long time.

"He picked up hers separately?" LeAnn asked, breaking into his thoughts.

He and Jordan shrugged.

"I swear, if he was sleeping with Alanna, I'll shoot him myself and then shoot her. That's disgusting. Practically cross-species. I'm not sure Alanna has a species. She probably crawled out of a crevice one day, and we're assuming she's evolved."

Jordan grinned. "Yeah, anyone interested in Alanna would have to be a totally worthless individual."

So help him, if Jordan outed his previous interest in Alanna, he'd shoot him.

LeAnn glanced between them, looking suspicious.

Luckily, Travis was so tired that he couldn't even drag up the energy for an expression. "Who else was here recently?"

he asked LeAnn.

"Hm. A couple other females, and then there are several older scents from males, but the strongest are Troy's and maybe Liam's." Shading her eyes, she scanned the woods. "They had to remove the body, right? So if we follow the scent of death and sex, maybe we can see where they took it." She winced. "That sounds disgusting, but Merilee really wasn't…shy."

"LeAnn and I can check it out, Travis. You can stay here."

"Why?" He narrowed his eyes. Jordan had a mate, but still…

Jordan gave him a bland look. "Because you look ready to drop, and I don't want to have to drag your body along with us while looking for one."

"Oh. Right." He pulled out his phone. "I should probably warn the pack that we're almost certain Ross is still alive." He met Jordan's eyes. "You are, too, right?"

Jordan nodded. "It's insane. But she's right about his scent out here. I don't think you could get it this clear with his clothing so long after he last wore them."

"What about Alanna? What do we know about her?"

"I might be able to smell her, but if her lab coat was here—it could just as easily be that," Jordan said.

"We know she's wearing my sweater all over. If I ever find her in it, it's going to need to die in a fire," LeAnn grumbled.

"What precisely will be dying in a fire?" Jordan asked smiling.

Travis shot him a quelling look.

"Well, I certainly won't be rushing to take it off her first."

Okay, time to rein this in. They didn't have enough proof.

They needed proof. "Maybe we should keep our concerns about Alanna to ourselves until we have more evidence."

Jordan nodded.

LeAnn narrowed her eyes, but shrugged. She leaned in and put a hand on his arm when he lifted his phone. "Can you ask them, if it's at all possible, if they could not kill Ross until I've talked to him one last time if they find him?" She dropped her eyes and wouldn't make eye contact with him. "He's all I have left. Everyone else is dead."

"You have the pack now, LeAnn. You have me." If he said it often enough, maybe she'd come to believe it; maybe it would keep her here.

She glanced up, but then pointedly looked at Merilee's place. "Yeah, and the pack is all warm and fuzzy, and I'm a murderer's sister they decided to let live." Without saying anything else, she spun away and left the porch to walk to the rear of the house.

Jordan shook his head. "I wish she was in my pack. We'd take her in, but I think you'd go insane being separated from her, and you definitely need her here." He nodded at Travis. "Stay put. We'll be back shortly."

"Okay, but I can hear you if you put the moves on LeAnn."

"Eww," LeAnn said on the other side of the house.

"My thoughts exactly," Jordan said, grinning, and walked off.

Yeah, well, maybe they hadn't noticed, but LeAnn's near-fight with Alanna hadn't turned off all the males in the lodge. He wasn't taking any chances.

• • •

"What do you mean that you think he needs me?" she asked Jordan as they slowly walked along surveying the ground. She asked quietly, but there was still a good chance Travis heard.

"Well, first of all, scent-matched mates tend to go nuts if you separate them. I had my mate's sister-in-law at my place for a short amount of time after she scent-matched to Dane, and she killed my blender one day. Smashed it to tiny pieces. I thought I was next. And I'm not handling being apart from Christa all that well, either. If there was a blender nearby, it'd be dead."

That shouldn't make her happy, but it did. She didn't want Travis to be miserable without her, but she also did… sort of. That most likely meant she was an awful person. But whatever. "Is Christa like you?" She hated to admit to it, but Alanna seemed more like an Alpha than she felt. She'd definitely never say it out loud.

Jordan grinned and pulled out his phone. "No. Not at all. She's small, human, and beautiful." His background was of a younger woman wearing a red-hooded coat with a flirtatious grin on her face. She looked tiny. Like half his size. She also was more cute than beautiful, in her opinion, but she was *very* cute.

"Not at all what I was expecting."

He pocketed his phone. "Not at all what I was expecting, either, but she's perfect for me. And your mate keeps dragging me here away from her."

"She's cute."

He nodded.

"She's an Alpha?" If his mate could be an Alpha and she wasn't a Lycan—maybe LeAnn wasn't as far off as she'd thought.

"Yeah. She keeps me in line, and she's better with a gun than I've ever seen." He pointed down at the ground. "Those look like drag marks, but I think we're going to lose them when we go through this grass. And I can't smell much of anything due to the moisture. You?"

"No. Here and there I catch the scent of something, but that rain was timed well for our psychopath, and this misty stuff has never really stopped. I swear it's raining more than not up here."

"It's our rainy season. It'll dry out a bit more in the summer. This would be much easier in June or July."

They tried to follow the marks left in the ground, but it was wishful thinking in her opinion. She sighed. "I'm much better in an urban environment. Ross gave me a crash course on tracking over near White Pass but there are so many other scents that smell…earthy. And it's so humid here."

He cleared his throat. "How close were you and Ross?"

"I've known him about five years, I guess, but I never really knew him. He seemed to want to hang on to the fact that he was an only child. His mother died and left him alone with my father, and it sounds like I didn't miss much by never having met my dad."

She crouched down and pointed to a black plastic scrap. "Wrapped in plastic. That's why we can't smell Merilee anymore." She stood up and redid her haphazard ponytail while Jordan examined the ground. "I feel like I was too late everywhere I go. I was too late to be a family for Ross. I was too late to stop him from this. I've been too late before. Now we're too late to make much of anything with this trail."

"Travis isn't wrong that the pack can be your family."

"Alanna and I are well on our way there."

"No, not Alanna, and I've already told Travis she has to be tossed out on her ass."

"Because of me?"

"Yep. When she goes into heat in March, one of you will be dead by the time she's done."

And they really had enough death on their hands already. She shuddered. It was freaky to hear about her "going into heat." If it wasn't a serious matter for them, she might be tempted to score one on Alanna for that. Instead, she asked, "One of us?"

"I'm betting on her being dead—for what it's worth."

She smiled at Jordan. "Thanks."

He shrugged and went back to scouting the area, though his scowl spoke to how successful he was.

"My mother was a real piece of work, but she used to say, 'There but for the grace of God, go I.' Mostly when she wanted to point out how miserable someone else was, but I'm wondering if I'd been stuck with my father instead of her…if I'd be as messed up as I'm starting to think my brother was."

"I think we all have a choice in who we're to become and how events shape us. I was a real ass two years ago, and some might argue I haven't changed, but I nearly killed Dane— Christa's brother—twice actually. But the whole experience that set your brother on his course changed mine. If Christa would have met me two years ago, she wouldn't have wanted anything to do with me."

"Oh, hey, I've got some drag marks again here," she said, pointing.

He walked over and they followed them for about ten

feet before they lost them again.

"Why else do you think Travis needs me? You made it sound like there was more than one reason."

"There is, and the second is more important. Lycan packs are only as strong as their leaders usually, but this pack is the least unified pack I've ever seen—and it's partly because a large percentage of them see themselves as leaders rather than followers. They don't see themselves as a pack, and they need someone strong to get them acting like a pack."

The rage built inside her faster than ever, and she fought back the urge to snarl. She saw red. No one challenged Travis like that. "Travis is strong," she ground out. She didn't like where he was going with this. Maybe he still was a real ass.

Jordan cut her a look and then stopped walking to gaze into her eyes.

Clenching her fists, she forced her temper back and took a deep breath. The darker side of her held on for a moment and then slipped away as she exhaled. "Travis *is* strong." It bore repeating.

Jordan shook his head with a half smile and went back to scanning the ground. "No, you misunderstood me. I meant this pack is too much for a single Alpha, and they *see* him as weak because he's behaving like a human leader rather than an alpha Lycan. He's organizing them rather than dominating them. He's always had a problem with that. He likes to control situations rather than commanding people. In another pack, that might be fine, but he's on shifting ground with this one. If he's not going to kill those who oppose him, he needs a second Alpha to bolster his position."

"I thought that was the problem with Troy." It sounded

like the last thing Travis needed right now was a second Alpha. She shook out her arms. Her temper didn't leave her feeling so jittery normally. She'd nearly lost it with Jordan—over nothing.

"No, an alpha *female*. He needs an alpha female who'll respect him and support him so that when he lets another challenger live—which might be a matter of time here—it's seen as merciful rather than weak. If you continue to refuse the scent-match, you're weakening his image. His mate is refusing his advances. In animals and in humans, that suggests something is faulty with him, not you…and we're a little of both of those. Troy would have probably held off longer, but Travis was forcing them to accept you as pack to keep you safe, even as you weren't accepting him. He needs you to step up and be the alpha female or he's going up against challenge after challenge."

She knew it'd been partly her fault, even if Travis had acted as if it was inevitable. That didn't sit well with her, but what could she do? Travis seemed to want her here. He'd gone searching for her last night.

Well, she could accept the scent-match.

It was so final. It was closing her escape hatch. She always kept track of her way out whenever she got into any situation.

But Travis's life was more important than this stubborn instinct she had. Not that self-preservation was such a bad thing. Maybe she could take Travis with her when she ran this time.

"Maybe he ought to walk away from this pack." Not that she'd ever taken the easy path before, but this time the other option had sharp teeth and claws.

"Have you met Kurt?"

"Who?"

"Short, sort of nerdy guy who was in the back of the group? He came from my pack. I think he was hoping to meet someone in this pack."

"If you're trying to hook us up, you better hope Travis has fallen asleep."

He laughed. "No, I'm asking because he told Alanna to leave you alone. He's never spoken up at a single meeting I held. It was unusual. I was proud of him. I wondered if you'd met him because of that."

"No. I didn't." It stunned her. Her mind went blank and she just stood there, blinking. Now she was curious who the guy was. A guy she didn't even know had stood up for her? Maybe this sort of thing happened in packs. So weird.

"How about Tasha? Have you met her? She's your height. She used to be a twin. She donated a kidney four years ago to try to save her twin, but her sister died anyway. She's much slower than she used to be, but she doesn't regret it. She was directly in back of you. You nearly plowed her over when Travis tackled you."

"There was someone in back of me?"

"Yep. She voted for you to live, too. No hesitation. Even after you nearly caught her with your elbow. In fact, she looked impressed." He crouched down again, and when he stood up, he picked up a stick and threw it…like they were on a nature walk, rather than chasing a killer.

"I haven't met her." Another person. Another stranger. Nobody had been on her side before Ross had come along. But these people weren't even related to her. It was… disconcerting, almost uncomfortable.

"Nope. You've met the standouts who are the loudest and most unlikable."

"Merilee wasn't too bad."

"And someone killed her because they saw her as weak. This pack needs someone to lead and protect them. They're looking for someone to follow, and the pack is too unwieldy and stubborn for a single Alpha."

She shrugged. He made it all sound nice like she could be important. There was one huge flaw. "That doesn't mean it's me."

"You'd rather see Travis with someone else?"

She rolled her shoulders in discomfort while wrinkling up her nose. No. Really no. That dark side of her growled its displeasure.

"Alanna maybe?"

And then she did actually growl. Holy freak. Her eyes widened and she glanced at Jordan to see if he'd noticed.

He was looking away rather than at her, but she could see his shoulders shaking.

She narrowed her eyes. "You only picked her because you know I hate her."

She could still hear the amusement in his voice as he said, "No, I picked her because she was Travis's most logical choice for an Alpha before you showed up. And Travis isn't going to want anyone else anyway. Scent-matched is scent-matched. He only wants you or no one. So even if there was someone other than Alanna who could be Alpha, he wouldn't be interested." He laughed. "Did you know that one of the females in this pack refuses to go on patrol if it's too muddy?"

"On patrol?"

"We protect our lands. Lycans watch their territory and their own very carefully. If this pack were closer and more protective of one another, Merilee might still be alive."

"So if I became pack, I'd do that? Patrol? Even though I'm not a Lycan?" She'd been doing that on her own occasionally. In the cities she lived in. How fantastic would it be to do it as a job? She could actually feel like she was contributing.

Jordan turned and frowned at her while seeming to examine her.

"What?"

"You've never shifted in your life?" he asked.

"No! Why does everyone assume I'm lying?"

"Because you have the abilities of a Lycan and you smell like a Lycan."

She sniffed her shoulder. Nobody had ever mentioned that. Which was probably good. Who knows how she'd have handled being told she smelled like a wolf outside of this scenario.

Jordan gestured behind them. "And there was a moment there when you thought I was calling Travis weak, I thought for sure…"

She sniffed. "You almost saw the nasty end of my temper, but I wasn't about to sprout hair and howl at the moon."

He didn't seem so sure.

"You'd think I'd know, right?" It'd be hard not to notice a thing like that.

"You'd think so. It's hard to believe that you can't. Have you tried?"

She rolled her eyes. "Travis asked me the same thing."

He shook his head. "Well, assuming through some weird

genetic fluke, you can't actually shift, even if you can do everything else, I'd bet you'd still do patrols somehow. Some of my two-footers do patrols, and Dane is a two-footer and Beta for my pack—Alpha when I'm gone."

She inhaled. "I smell an engine and gasoline. But it's faint." She pointed to the left. "Tire tracks. Looks like someone parked right here and took the body this way."

A mist was falling again, and the scent was already dissolving.

Jordan eyed the faint trail left from whatever vehicle had been here. "I can try following it, but I'm wondering if the rainy season is screwing us." He turned to look at her. "You should come spend a day here and there up in Glacier Peak. I'll teach you how to track better outside. The bears come out soon—and they're fun to track."

"She's not messing with bears!" Travis called from the house. Wow, he really did have incredible hearing, even if they hadn't gone very far.

"Busted," she said, grinning.

"Ignore him. You're Alpha and he could use the practice anyway. You can both come. We'll even drag along my in-laws and my mate and have a picnic."

"So, it's like that teddy-bear picnic song only with real bears."

"Surly bears. They're the most fun."

"She's not messing with surly bears!" Travis yelled.

"I'm Alpha! You can't tell me what to do!" she shouted back.

"Damn straight," Jordan said.

She high-fived him.

Chapter Ten

She had that hunting knife out on the dining room table, and she was spinning it in circles while staring at it moodily. "I feel so useless." She'd come back from tracking looking pretty damn pleased with herself and almost, well, content for it having been a fruitless search, but her temperament couldn't hold up to the forced reliance on others' searching.

"We need to wait for some of the others to check in, and some of them are out on four feet so we haven't heard back."

She picked up the knife and pointed at him with it. "You should be sleeping. I sent Jordan home to take care of his pack, and he listened. You. Need. To. Sleep."

He stared at the knife with raised eyebrows. "I can't imagine why I'm not. I'll get right on that." He didn't add that Jordan wouldn't have gone along with her edict if he hadn't already been intending on going back. It was probably validating to let her think she had some authority over Jordan.

Sheathing the knife, she said in a calmer voice, "Travis, you can at least sleep in between phone calls. You're going to start seeing pink elephants soon."

Oh, that already started. He could get where she was coming from right now with her moodiness—there was nothing worse in tracking than losing a trail to the elements.

Getting up, she grabbed his hand and towed him to the nearby couch. "You need to be ready for when something actually does happen." She sat down and patted her lap. "Lie down."

Blinking, he lay down with his head on her lap. Okay, this wasn't relaxing at all. He could really smell her sweet honey scent. He opened his mouth to tell her that when she started running her fingers through his hair, her nails raking his scalp lightly. *Mmm, that feels good.* This might work.

"Did you hear Jordan telling me about people in the pack?" she asked.

"Mm. Yup."

Her hand stopped.

He smiled and said, "Yes," while closing his eyes.

"Was he trying to con me into staying?"

"What do you mean?" That had obviously been what he was doing. Travis was hoping it'd worked. She seemed less averse to being Alpha.

There was no way he was taking her on a bear hunt—even if she was Alpha.

"Do you have someone in your pack named Kurt?"

"Yeah. And he's never spoken at a meeting I've held, either. You'd like him…but not too much or I'd have to kill him."

She laughed softly. "What about the others?"

"You can't like any of them too much, either—because jealousy is an ugly thing."

"No, I mean how are the other members of the pack?"

"When you become Alpha, there's this heavy responsibility that you feel for your pack—even the ones you'd like to shake. I like some more than others, but I sense potential in all of them. It's just…a huge group, and the morons won't form pairs and start families. It's relationships like those that build a pack. Instead I'm running a fraternity, and I swear this week feels like a hazing gone wrong."

"What if I asked you to leave the pack?"

It cut into him, and he felt a sharp ache in his chest. Being an Alpha was a part of him now. On the other hand, this was LeAnn. "Would you ask me to do that?" When they'd talked about it prior to the challenge, it'd felt like just words. This time, it felt like a real possibility.

"Of course not. How much of a girl do you think I am?"

He opened his eyes to stare at her. That was the weirdest question ever then. "I think I'm hearing things."

She leaned over him. "No, you're supposed to say, 'Yes, LeAnn, I would do anything for you.'"

"Of course I would."

She huffed out a breath. "That was weak." She kept running her fingers through his hair. "What would you do if I accepted the scent-match right now?"

"Are you?"

"I don't know. These are all hypothetical questions."

He blinked. Hypothetical questions were practically his worst nightmare. Questions about possibilities that might or might not exist and you might be held to your answers either way? What strange torture was this? If not for the fact that he was amazingly comfortable, he'd be running from the room screaming.

"Never mind. We could talk about volcanoes instead."

He kept blinking. This felt like a trick, too. It had to be. That was too strange a conversation jump, even for LeAnn. On the other hand, it was volcanoes. What could go wrong in a conversation about volcanoes? Unless one was erupting right beside you, it was a nice, safe topic.

He opened his mouth to talk about volcanoes and she asked, "Were you interested in Alanna before I came along?"

Okay, that was definitely a trick question. Maybe if he pretended to be asleep she'd stop asking questions. Maybe she wouldn't notice if he didn't answer the questions.

His phone rang, and he answered it quickly. Saved. Hopefully she'd forget that last question by the time he hung up. It was Kurt's group. He'd even paired up with two females—which was also unlike him. Maybe defending LeAnn had given him some much-needed confidence. If he had defended her. Jordan might have been making that up to convince LeAnn the pack wasn't as bad as she thought.

"We didn't find anything, but, uhh…a bunch of us have talked about staying in the lodge tonight. Safety in numbers. With it being a Friday—most of us don't have work tomorrow anyway."

"That sounds like a good idea."

He could hear the smile in Kurt's voice as he said, "I thought so."

"Report in and tell me who ends up there and who's still at their places."

"Me?"

"Yes."

"Okay."

"One last thing...did you ask Alanna not to bother LeAnn?"

There was silence, and then Kurt said, "Yes."

"Good. I'll wait for your call." When he hung up, he smiled at LeAnn. "Well, I'll be damned. I never would have guessed that."

She'd stopped running her hands through his hair and was staring at him.

"What?" he asked finally. He couldn't read her expression. This could be bad. It could be very bad. He never knew when she was two seconds from making a run for it. Maybe he should bring up volcanoes again.

"I think I want to accept the scent-match."

Or good. Very good. Sitting up, he dragged her across his lap. She gasped, surprised, right before his mouth covered hers. Too far away. He pulled her into straddling his lap as he tightened his arms around her.

He needed her. He wanted her. It was finally okay to have her. She was his. The pack would know she was his.

Mine.

She laughed against his lips. "I thought you were tired."

"Second wind." He slid his hands up her back. She even had a perfect back. Her skin was so soft.

Still too far away. He tipped her onto her back, pressing her into the couch with his body.

LeAnn cupped his face. "Don't you think you should get that?" she asked between kisses.

"What?" He kissed a path down her neck. Hell, why was she wearing so many clothes? He'd have to stop kissing her to pull some of them off—unless he tore them off. How much did she like this shirt?

"The phone."

He stopped and stared at the glowing display on the side table where his phone was hopping around as it vibrated. Outside the pound of his pulse, he could hear it ringing. He should answer it. He could at least see who it was. It might be important. It might be life or death. Literally. And he went back to kissing her neck. *Mm.* She smelled amazing. He licked her skin—she tasted sweet as honey, too.

"Oh, whoa…but also…" She reached out and grabbed the phone. "Hello."

He paused on her collarbone.

"Uhh," the voice on the phone said.

"What is it, Liam? Travis is busy."

He smiled against her skin. She sounded breathless, and Liam could probably hear his heavy breathing a foot away. They wouldn't be fooling anyone.

"Troy didn't leave. In fact, he took his tracking device out and, from his scent, I think he's heading toward Travis's."

His heart stopped. *You have to be kidding.* "What the hell?" He sat up, grabbing the phone from her hand.

The window behind the couch shattered as a bullet whizzed by his head. Jerking back, he growled. Seriously? He ducked down, dragging LeAnn onto the floor in front of the couch. In a crouch, he tugged her behind him to the nearby oak dining room table. He tipped the table onto its side and pulled her behind it, out of sight. If that had even grazed LeAnn, he'd have ripped Troy to shreds. He might anyway.

"Was that a gunshot?" Liam asked.

Hell yeah it was. He should have killed the bastard after

the challenge. "Yeah. Apparently, Troy has decided not to honor the terms of the challenge," Travis said as he pulled out his gun. Another shot through the window.

"I'll see who I can gather, and we'll come at him from behind," Liam said quietly before hanging up.

They couldn't see Troy from behind the table, but he couldn't see them, either. They'd both be firing blind. Unfortunately, Travis's living room didn't provide much other cover, and the attached kitchen wasn't any better. An open floor plan had seemed like such a good idea when he was looking at houses. The real estate agent had failed to mention it wasn't ideal for a hostile situation with gunfire. Running for the hall would leave them too long in the open. Damn. They were trapped.

"Stay down and stay silent," Travis hissed. They had to hold their position until reinforcements arrived. Hopefully his mate could be levelheaded and calm in a tense situation.

LeAnn nodded, but reached out and grabbed the cord of the nearby lamp and yanked it from the wall, plunging them into the dark.

Hell, he loved this woman.

It was bad luck that the pounding of his pulse was making it difficult to concentrate, but what they'd been doing gave him a lot of motivation to survive this standoff. This waiting sucked. It wasn't like him to be in a defensive-only position. Travis listened for a moment before popping his head up and taking a shot.

Troy swore and moved. Travis had gotten close, but hadn't hit him.

He bounced up again and fired, hitting the tree Troy had ducked behind. Travis growled as he took cover.

Troy fired directly through the table a few times, but LeAnn dived to the ground, and they passed far above her.

Okay, now he was really mad. This was probably similar to the blind rage he'd seen between the two women earlier, but it seemed much more reasonable in this case. As he raised up and fired two more shots, LeAnn crawled quickly behind him.

He turned to glare at her as he ducked back down. What was she doing? He'd told her *specifically* to stay down.

She glared back but got up from the ground and ran at a crouch toward his slim gun safe on the nearby wall. Oh, hell… He had to go and find himself an Alpha, didn't he?

Troy took a shot, but Travis jumped up from behind the table and fired on him, making him dive for cover.

"This was a bad idea," he whispered to LeAnn as he moved toward her. He threw off a blind shot at Troy to keep him behind the tree while they were exposed like this.

They didn't have time for her to… LeAnn opened the gun safe within seconds. Well, that was nice and secure. She tossed him his rifle and ammunition.

"Yeah, tell me that again after I've saved your ass," she said in return, grabbing the handgun he kept taking from her and putting away.

"Do you know how to shoot?" he asked. She said she'd killed that criminal, but…

Troy let loose another barrage of gunfire that had them diving for the safety of the table.

A moment later, LeAnn bobbed up and fired three shots before crouching back down. "Does that answer your question?" she asked.

Okay, fine, she could shoot.

LeAnn listened and swore. "I was hoping that one hit him, but he's fast."

"It's your fault Merilee is dead!" Troy yelled.

"Jordan was right—this whole pack is full of psychopaths." He popped up and fired off a shot before dropping the handgun and grabbing the rifle she'd gotten for him. "Damn, he's fast."

"I know, right?"

She gave him a pointed look as he loaded the rifle.

"Out of bullets?" Troy shouted, laughing.

She bounced up and fired off a couple shots, which had Troy swearing. "Yeah, we are, Troy. Come in and get us."

"Cute," Travis said.

"Oh, I know."

He pulled up and fired. "If he'd waited until we were done to interrupt us, I'd feel a whole lot less like killing him." Though, really, their first time might take quite a while, and he wouldn't have wanted an audience out there. Actually, considering how much he wanted LeAnn, their first time might have been fast and hot, but then he'd have wanted a second time right away, and *that* would have taken longer.

"Ow. Damn," Troy hissed.

"Nicked him," Travis said. "I think I got his shoulder before he could yank it out of sight."

"Still feeling the love of the pack?"

"No, but we will be in a couple minutes." He shoved her backward as Troy fired again. The table absorbed some of the speed, but the bullets still sprayed the floor between them. His living room looked like a war zone with the busted glass everywhere, along with pieces of furniture.

Both he and LeAnn bounced up at the same time, firing.

More swearing from Troy.

"Yes!" LeAnn said as they dropped back down to the floor.

"I got him," they said at the same time before scowling at each other.

"Oh, that was me," LeAnn said.

"No, I'm sorry, but that was me." He wasn't going to give up his hits because she was a woman he wanted in a filthy way—one he wanted even more now that he'd seen her fire a gun. "Troy, was that last hit from a rifle or a handgun?" he yelled.

His answer was more swearing.

"It was from a rifle," he translated for her.

"Oh, sweetie, if you really need this to boost your self-confidence, I'll give you this one," she said, giving him a long look.

"Honey, that wasn't a gun in my pocket a few minutes back. Trust me, I have a lot to be confident about." He gestured toward the other side of the table with his head. "Including that last shot."

She pulled her shirt off. "And they're real, babydoll."

He stared.

"And that last shot was all me, too."

"Put your shirt back on." How was he supposed to concentrate with her there in only a bra? A black lace bra. He'd seen her naked, but this was somehow showcasing rather than concealing. And he hadn't seen her naked since he'd gotten to know her…and knowing LeAnn had made her fifty times more sexy. Wow. Yeah. There was no way he'd have any kind of accuracy with her undressed. He picked up her shirt and tossed it at her. "Put it back on."

She brushed it off her. "No."

"Yes."

"No."

"Next shot counts for both."

"Fine."

"Put your shirt back on."

"Why?" She raised her eyebrows.

"You're not supposed to take off layers of protection in a gunfight." Yeah, his ability to think was being severely hampered but the vision of her…in lace…and, wow.

"What do you think my shirt was made of—Kevlar?"

Shaking it off, Travis slid up and then back down again. "No shot. He's behind that tree out there. I think he's reevaluating the poor choices he's made in his life up until now."

"Shut up!" Troy yelled.

A single shot tore through the table and caught the edge of Travis's arm before he could move.

"Hell," Travis muttered, scrambling sideways. It stung, but it was nothing. The tear in his side from the previous night was far worse.

"Did he hit you?" LeAnn asked, her mouth dropped open. "Oh, no he didn't!" He should have known what her reaction would be from earlier with Alanna. She jumped up and emptied her gun into the trees.

"Was that really necessary?" he asked when she dropped down beside him.

"Yes." She grinned. "I think I got him."

More swearing from outside.

"Damn."

"Was that for your arm or because I just took that?" When he didn't answer, she continued, "I guess I can use your rifle."

"Hell no."

She was back to looking at the gun safe.

Then he heard it and relaxed against his bullet-riddled table. The pound of feet. The pack had come.

He heard more swearing and then a snarl as Troy shifted and ran.

Travis grabbed LeAnn and pulled the side of her head against his chest in a hug while he covered her other ear just as they caught him. Pack killings were ugly—and loud...far too loud. The revulsion hit him hard and fast and he tightened his arms around her. Troy still felt like pack, and this was so senseless. It shouldn't have gone this way, but the moron had left them no choice.

"What?" she asked.

After a moment, he released her and answered, "Nothing. It's over." He grabbed her shirt from beside them. She felt like heaven with her skin against his, but no one else was seeing her like this. She was accepting the scent-match, which meant they were married, and no one was seeing his wife in only a bra...other than him...later.

"What happened?"

"Pack law."

She swallowed and nodded and hugged him tight.

He winced and tried to get a look at his arm. It was nothing. He'd live. And he hugged her back.

"Just so we're clear, I won, right?" she asked.

"I'll give you this one." It'd put her in a better mood for later, and he wanted her in a very good mood.

"You'll *give* me this one?"

He laughed.

• • •

LeAnn studied the wound on Travis's arm. He sat on the counter in the bathroom off one of the lodge's upper rooms.

"It'll fall off if I shift," Travis said, staring down at where she'd put the bandage on his bicep.

She rolled her eyes. *Idiot man.* "Well, don't shift." Biting her lip, she nodded at the bandage. "You should really have that stitched. Maybe we should ask Alanna." It cost her so very much to suggest that. And no one would ever appreciate how much.

"Hell no. It's not even as bad as the one on my side."

She leaned forward and pressed her forehead against his. "You're not filling me with confidence." That one on his side was pretty bad. Tipping back, she pulled up his shirt to look at it.

"Here, I'll help." He pulled his shirt off and tossed it to the side before giving her a hot look. Lifting his hands, he cupped her hips before slipping them up and underneath her shirt and around her waist.

He had to be kidding. Half the pack was staying the night in the lodge, but his place no longer had a back sliding-glass door, and he refused to stay at Ross's place when her brother might possibly be on a psychotic rampage. But he was feeling amorous? *Here? Now?*

"Travis." She looped her arms around his neck. "You need sleep." Not to mention that she hadn't planned on the whole pack knowing firsthand that she was accepting Travis as her mate.

He leaned forward and kissed her neck.

His mouth was so warm, and he smelled so sexy and heavenly. Yeah. Still no. She could hear a few other couples getting it on in the lodge, and that was already too close to voyeur for her. Sometimes having great hearing really sucked, and it's not like the walls were helping. She'd wanted to yell, "Get a room!" like twenty times, but she also was very happy to have one of the few rooms above the large common area. Being with the Alpha definitely had its perks. He'd pointed at the one he'd wanted, and they'd all nodded.

She cupped his face and pulled him up to stare into his eyes. She had to stop him while she still could. Her body was starting to say "yes" in a real way. "Travis, we're going to get some sleep."

He scowled…which made her grin.

"Is this your way of telling me you're only interested in me for my body?" Not that she thought that. Okay, maybe she thought that. A little.

The frown fell from his face.

Crouching, she grabbed his shirt and handed it back to him before exiting the bathroom.

"You know that's not true," he said, following her and pulling on the shirt.

"Do I?" she asked, sliding into the bed. He'd said that he "wanted her" a ton of times, but that was a far cry from other emotions. She wanted chocolate cake right now, but she wasn't about to go all primal on a slice of it. Well, maybe. That was a bad comparison. The point was that she didn't know if he felt anything more than "want."

He flipped off the light as he headed toward her. Crawling across the bed, he kept their gazes locked. "Yeah. You do." He stopped right above her, though he slipped under the covers, too.

"I guess I asked for it. Showing up naked that first time—it probably gave you the wrong idea."

"You had a knife. Up to my neck. I think I got the right idea."

"And what idea was that?"

He lay down beside her and pulled her up against his side. "That you'd be a helluva lot of work, but you'd be worth it."

"You thought that?"

"The knife said that."

"Yeah?" That sounded like more than "want."

"Mm-hm. You know what else I thought?"

"What?" she asked, yawning.

"That you had the hottest body I'd ever seen, and it might be worth dying to touch."

• • •

LeAnn heard both their screams—her mother's and the little girl's—but it was her mother she saw, pointing at her. The world was drenched in anger and heat.

She wanted to rage. She wanted to scream herself, but she couldn't move. She looked up from the ground at her mother and she heard a growling monster come from behind her. Its teeth snapped and claws scrabbled across the floor as it moved.

When LeAnn turned, she saw the little girl screaming and screaming.

Moaning, she struggled to get free, trying to get away from the monster that lurked in the room. LeAnn was trapped in this body. This was not her. It couldn't be her. Why could she not move?

When she turned back, her mother's fear had melted away to anger, and she darted forward yelling, "You're just like him. A monster."

LeAnn tried to deny it. Why would her mouth not move? Why would her legs not work? The growling and snapping of teeth filled the room. If only her hands could cover her ears. The vicious clacking of those jaws would end. If only she could see the monster…

"You are a monster," her mother yelled again. "Stay away from me. Stay away!"

I'm not a monster.

The young girl screamed.

I am a monster.

"Shh, LeAnn. Shh. You're safe now. I have you. You're not alone. I'm here. Shh, honey. You're okay." His warmth enveloped her and his scent filled her nostrils as she inhaled. His voice promised security…and acceptance.

The sharp red rage the color of blood receded. The beast inside her retreated.

With a sigh, she drew closer to the only thing that mattered…the peace in the middle of the madness.

I am not a monster.

Chapter Eleven

He jerked awake and searched the bed beside him. Empty. Then he heard her laughing elsewhere in the house, and his body flushed with heat and want. *Mine.* Taking a deep breath, he forced it back, because there were definitely others with her…making her laugh. Meanwhile, he'd woken up alone. He took another breath and exhaled slowly.

She was his.

She was accepting the scent-match.

Everything was better today. The world was brighter. Finding balance seemed more plausible. She was accepting the scent-match, and she sounded happy.

After her nightmare last night, it was good to hear her so lighthearted. Her body had shaken and she'd twisted and arched her back as she moaned. Maybe he should have done something more than just hold her and rub her taut muscles while reassuring her with his voice. It seemed to have worked. That was something. And she was laughing this morning.

Life is good.

There is no reason to fly into a jealous rage and kill whoever is making her laugh.

He dragged a hand through his hair. Okay, they had to have sex soon, or he'd get homicidal. This was probably how it started. One day, you were a sane, rational person, and then, less than a week later, you were mentally tearing the head off anyone who dared talk to her.

His life used to make sense.

She laughed again.

His body flushed with heat. Hell, he wanted her. She was his.

Making sense was overrated.

Travis pushed out of the bed and went to go find his mate, pocketing his phone on the way.

LeAnn was downstairs in the kitchen with six of his pack making breakfast. The smell of bacon was as mouthwatering as her scent—which called to him despite all the other scents around. Everyone quieted and lowered their heads when he walked in, and it dampened his irritation. Striding through the gathered Lycans, he went to her side at the stove and wrapped an arm around her as he kissed her on the mouth. It was possessive and arrogant, but he didn't care.

When he pulled back, her lips tipped up in a half smile. "Good morning. I was about to bring you some breakfast as soon as the bacon was done."

"I heard you down here laughing." He hadn't intended for it to sound like an accusation, but it did.

She nodded at the Lycans behind him who'd gone back to eating. "Kristin was telling me that you guys have some raccoons getting the best of you. She said they're harder to deal with than the bears."

He smiled and relaxed. "Did she tell you about Ugly Bart?"

"She was starting to." She fed him a piece of bacon from the nearby plate before transferring the remainder from the skillet to the plate.

"That thing's days are numbered," Travis said, leaning against the counter beside LeAnn.

Kristin continued looking down as she said, "I can't figure out how he manages to break into all our garbages in one night, let alone with one eye."

"And he doesn't even want the garbage," Grant added, sliding closer to Kristin. "He just wants to dump all the damn cans to annoy us." Things had changed between a few of the couples. The dynamic had shifted. They weren't squandering the opportunities or chances at relationships.

Kristin looked up at Grant and smiled and winked.

Travis turned his attention back to LeAnn, who was humming under her breath.

She glanced up and caught him staring. Grinning, she fed him another piece of bacon.

"Is all the bacon for me?" he asked, nodding at the two dozen pieces of bacon.

There was a chorus of disappointed groans behind him.

Shaking her head, she grabbed the plate of bacon, sheltering it with her body, and twisted to set it on the island with plates of eggs and hash browns. "Quick, I'll hold him off," she said, turning back to him and wrapping her arms around his waist.

He winced when her arm rubbed against the healing

gouge in his side, but hugged her back. He could get used to this. The last few days had been intense—days spent waiting for the next thing to go wrong.

"What are the plans for patrol today?" Liam asked, walking in. He sounded far more somber than he ever had, and he kept his head bowed in deference. He'd led the pack in killing Troy and overseen the cleanup, and some of his disregard for authority had died with his friend. Liam had watched over the lodge for part of the night after he'd returned. "Oh! Bacon!" Well, okay, that was less somber, but it *was* bacon.

"I should have had him grab more bacon," LeAnn said. She looked up. "I sent Kurt out for food for all of us. I failed to consider how much a hungry bunch of Lycans might eat."

She'd organized breakfast. And the pack was following her directions. All this hell might end up being worth it.

"As far as patrols go," Travis said, "I think it's time to figure out where Ross stashed the vehicle he was using and where he's holing up at night. Jordan and LeAnn found some tire tracks yesterday behind Merilee's that I want to take a closer look at—providing the rain hasn't washed them out." He'd been too tired yesterday to follow some of the more obvious plans of action, but with a mostly uninterrupted night's sleep and LeAnn in his arms, his brain was much sharper, even if her scent was playing havoc with his libido. She smelled like bacon and herself, and he was only a man.

Liam nodded as he dished himself food.

"Someone should check on everyone who wasn't here last night," LeAnn said. She left him to go fix a plate of food, too.

He should really grab his own food before it was all gone, but this rare harmony among pack members was a relief. It felt like they *were* a pack. Finally.

"We should get a head count every night until this is resolved," Travis said. "Resolved" was a strange word choice, but the fact that they were hunting down his mate's brother made him temper his words more than he ever had.

LeAnn turned and handed him the plate she'd filled, along with a fork, before going to get her own food.

He fought a smile as he noticed all the quick glances from the pack. LeAnn had inadvertently acknowledged him as Alpha—her Alpha. Also, she'd gotten him even more bacon. Life was very good.

His phone rang, and he frowned at the number before answering, "Hello." That was strange. Maybe someone in the pack had picked up the phone, not realizing it was Troy's.

Ragged breathing met this, and the pack went still in the kitchen.

"Who is this?" His tolerance for playing games was at an all-time low.

"I know what you're doing. Leave my sister out of this."

Blood thrummed in his ears as the threat registered. The wolf surged up inside him. Nothing could happen to LeAnn. Nothing.

There was a crunching sound that probably indicated tracing the phone would be a dead end.

LeAnn's plate shattered as it struck the floor.

• • •

They were back to looking at her like she was an outsider

who didn't belong. It was just as well she hadn't started eating, because her stomach clenched and ached. She was never meant to belong anywhere. They couldn't actually accept a traitor's sister no matter how much Travis fought to claim her as pack.

I'm not pack.

"You're okay?" Travis asked, crouching beside her as she cleaned up the broken plate. "You're okay." And he was up and moving before she'd even answered.

She opened her eyes wide and blinked them furiously without looking up. Yeah, the pack wouldn't see her cry over this. She dumped the remnants of her breakfast in the trash while Travis started arranging groups to go check on others. He was taking Liam and Grant with him to go circle Troy's place and see if they could catch Ross.

She stood in front of the sink washing her hands mindlessly as she stared out across the forest. The murmuring voices of the pack wrapped around her.

What the hell was she doing? Just like that, they'd remembered that she didn't belong and that her brother was the monster hunting them.

And what did Ross mean? Was any of this because she'd come here and stepped into the life he'd thrown away? It didn't make sense he'd kill Merilee, but maybe Ross had long since stopped making sense.

"You shouldn't come with us," Travis said, touching her back. He'd moved so quickly and silently.

No. Of course not. Even though it was her brother and she was good at tracking him...no, that wouldn't make sense for her to come. She wanted to shake Travis. Then again, maybe he didn't want her to come because they'd be killing

Ross. Hell. "I can't come?"

"Some of the others are staying," he said, rather than explaining.

She shrugged. What did he want her to do? Accept it? Be all *woo* and *yay*? He was immediately back to keeping secrets and shutting her out. It felt like he didn't trust her, either. Then again, Ross *was* her brother.

But maybe that was the reason she should come. She could reason with Ross. He might listen to her.

She definitely wasn't going to beg to come with him, not in front of the pack.

"We need to go so we don't lose the trail." Travis turned her toward him, but she stayed staring straight ahead—at his chest.

Screw it. "I can help you. I'm good at tracking, and I'm the most familiar with his scent."

Travis lowered his voice and said, "I need to know you're here so I can concentrate."

She stared at him. Did he even realize what he'd done? And in front of the entire pack. Her worth was solely in being his arm ornament apparently, and he didn't trust her to stay out of his way and out of trouble.

"It's fine," she said finally when it seemed like he wouldn't leave without a response.

"We're going on four feet, so you can hang on to this for me." He handed her his phone.

Oh, great. As far as consolation prizes went, being keeper of the phone wasn't stellar. *Here, wait at home for me, little woman. All you're good for is sex and sandwiches.* Okay, maybe it wasn't like that. It just felt like that.

It also seemed to reiterate that she was the only non-

Lycan in the house. She wouldn't be changing form, so she might as well be of use in some other way.

She didn't fit, didn't belong.

. . .

"I'll be back." He kissed her mouth firmly.

Heading out the back door, his heartbeat was picking up as his Lycan side anticipated the hunt, but there was a niggling sense that he was making a mistake. He shouldn't be leaving her. She *was* the best tracker in the pack. Still, he had to keep control. There'd been too much death already. He wasn't about to lose her like he'd lost his brother.

Travis let the change take him, and all the worries and concerns began to recede as the wolf took over, but he stopped just off the porch and looked back through the kitchen window.

Mate.

Mine.

Safe.

His mate stood there, with her back to the other female in the room. Her hand came up and brushed at her cheek, then she briefly covered her eyes and took a deep breath before turning around.

He sensed the others turning back to look at him in question.

An Alpha didn't second-guess his choices. An Alpha was firm and always in control. With a howl, he took the lead and bolted into the forest with the others following him. He could come back to thoughts of his mate after he'd caught the enemy.

· · ·

"Well, this is lame," Kristin said, echoing her thoughts.

If only she had that map from Ross's house. Staring at it made her feel connected to this place. It helped calm her down and to concentrate. At least she'd had the knife when they'd come here last night.

Travis's breakfast was cooling on a plate where he'd left it. "Should we save the food for them?" she asked Kristin.

"Probably. They'll burn off a lot of energy running." She looked up to see Kristin staring in the direction they'd gone with a frown on her face. "I wish I could have gone. I got left behind at Glacier Peak, too. The only female Travis took was Alanna."

It actually made her ill. She'd been left behind because she didn't belong on a hunt of her brother—her murderer brother. But Alanna would always have a place in the pack.

"Uhh, because she's a doctor," Kristin said quickly. "Not because Travis liked her."

Alanna should have been Alpha. In fact, she was beginning to suspect she'd taken Alanna's place. Alanna would get to go with Travis places because she was a doctor. She'd always have that over LeAnn.

She was still a whore who should be throat-punched at the earliest opportunity.

LeAnn fake-smiled at Kristin…who wasn't meeting her eyes and looked appalled. After yesterday, the pack most likely expected any mention of Alanna's name to be met with screaming and swinging punches.

LeAnn busied herself with putting away food, trying not

to bump into Kristin as she did so. One of the other male pack members had been left behind, too, but he'd gone to email out updates to others in the pack. Somewhere else in the lodge, another female member was taking a shower, totally oblivious to all that was happening.

As if she'd been summoned, the front door opened, and she could smell Alanna's scent even before she asked the other male, "What's happened? I saw a bunch of the pack heading off in all directions."

Kristin's eyes widened, and she briefly met LeAnn's gaze before looking down.

Great. Kristin was acting afraid of her, and she was worried there'd be an all-out girl fight in a second. She might not be wrong. Especially if LeAnn stayed. Then Travis would get back and be disappointed that she'd killed their only doctor who probably still was a murdering hag…but she *was* a doctor.

What the hell was she doing here? She didn't belong. Nobody really wanted her as Alpha, aside from Travis, and he clearly didn't see her as an equal.

"I left a map at Travis's. I'll go get it." And leave. Her car and her keys were at Travis's house. The map could be a damn memento of her time here. Maybe if she left, Ross would lay off everyone and leave the pack alone.

"Uhh." Kristin looked back and forth between her and the front area where she could hear the pack member filling Alanna in.

"It's fine," she said again. She'd said that so many times today, she ought to sew the stupid phrase on a throw pillow and be done with it. Then she went out the back, too, before she was forced to kill Alanna.

The air was still moist and thick but it was less cold—which was good because she didn't want to go back inside to get the keys to Travis's truck. Luckily, the lodge was close to Travis's place, which was most likely not a coincidence.

There were piles of clothes on the porch, left from the men shifting, and she walked over and bent next to Travis's and lifted his shirt to her nose. Mm. If she'd ever done a thing right in her life, maybe she'd deserve him, and he smelled amazing. Shaking her head, she dropped the shirt and left the porch.

Leaving would make her seem like a crazy freak after she'd told Travis she was going to accept the scent-match.

That was before he'd gone to hunt down her brother. Without her.

Ross looked like a good suspect for Merilee's murder—even though she couldn't imagine Ross killing an unarmed woman. All the evidence either pointed at him...or his sister. And she'd conveniently forgotten that. And now Ross had proved he was alive.

Damn.

Who'd have guessed breakfast would be so eventful? Other than, of course, being the most important meal of the day.

And she hadn't even eaten anything.

The walk was helping to clear her head...sort of. The longer she walked, the more she realized she'd jumped to accept the scent-match and join the pack somewhat rashly. It was easy to be all "rah rah pack" when they'd just killed a murderous psychopath for you, but would probably be less so when the other murderous psychopath was your only relative.

Not that Ross didn't deserve it.

But it wasn't as if the pack would let that go. She'd always be the murderer's sister here. And anything other than that was wishful thinking.

Hell. What had she been thinking? Her…and the sheriff…who was hunting her brother? That was insane.

As she came up behind his house, she could smell Troy… and death and a lot of blood. She was near enough to where the pack had killed him, and even if they'd taken and buried the body it nearly overwhelmed her—the area would smell like this for a good long time. This is what was waiting for her brother, her only relative. Closing her eyes, she dropped against the trunk of a tree and took deep breaths. Her inhale brought another scent—her brother's. Ross had been around here. Death. Ross. Blood.

It might all end like this as soon as today. They might have already caught Ross even.

If they did, would it be another pack killing?

Ross would be ripped to shreds before she even got to talk to him?

Her stomach turned. She took deep breaths to avoid gagging.

What would Travis say if that happened? *Sorry, LeAnn, it's the pack way. The pack protects its own.*

The pack did.

She was never going to be pack no matter how her mind tried to spin it. Not with how fast they were to go after her brother.

Tears spilled down her cheeks despite her keeping her eyes closed to hold them back. Ross's cryptic words to Travis came to her then. What did he think Travis had done? Her brother might try to kill Travis now, too. All because she'd come here, looking for answers.

Sniffing, she opened her eyes and rubbed the tears from her cheeks. That was a pointless road to go down. She knew that from her past. You couldn't change the past. You couldn't arrive somewhere sooner. You couldn't stop someone from doing something they'd already done. You couldn't magically erase all the wrongs you'd committed by a few good deeds.

It had happened. It was over. And you picked up the pieces and moved on.

If Ross lived, LeAnn was putting Travis on his hit list if she remained. And coming here had put Ross on Travis's. Wow, she was a terrible sister. Not that her brother didn't deserve it, but…wow. It might even be her fault that Merilee was dead. The obvious motive with her death was to frame LeAnn.

There were bullets embedded in the trees she walked past, and the smell of blood was there, too. Her pulse roared in her ears, and the scent of blood and death sucked all the available air from around her. Her vision faded…

Stopping, LeAnn blinked rapidly. It was fine. She was fine. She breathed in and out through pursed lips. This was a different time and a different place. Sometimes, killing was justified.

Still, there was so much blood.

And Troy was a bastard, but…

Shaking her head, she moved on. Once she wasn't quite so close to the scent of blood and death, she'd be able to think again. Already her head was clearing. She had to be rational about this.

She had to get out of here. The pack could go back to the way it was. Life could go back to the way it was. She'd never hear firsthand how her mate had killed her brother or vice versa. If she left, it'd draw Ross after her, possibly. It was win-win for everyone, except maybe her.

And heaven knew, she didn't deserve nice things.

Someone had boarded over the back entryway, but this was her third time breaking into Travis's house, and even if he'd rehidden his spare key every time, keys called to her. She could smell them easily, and she'd never lost her keys even once. Travis'd buried it under a rock this time. It made her curious if he'd be able to find the key if she hid it somewhere else. Ross couldn't find keys like she could, so it wasn't a superpower everyone related to Lycans lucked into.

"Easy peasy," she said, wiping off the spare key and using it before pocketing it. She'd hide it much better before she left.

Stepping into his house, she took a deep breath. Much better. Her. Travis. And then the smell of a lot of gunfire. Speaking of which… She walked by Travis's destroyed couch to his gun safe. It didn't feel right walking around this area without a gun right now.

Opening up the gun safe, she picked a handgun and loaded it. It wasn't her favorite by any means, but someone had killed Merilee, and right now the only ones off her list of suspects were her and Travis…well, and a few of the pack she'd met that morning. Kristin was even a vegetarian, for crying out loud. Vegetarians were probably the least murderous demographic out there. Second only to preschool teachers and obstetricians.

She picked up the map from the counter. *Something to*

remember Travis by. Her keys were there, too. Right beside a notepad.

Before she lost her nerve, she set down the map and grabbed a pen.

How did you say "good-bye and don't follow me" while still leaving it open to him doing that, if he cared? He shouldn't follow her. It wasn't safe. Besides, chances were, the pack would say good riddance.

Dear Travis,

My family and my past will always come between us. I'm not right for you. I don't belong in your pack. I can't change what Ross did, but maybe if I'm not here he won't bother with you or the pack. If you didn't kill him already. That's probably why you didn't want me to come this morning. If you did kill him I guess that would be between us, too. If you did, I understand. You have to do what is right for the pack. They're more important. But I don't belong here either way. I want you to know

She tapped the pen. Should she really tell him how she felt about him? And how did she sign it? "Love, LeAnn"? She'd never even told him that she loved him. Tears dropped down onto the paper before she even realized she was crying.

She loved him.

She'd never told him.

Why hadn't she told him?

Of course he'd never said it, either. Which made her cry harder.

Gah. Where was a tissue when you needed one? Ugh, she was a mess. She was such an ugly crier. Alanna probably looked beautiful when she cried. Yet another reason to hate her.

Grabbing a paper towel, LeAnn wiped her eyes before blowing her nose.

She'd cried more in the last week than she had her entire life. So much for being a badass Alpha—see, obviously she wasn't meant to be an Alpha. She couldn't even write a damn good-bye letter without sobbing all over it.

Leaning over, with her elbows on the counter, she cupped her hands over her eyes and took a deep breath. And then another. It'd all gone to hell so fast.

And his scent hit her. Her eyes widened and shivers of awareness skittered across her skin.

He's here.

No! Not now!

Then an arm circled her as a needle pricked her skin.

She jerked and screamed.

No!

She wasn't going this way! She wrestled with the arm around her, swinging them around and slamming them both against the counter, knocking the keys and the map to the floor. Her shoe caught the dropped syringe and it skidded across the floor. And then a heaviness hit her like a wall, towing her under into the blackness.

Chapter Twelve

He shifted on the lodge's back porch with a growl still in his throat. It was hard to leave the beast behind after another unsuccessful search. When he picked up his shirt to put it on, the scent of LeAnn wafted up, making him smile. Sleeping with her in his arms had mixed their scents together—his shirt smelled like them. It was a good scent.

He inhaled again and frowned. Actually the back porch smelled like LeAnn, too. That was…a concern.

Kristin was right next to the door when they stepped in, and she was having difficulty maintaining deference as the scent of anxiety poured off her. "LeAnn left to go get a map from your place and hasn't returned. I was about to send Nate to get you."

He sucked in a breath. "What? When did she leave?"

"Two hours ago."

His mouth went dry. This couldn't be happening. It was like juggling grenades trying to keep everything in control.

He'd counted on her to be here. Two hours? "And you let her go?"

"She's Alpha," Kristin said, crying. "And Alanna had just walked in the front door. I think that's why she left. Maybe she thinks Alanna is still here and that's why she hasn't come back."

He inhaled and forced himself to calm down. If the pack was starting to accept LeAnn as Alpha it was a good thing—even if it meant they'd not struggle to question her decisions, and he'd noticed that Kristin was showing LeAnn deference. Kristin would be one of the first…it fit with the natural hierarchy. *Dammit.* Maybe he should have left someone else here. Though anyone keeping LeAnn somewhere when she was determined to leave would have their hands full, and having her and Alanna in the same place might have gotten…messy.

"But Alanna's not here?" he asked Kristin.

Kristin relaxed and let Grant pull her into his arms. "She left right after LeAnn did. She said she was following you to Troy's, and I thought maybe it was just as well LeAnn had left before she said that." She bit back another sob and said, "I also messed up and mentioned that Alanna was the only female in the pack you took with you to the fight in Glacier Peak, but I made sure that she knew it was because Alanna was a doctor."

He winced. *That had probably gone over like a house fire.*

"She seemed like she understood," Kristin said.

He nodded and smiled tightly.

Kristin turned in Grant's arms and continued to cry into his shirt. Yeah, he should have left someone else here, too.

Though he'd have had a hard time trusting anyone more dominant…and male. And they still didn't know who'd killed Merilee if it wasn't Ross. Though it definitely wasn't Kristin.

"I'm going to go look for her at my place after I try her phone." He patted his pockets. "Wait, I left my phone with her."

Grant reached into his pocket and pulled out his phone, tossing it to Travis. He dialed her phone first, and they all looked up at the ceiling as it rang up in the bedroom they'd used. Hanging up, he called his phone. It rang and rang…and that wasn't good.

He shifted back and bolted out the door. Minutes later, he'd reached his place and found LeAnn's scent.

Mine.

Mate.

And then the scent of someone else. His lips pulled back as he growled. He didn't like this scent near his mate.

Liam had followed and was staying off his property out of deference. Travis turned and jerked his head in acceptance before he shifted back beside the door.

"Ross again," Liam said as Travis tried the door. Unlocked.

They went inside. Her keys were on the floor along with the map, but she'd left a note. Travis pulled the notepad toward him.

His stomach clenched, and bile rose in his throat. What the hell? No. No, this couldn't be happening.

Liam cleared his throat and stepped back, reminding Travis of his presence.

His alpha side reared up. His brain told him he should brush it off. He should act like he didn't care. Travis slammed a fist against the counter.

Why didn't I take her with me?

If she left, being an Alpha would be all that he had. His job and his place in the pack. Things would be back under his control…but he'd go slowly mad for wanting her. And that wasn't just the scent-match.

She'd turned his life upside down. She was crazy. She made him crazy. He couldn't live without that. He could convince her to stay—to come back and stay.

He was a damn genius, but ever since she'd put that knife to his throat he'd become a drooling idiot. He needed his damned wits, just for a minute, so he could fix this.

Suppressing the wolf inside him, he reread the note. "The note's not finished."

"Maybe Ross interrupted her," Liam said…and Travis wanted to punch him, even if he might be right. That was a possibility.

There were spots on the note. She'd been crying.

Well, why the hell is she leaving if it makes her cry?

He tore the note from the pad.

Think, dammit. Think!

He stooped to pick her keys up. "If she left, why are her keys and her car still here?"

"Maybe she left *with* Ross."

It was a sad state of affairs when Liam had become the voice of reason.

Travis took her keys outside to her car and opened the trunk. "Her stuff is here. Something is…off." And it wasn't just because he wanted it to be. She wouldn't have left without all her stuff, and why had the keys been on the floor?

Wait, didn't Kristin say she came here for the map? He stalked back inside.

Travis picked up the map before tossing it in frustration.

He inhaled and exhaled slowly. He was acting like a lunatic. Then he inhaled again. "Can you smell that?"

Liam sniffed and looked around. "There's another scent in here."

They walked toward the couch, following the scent.

Travis dropped down and dragged a syringe from underneath it. He winced and fought a snarl.

This was bad. This was very bad.

"I don't think LeAnn left here by choice," Travis said.

"So Ross grabbed her?"

"He must have."

His heartbeat picked up, and panic muddled his thinking. He'd done this. He'd told her she couldn't come earlier because she would cloud his control of the situation. He'd wanted her to be one of the elements he could control rather than letting her make her own choices, like an equal. He'd driven her out of the damn lodge and made her think leaving was her best option, that she meant nothing to him or the pack. He'd practically pushed her out the door. And now she was gone.

It's all my damn fault.

LeAnn wasn't another variable in a scenario to be manipulated. She was the woman he loved. Even his Lycan side had realized he'd screwed up—that's why he'd turned and watched her through the window.

And she'd been upset.

And he'd left.

What an ignorant bastard he'd been…what a jackass…

He breathed deeply, trying to calm down…and not because he was Alpha, because he was LeAnn's mate.

They moved outside and looked at the dirt near the

door. No drag marks. Damn. He'd picked her up and carried her. *But then why*—

"Would Ross hurt her?"

"I don't know."

Travis looked down at the note again. *Damn.*

Concentrate, Travis. She needs you. You can throw yourself at her feet and grovel later.

He wiped a hand down his face. "Okay, this is what we'll do." Walking back inside, Travis went to his phone. "I'm going to have a friend of mine run a trace on my cell phone. You'll go back and gather who you can to send out on search parties...except Alanna. If you can find Alanna, she's to stay at the lodge—by force if necessary."

"Alanna? You think Alanna did this?"

He shook his head. "No, but something that LeAnn said yesterday about Ross having Alanna's lab coat has been stuck in my head, and I keep coming back to it." Plus, Merilee was shorter and lighter weight that LeAnn. But there'd been drag marks to follow at her house. If Ross had killed Merilee, he'd had someone else dispose of the body. "I'm going to follow this scent trail here. I'll have my hacker guy call Grant's phone to check in if he can trace mine." He nodded at the door. "Go!"

Liam shifted and was gone.

His hand paused on the phone for a second, and he stared after the other man. This switch from enemy to ally was a little quick... Shaking his head, he picked up the phone. He was trusting his instincts.

And his instincts said to dump his pride and make a couple phone calls.

Jordan answered with a groan. "Do you want to come

on our honeymoon, Travis? I'm starting to wonder if you can live without me."

"I need your help tracking Ross in case I can't find him right away."

"Your mate is as good as, if not better than, me at tracking. Trust her to be able to drop her emotions and help you."

I'm an idiot.

He shook it off. He'd have to work out his control issues when he found LeAnn. And he would find her.

"He's *got* LeAnn. He grabbed her, and I don't know where he's taken her or if he'll kill her," Travis said through gritted teeth.

"I'll be there as soon as I can…but you owe me mileage." And he hung up.

One call down. One to go. Hopefully Ross hadn't smashed that phone, too.

• • •

Moaning, LeAnn tried to ease off her hands, which she was lying on, only to discover they were zip-tied together. It smelled dank and musky like an animal's pen.

Where the hell am I?

Her head ached, but she opened her eyes. Above her were rafters. No, floor joists. She was underneath a cabin in a cellar, and that scent of animal wasn't just any animal—it was a bitch she hated and the killing machine she was related to.

Her brother paced beside her.

"You're okay, LeAnn," he said, turning to her.

"Everything is so far from okay." She wanted to laugh and cry at the same time. So much for leaving and dragging her brother away from the area. And he'd brought her to a place that screamed he was in league with the person she despised. "Though I've always wanted to sleep on a dirt floor on top of my arms in a place that reeks of a woman I'd kill in her sleep. That has its charm."

Ross stilled. "Alanna?"

"Yeah, Alanna. If she's here, I swear I will get to my feet somehow and kick her to death."

"She said you were jealous of her." He said it curtly, matter-of-factly.

"I am not." Okay, she was. The woman had that stupid medical degree. You couldn't really compete with that at the drop of a hat. And even if she was a veterinarian, that worked out great for a group that was half wolf.

"She said that's why you killed Merilee."

She squinted at her brother. Granted she was a little groggy, but that made no sense.

She wriggled onto her side, and her arms protested being woken up. *Ouch.* This blew. Her arms stung as the circulation returned, like they were still being jabbed by needles, and the damn things were zip-tied. She was dirty. Her hair felt like a knotted mess. All while she was in Alanna's cellar. Could this get any worse?

Wait. It could. Instead of getting out of here and taking herself out of the equation as a source of tension, she was square in the middle, and her big dope of a brother might not realize it, but she did: someone was going to die for this. There was no way Alanna would let LeAnn live now that she'd been here and her brother had opened his mouth. No way Travis would let her brother get away with kidnapping her. Even the pack had a dog in this fight. She hadn't officially turned down the position of alpha female, so Ross had snatched not only his sister, but the pack's Alpha, and as much as they hated him, they'd use it as an excuse to kill her brother.

I've ruined everything.

She laughed, and it wasn't a "ha ha funny" laugh; it was a "holy hell, if I'd stayed put like Travis had ordered me to, maybe nobody else would have to die" laugh.

"I didn't kill Merilee," she said. "And apparently neither did you. Alanna did." Which was bad. She could reason with her brother, but there was no reasoning with that other psychopath. *How many are we up to now…three?* And if Alanna arrived while she was still zip-tied…it was bye-bye LeAnn, and then that freak would pop some popcorn and watch as Travis and Ross tried to kill each other. Why hadn't she stayed put when Travis asked her? She could have pitched her fit later and gotten the sheriff's escort to the airport. Not to mention it was a little gutless to dump him and slink off with her tail between her legs. Not that she had a tail.

"It's not your fault. Travis is filling your head with all these ideas, and I didn't explain about pack rules like I should have. But you never said you wanted to join a pack."

"Ross, I didn't kill Merilee. And cut these damn things and let me loose." She'd really screwed up. This was what you got for being a coward and running off when things got difficult.

Her brother shook his head. "You did kill Merilee. It's hard to fight your instincts, and you don't always realize when you do things, but I got there too late. And I'm sorry. I could have stopped you…explained."

"Explained what?" she asked, pulling up to sitting… with difficulty. "That you don't kill people? Thanks. I got that. I didn't even need to be told that like *some* people in this room."

"That was different. And a mistake…I see that now. But Colby wasn't pack. And Glacier wasn't pack anymore. You don't do things like *this* within a pack. That's why Dane and Jordan needed to die…why they all maybe should have. Sammy was pack, and they didn't try to help her, and they'd let her be killed, and no one cared. But maybe it wasn't my place to do it, and I never meant for anyone from this pack to go over and be killed. It was mostly about Jordan and Dane. I couldn't seem to stop it once it started." He gestured around wildly. "And then the poachers came, and they were much better at planning. And I knew what to do, knew how the pack would act—or how I expected them to act. For once, I was in charge. It was like I was Alpha. But I'd never meant for it to get that big."

"I've got no idea what you're talking about. But I've met Jordan, and you're a moron." Even if she didn't understand most of that rambling nonsense, he'd mentioned killing Jordan, and Jordan was—Jordan. The only one she'd be more surprised about being on a hit list would be Travis.

"That's because you don't understand what being in a pack is like."

Okay, that was enough. "And I probably never will. You know why? My older brother is a raging psychopath who murders people. It's a little hard to recover from that first impression, Ross, but they've already voted once not to kill me, so I was starting to do okay." She had been. In fact, this morning while they'd been making breakfast, that was about the closest she'd ever felt to having a family. They'd been laughing and joking around. It'd been like having a houseful of siblings. For one bright and shining moment, she hadn't felt adrift and alone. She had the pack, and she had Travis. And then it had all turned to ash in front of her.

"No…no…you don't belong here, LeAnn. That's why I've had to stay around. Imagine how…aggravating it was to go back for my new ID at my place and to find you. I could have left, but no, my sister had to show up and ruin things. You shouldn't have come. You don't belong here."

No. He wasn't allowed to say that. She could say that. And Travis could say that. But Ross couldn't make that decision. "Travis wanted me here…which is pretty damn forgiving of him, even if he didn't have this scent-match thing forcing the issue." Maybe he felt something outside the scent-match. He'd acted like he did. And if he did, maybe this morning he'd been trying to protect her from this exact scenario. Maybe he'd understood Ross a bit more than she did.

Ross'd gone back to pacing but he froze again. "So, you *have* scent-matched?"

"Yes." And it felt good. She had someone—who belonged with her. They were matched. A matched set.

"Oh, that's no good. That's not good at all. Alanna said that, but I was hoping she was mistaken. That means we *will* need to kill Travis before we leave, or it'll make you crazy."

It knocked the breath out of her. No. Not Travis! "What! No, you killing Travis would make me crazy, and I'd kill you first, which would make us some creepy Shakespearean tragedy or something. Maybe. I can't remember if siblings killed each other in Shakespeare." *Oh, hell, why didn't I try harder in school? And Travis spends hours studying volcanoes. He was probably wondering if I'd need cue cards in our conversations.*

She took a deep breath. "Okay, what the hell did you drug me with? Because I swear this pounding in my head is making me sound even weirder than normal. I don't even know what I just said." He *was* planning on killing Travis? That was...insane. This had to be some sort of nightmare.

She kicked out with her legs, drawing his attention, and ending that eerie pacing he kept returning to. "Ross, you've got to cut me loose."

Shaking his head again, Ross crouched in front of her, and it hurt, even in the dim room, to see the feverish look in his eyes. He'd definitely snapped. "This is not your fault, and we can fix this."

She sighed. "It's a little my fault. And we can't fix this. I don't know what sort of garbage Alanna has been telling you, but she's lying. She killed Merilee and staged it so everyone thought I had killed her, so the pack would kill me and she could have Travis. They all seemed to think I was going to pick off the females one by one, and that's what she wanted. She wanted to be Alpha, and I think she likes death...well, not her own, but that's tough luck." It probably didn't bode well for her own mental health that she was really starting to look forward to killing Alanna. *If I can get free...* She twisted her hands and jerked them apart, trying to stretch the zip ties, but there was no give. Stupid zip ties.

Ross shook his head back and forth and then kept doing it as he stood up and said, "No...no...no... She wouldn't have a reason to do that. She was already Alpha if she wanted it.

She could have *been* Alpha when the pack first arrived. She was already here. She's from here."

"She's from here? So she was just hanging out…a lone wolf…waiting for a pack to lead?" That was weird. Maybe the pack showed up and took over her territory, and that's why she was a psycho freak. Obviously she didn't play well with others, so there was that.

"Yes, and Travis was interested in her from the beginning. If she'd wanted to be Alpha, she could have been a year ago."

"Travis was interested in her?"

Her brother nodded.

Ow. She jerked at the shaft of pain in her chest. If he'd driven a spike through her heart, it would have hurt less. She stopped struggling.

And thought back.

Had Travis ever believed her about Alanna? *Does he still want that skanky troll, but got stuck scent-matched with me?*

It stole her breath, and her shoulders drooped in defeat. That hurt. Even if she'd suspected. Even if she'd known that Alanna would make a better Alpha, it stung like a knife in her heart, and she couldn't breathe. LeAnn closed her eyes against the tears gathering. She wouldn't cry. Not here in this basement that smelled like that whore. Not while she was being held captive by her ranting, psychotic sibling.

Her eyes flew open.

In fact… No. She yanked at her restraints again. Even if Travis had been interested in Alanna, she'd ruined her chances with him by killing Merilee. There no way LeAnn was going to sit back and die so that the local freak show could take control of the pack. No way. And she was going to save her meltdown for when she escaped to some-place more pleasant, and she was also going to punch her brother in the face for bringing her here.

Ross went on as if he hadn't dropped a bombshell on her heart. "So Alanna had no reason to kill Merilee. We all knew she was Alpha. You were just…a snag, but she said you weren't pack—that no one would accept you as pack, so I thought we could leave after I'd gathered my stuff. Then Alanna said it was a scent-match, but that Troy had chal-lenged, and we both knew that Troy would kill Travis if he won, so that would solve that, too." He went back to that stu-pid, stupid pacing that was making her sick. "But Travis won, and you killed Merilee, and it's just very screwed up. Maybe if I get you somewhere safe, I can come back and kill Travis."

She had a wall at her back, and she leaned against it. If the pounding in her head eased up, maybe she'd be able to reason with Ross, but it was doubtful. She was not going to let him kill Travis. Over her dead body would she let him kill Travis. No. No way.

"I *am* pack," LeAnn said. "And no one is killing Travis."

Ross shot her an indulgent look that made her narrow her eyes. Okay, so he didn't believe her, but she was starting to believe it herself. No one was killing Travis. And she *was* pack. They'd been eating bacon together this morning—like a pack. Bacon that she'd asked someone to go get and they had. She hadn't even needed to chip in money for the bacon. You did that for family, for pack.

"So, you've been talking with Alanna all this time?" she asked. "She's known where you are?" It was time to get the lay of the land for when she broke free, because she was going to break free, if for no other reason than to prevent

Alanna from getting what she wanted. *And to punch that bitch in the face.*

Her brother did some sort of nod and shrug gesture combined and kept pacing.

"Are you sleeping with her?" *Please no. Please, please no.* That was so gross she might need to throw up before they could continue the conversation.

He stopped. "No. LeAnn, she's Alpha. She takes care of the pack like an Alpha should."

"She's not Alpha. I'm Alpha." *Probably. Close enough.*

Ross talked above her. "She should only be with the Alpha, but she wasn't sure that Travis was right for Alpha, and that's why she was waiting." He shook his head. "See, this is what I'm saying. You don't understand pack. I'm not an Alpha, so I was only meant to serve her."

Well, that was a small relief. It wouldn't improve her situation to be surrounded by vomit. It was still freaky that he'd turned minion to the Queen of the Damned, but slightly better than him swapping bodily fluids.

She shuddered. *Ow. Hell.* That hurt.

"And you're not Alpha…which is why you messed up and killed Merilee."

"I *am* Alpha, and I did not kill Merilee." She could have taken down Alanna in that fight, even though she'd cheated and shifted…so that was probably further proof she was Alpha.

"I was there, LeAnn. I was there right after you killed her."

"That was Alanna. Alanna did that and made it seem like I did. Look, whatever. Did she know what you were going to do with Glacier Peak and the poachers?" Her brother had never seemed to be that proactive. He'd never even asked out that chick he was hot for two years ago.

Ross froze and stared at her...and pointedly didn't answer.

Hell. That hag was going to die.

"It was my idea," he said finally.

Like hell it was. It was put there by Alanna—who might have seen herself as Alpha, but she hadn't wanted it until Travis wasn't available. Alanna was a manipulative sicko. She'd seen an opportunity since Ross was already a bit around the bend, and so she got the entertainment of watching a bunch of people kill each other. If she was there as a doctor, she got ringside seats.

That woman should not be a veterinarian. She had a God complex and a fascination with murder. The poor pets in this area were probably getting crappy treatment—that much was certain. Even if everything else *was* guessing, she had to be a lousy vet. It was just as well she hadn't stitched up Travis. She'd probably have done a crappy-ass job.

"You shouldn't have shown her the lab coat, LeAnn. She was very angry about the lab coat." Annnnd he was back to pacing.

"I'll bet she was."

"It seemed like I needed one more scent, and I was there. But I should have asked her, told her. But I knew they wouldn't suspect her." He frowned. "She was mad."

"Oh, she's mad all right." It was a weak comeback, but her head was still working on clearing, and it was hard to think in a room with someone ranting. And pacing. She took a few deep breaths and then coughed again. This place was nasty. She was going to get like black lung or something.

You'd think a doctor would take better care of her place, and this nasty room smelled too much like Alanna to belong to anyone else.

Then she could smell something beyond the basement, Ross, Alanna, and her. Metal. A key. She still had Travis's spare key in her pocket. She shifted back and forth while leaning back. It dropped to the floor with a muffled *ting* before she flattened it with her tied hands.

"What was that?" Ross whirled around.

"What was what?" She shifted sideways slightly and grabbed the key, angling it up toward her wrist. Hah! She was so going to get her not-quite alpha ass out of here.

"Nothing." He sighed. "So, we'll wait here until it's dark, and then we'll leave. If Alanna comes back, she can help us plan. She was the one who told me this morning I needed to get you out of here…but I'd still need to kill Travis. She's good at planning. She can help us."

Yeah, Alanna would help him dig her grave. Plan? Sure. Right. That's what she'd do. She could picture it now. *Oh, sorry, Ross, this gun went off, and I accidentally shot your sister in the head, but it's cool because I'm your Alpha, and I'll take care of you. Find a shovel.*

"You know, Alanna stole both our clothes and has been making it look like we're both guilty as hell," LeAnn said. She wasn't sure why she was still bothering. Ross was thoroughly brainwashed, but her talking would cover up the key sawing at the plastic.

He shook his head. "You don't know what you're saying."

"And we're not going to be able to sneak out of here. Travis was already out looking for you. The entire pack is probably looking for you now, because I don't know how long I was out, but I bet they've figured out I'm missing." Though Travis might assume she'd taken off. Or the pack might think she was in on all of this with her brother.

She'd finally gotten the key in the right place, and she began scraping it against the zip ties. Every time Ross turned toward the single, poorly-boarded-up window, she saw the flash of her gun on his hip. She'd get free. Get the gun. And somehow manage to subdue Ross. Her planning sort of fell apart there because Ross could shift and take off, but she'd deal with the details when she got there. If anyone heard some of the stuff that Ross was saying, it'd implicate the hell out of Alanna, and maybe Ross would get a less brutal killing. It was worth a shot.

Besides, on the off chance Travis was coming, she didn't want Ross shooting him. So she needed that gun at the very least.

"No. It's all going to be fine," he said. Then he stared at her. "They were looking for me?"

"Yep. Wherever we are, I'm sure they'll find us soon."

He spun and grabbed something from a nearby table. A rip of duct tape later, she was wishing she'd kept her mouth shut.

"It's only until tonight. Then we'll leave."

Like hell they would. She was going to get free and prove she could be Alpha by making a stand. It was time to stop running away and to fight for what she wanted. She kept sawing at her zip ties.

• • •

Travis stopped by Terri's car and shifted. One rock later, he'd grabbed the phone from her passenger seat.

"Tell me something," he said, after he called Grant.

"Your hacker called, and we're looking it up now. It looks like your phone is… Damn…we need a faster internet connection here."

He leaned against the car, taking deep breaths. He'd never run this all out before. He was in the right area—he was sure. He could track LeAnn's scent much better than anyone else's. Even the constant rain wasn't enough to dampen his ability to find his mate. "Tell Terri that I owe her a new car window."

"You're over near Terri's?"

"Yes."

"It's coming from a quarter mile southeast."

"Okay, start calling it, and I'll look for it. Did you find Alanna?"

"Yeah. She's supposed to stay here?"

"Yes, she doesn't leave." He heard swearing in the background. Alanna wasn't too pleased about that. "Send anyone available to help me search this area."

"I'll have Liam go grab whoever is nearby—he just came back."

He hung up and dropped the phone back on the seat. He could come back here if he needed to check in. Shifting, he ran toward the southeast where he could hear the buzzing of his phone. He nearly ran over it before he realized this wasn't the end of the hunt. This was where his phone had dropped out of LeAnn's pocket.

"Hey," he said, shifting and answering. "My phone is here and I think I've caught their scent again. I'm heading east toward what looks like a half dozen empty cabins, but there might be more."

"He carried her that far?" Liam asked in the background.

"He had a car," Travis said, trying to catch his breath. He definitely wasn't leaving anything for the return trip. "I can smell gasoline, too. Okay, I'll focus on anything with a garage or a car nearby."

"Heading that way," Liam said.

He hung up, shifted, and ran. *Mate. Mine. Mate.*

The Jeep was parked behind a set of cabins that smelled faintly of Alanna. She'd lived in the area prior to the pack arriving, so it was possible she owned property they didn't know about. It was also possible that Ross had found these cabins empty and decided to use them, but he was taking a pragmatic outlook on this. Alanna was somehow involved.

He shifted and circled quietly.

LeAnn was in one of those cabins, and he had to believe she was fine. She had to be. He still felt the pull of her scent, so he knew she was alive.

Then he heard Ross's voice.

"What you don't understand is that pack is more important than anything," he said. "It takes over your head, and it's all you can think about. So it'll be hard to kill Travis, but it's right."

It was going to be damn hard to kill Travis. He wanted LeAnn, and she'd agreed to the scent-match last night. He might have to convince her again today—and every day, but he lived for a challenge. He wasn't about to die now.

There was a stomping sound and mumbling.

"Well, you wouldn't keep quiet, and I need to think. Maybe if you promise to keep quiet, I'll take off the duct tape. Do you promise to be quiet?"

Travis grinned. That was undoubtedly the sound of a lot of profanity. He followed the muffled swearing to one of the cabins that appeared to have a den underneath. They'd all had to make do with not having basement dens because the area's houses weren't built with Lycans in mind. This one seemed to have been—which would make sense if it'd belonged to Alanna's family. While there was an entrance inside the cabin, dens had a swinging door entry usually, but it was often hidden and gave with force. It was Lycan-sized, so he'd probably taken her in through the cabin, but no matter how quiet Travis intended to be, it'd be impossible to be quiet enough to enter from inside the cabin. He had to use the den entrance.

If he waited for the others…

No, Ross was insane. He didn't want LeAnn in there with her psycho sibling any longer, and the presence of a lot of the pack might make Ross panic and become violent. He wasn't betting LeAnn's life on Ross's sanity.

This was reckless. This was impetuous and crazy as hell, but he loved LeAnn and he had to go in. Some things were worth getting killed over.

He had one chance to get this right before he gave away his game by slamming into the side of the cabin.

Shifting, he kept clear of the window as he sniffed the wooden slats surrounding the cabin's den.

Someone had passed through here. Not his mate, but another Lycan. He stared at the wooden slats.

"Did you hear something?" a male voice said inside the den. Ross. Family to his mate and enemy. Threat to his mate.

Mate.

Mine.

He slammed through the slats and skidded into the basement.

Ross turned and grabbed a gun from his belt, but Travis lunged, knocking it from his hand. Ross shifted and snarled, going for Travis's throat. Travis threw him off and turned to attack. Ross moved erratically, diving in again. Travis dived out of the way, but scrambled to stand between Ross and his mate, growling.

Plastic snapped, and his mate bounded to her feet before running to grab the gun. Yanking the tape off her mouth as she turned, she yelled, "Son of a…holy hell…that hurts."

Ross used the distraction to jump on him, sinking his teeth into Travis's neck.

"Ross! Stop! Ross, I don't want to shoot you!" she screamed, following their movement with the gun.

He bucked Ross off, but the other wolf recovered and dived back at Travis with a snarl. They rolled across the floor, snapping their teeth and missing.

"Stop! Ross! Stop!" She fired up into the ceiling, but neither of them stopped.

His blood was pounding, and he couldn't stop, not until his mate was safe. She was his. She belonged to him. And he was going to rip the throat out of this threat. He caught a hold of the other wolf's shoulder and bit in, tearing through flesh as blood spurted into his mouth. Ross slammed him into a nearby wall, knocking him off.

"Stay back! Travis! Stay back!"

He couldn't tell who she was aiming at. The blood in his mouth was her family's. He turned to look at her right as the other wolf leaped at him. The gun went off, and Travis was slammed hard against the floor.

"No!" his mate screamed.

He lay there disoriented, staring at his mate, as blood dripped down and around him. So much blood. Blood that smelled wrong.

She fell to the ground, dropping the gun, and crawled toward him.

"I'm so sorry…I had to. I'm so sorry. You wouldn't stop."

There was a sharp pinprick in his shoulder, and it was hard to breathe, and he still couldn't make sense of things.

His mate reached him and pushed the weight off him, and the sharp pain of teeth pressed against him stopped, and he could breathe.

Her eyes darted between him and the other wolf, and the scent of her pain hit the air as she curled up around her legs, whimpering. Ducking her head down into her arms, she cried.

Travis shifted back and tried to adjust to his human mind-set and the things that had occurred, but his brain couldn't get past the sound of LeAnn crying and the smell of death that was all over him. He wiped his mouth on his arm. Blood. A lot of blood. And Ross and LeAnn smelled enough alike that the scent disgusted him more than normal.

"I killed him," she whispered. "I shot him. I did. I shot him." She scrambled to her feet and ran toward the den's Lycan entrance. It didn't give to her weight, and she fell to the ground in front of it.

"LeAnn," he said.

She growled at the side panel and then slammed both her feet against it, knocking it off its hinges. Then she was out in the fresh air, where he heard her gagging and dragging in deep breaths before she stumbled farther away and fell down crying.

Blinking, he turned to Ross and checked for a pulse that he knew he wouldn't find. She'd gone for the kill shot and stopped his heart.

Searching the cabin, he saw a duffel bag with Ross's clothes. Wiping his face and body on a shirt, he cleared off as much of the blood as he could before, despite the repellent feel of it, he dragged on a pair of Ross's pants. If he looked less like the wolf that'd forced her to kill her brother, this might go better.

He followed her out the entrance she'd broken and approached her slowly.

Her sobbing was hoarse, and she was sitting with her arms wrapped around her knees and her head ducked down.

He knelt down beside his mate. "LeAnn," he whispered. Swallowing, he put his arms around her and then sighed in relief when she turned into his body and wrapped her arms around him. Her sticky face pressed against his chest as she kept crying.

Others began arriving, moving silently. Liam got there first and went inside, following the scent of death. After checking the den, he pointed in the direction of the lodge, and Travis nodded in return while still holding LeAnn.

Shifting, Liam ran back the way he'd come and the others followed.

Her crying got softer and lighter, and he kept holding her. He loved this woman, and she'd killed her brother to save his life. Hopefully, she'd be able to get through that, and he'd be here to help her.

"Honey, it's okay." He kissed her temple. "I love you. I'm sorry."

She whimpered again and rubbed her cheek against his chest.

"I'm sorry you had to do that, but you're not alone. I'm here. And I'm going to help you."

She might have nodded.

"You're my pack. And you can't leave me. Not for that reason. Leave me because I forced you to shoot your brother, but not because you don't belong. You belong with me." He was rambling, but he didn't know how to make this better. She'd shot her brother because of him. She'd already been planning on leaving him.

She sniffed and tightened her arms.

"You're my Alpha. Jordan was right. I need you. You make my life crazy and out of control, but I think I need that, too. I feel things now. I'm not just pushing through a routine."

He rubbed his hands down along her back, wishing he could take some of her grief on. He could prove to LeAnn she had a place in his life and in his pack. He had to believe that. Without Ross between them, they could make this work.

LeAnn pulled back suddenly, banging his chin with her head and making his teeth snap together.

"Where's Alanna?" she asked. Her voice was scratchy and deep from crying for so long.

"She's at the lodge. I told them to keep her there."

She jumped to her feet and started north before spinning around and squinting. "Where the hell are we?"

"Five miles southeast of the lodge." He got to his feet, too. "My phone is nearby. We can call for a ride."

She'd been looking around, but spotted the Jeep parked

behind the cabin. She strode toward it.

"Do you want me to get keys?" he asked, following her. It was difficult to read her mood—especially since it seemed to have changed rapidly.

She didn't answer, but slid behind the wheel and reached under the steering column, yanking out wires. A minute later, the Jeep started up, and he climbed into the passenger seat.

She could hot-wire cars. That was good to know. Also very sexy. In a non-law-abiding way that he couldn't ever outwardly support.

They'd gone a mile on the bumpy almost-a-road that connected the cabins to the rest of civilization before he asked, "Are you okay?"

"No."

That really had been too much to hope for. And she hadn't started off all that mentally well—which he was fine with, but it probably didn't help for coping in emergencies. He cleared his throat. "I'm sorry about Ross." She'd stopped crying at least, but it looked now like fury was fueling her quick demeanor change.

She shrugged and scowled. "I warned him, and I'd told him before that I wasn't letting him kill you. He just *wouldn't* listen." She slammed a fist against the steering wheel. "Why wouldn't he listen? Because dammit he wouldn't! And it all happened so fast!"

"I'm still sorry."

The scowl dropped off, and she glanced at him. "Are *you* okay?"

He shrugged. He had a few nasty gouges to add to the collection, but he hadn't really noticed them until right now because he was more worried about LeAnn than anything.

"When we get to the lodge…this might get ugly," she said, biting her lower lip.

"I figured."

"Are you going to stop me?"

"Hell no. I'll keep everyone else out of the way and jump in if she shifts and you don't."

She threw him another look. "I can't shift."

"That's what you keep saying."

"Do you believe me?"

He could lie, but this was LeAnn, and his mate, and it didn't seem right. "Nope. I think you're a full-blooded Lycan."

She kept her eyes on the road as she tilted her head. "That would make me really insane."

"That's what I love about you."

She slammed on the brakes, throwing them both forward. "What?"

He turned to face her. "I'm okay with you being crazy. And hell, that probably means I am, too, but it works."

She shook her head. "Not that part…the love part."

"I love you. Everything about you. And I don't want you to leave."

"Because of the scent-match."

He wanted to shake her and hug her at the same time. "No, not because of the scent-match. Because I love you. The scent-match might have gotten us together, but there's a helluva lot more that'll keep us together."

She swallowed and frowned. "You said I was the last person…"

"I was an ass. You're the first person I thought of this morning. You're the first person I want to see every morning.

You're the only person I want. Ever. I want to be with you. I want to get married…even if you accepting the scent-match basically says that. And I definitely want you to accept the scent-match."

She blinked and stared at him, but then nodded. Then she squinted. "Did you say you loved me earlier?"

"Yup."

She narrowed her eyes.

"I mean…yes, I did."

"I thought so."

They sat there. In the Jeep. Their gazes holding.

Then she shook herself and said, "I love you, too. Did I say that before?"

"No. First time." And it made his heart pound, and his mouth go dry, and he'd never have expected it so soon after what had happened in the den.

"Oh. Because I do." She swallowed.

He sighed. "I thought you were going to leave me."

"What would you do if I did? If I left you?" Her defiant look said this was some sort of test. She'd left people before, and they hadn't bothered to come after her.

"I'd come after you. I wouldn't sleep until I found you and convinced you to give us a chance."

She looked surprised.

He leaned over and framed her face with his hands. "I love you, LeAnn. You belong with me and I belong to you. Do you understand?"

"I think so."

"Because I'm keeping you. We'll figure all this out together. I promise you I've got your back."

"Even if I go all…rabid and attack Alanna?"

"Yes." He grabbed her hands, bringing one up to his lips to kiss. He was keeping her forever. Jordan had been too late to help with the rescue, but maybe he could talk to him about marrying them. Soon. He wanted her as his…in every way. A marriage might help her see that she hadn't lost the only ties she had to here—and to see that the pack could be her family—and they could start their own family. He was definitely keeping her.

"Are you still doing the handcuffed thing?"

"Yes, and taking lots of showers."

She glanced down at their clothes and said, "It might take a couple to start off."

He grinned. She wasn't going to run. He wanted to shout and hug her, but he probably shouldn't make a big deal of it.

She cleared her throat. "You really won't be disappointed if I go all *Exorcist* on Alanna a few minutes from now?"

"Honey, I'd be disappointed if you didn't."

Smiling, she took her foot off the brake, and they jolted forward. And he held on tight. Because it'd be a shame to die in a Jeep after all they'd survived.

• • •

She'd tried to plan what she was going to say, but it all flew out the window when she arrived to find a lot of the pack gathered and Alanna, leaning against the wall, looking bored, rather than like a prisoner being held there. *Oh, it was on!*

"You!" she shouted, pointing, and the Lycans between them melted out of the way.

Alanna raised her eyebrows as LeAnn stalked toward

her.

Stopping ten feet from her, she yelled, "You freaking whore! You filled my brother's brain with lies about how the pack should have protected that woman he liked…" She snapped her fingers.

"Sammy?" Travis supplied.

"Thank you," she threw over her shoulder. She took a second look when she saw Jordan standing beside Travis, but she shook it off. "You convinced Ross that the Glacier pack had failed Sammy, and you twisted it and twisted it until he started the damn war you wanted."

"Why would I do that?"

"Because you're a sick nutjob who gets off on death, and because you like to manipulate people into doing whatever you want. And because you were here at Rainier, all alone, for all that time and this was your land, and Glacier Peak never invited you to their party or to join their club. Instead, suddenly they start a pack here and take over this place."

"I joined this pack!" she shouted, pointing at herself and standing up.

"Did you? Regardless, it was all fine and good because everyone thought of you as Alpha, and you were still pulling the strings and making puppets like my brother dance, and it was fun. Then I came here, and it wasn't funny anymore, and Ross lived through what happened at Glacier Peak, and he could tell everyone all about how you'd encouraged him to call in the poachers."

"I never did that! If he told you I did that, he's a damn liar!"

"My brother is dead! Because of you! Because not only did you do that, but you've been feeding him lies this whole time, and he believed you because he saw you as Alpha still. Of course he did. I was his little sister, and I didn't know anything about being in a pack. You told him that Travis had scent-matched to me in order to get him to kill Travis because suddenly you weren't Travis's first choice for Alpha." *Right. We'll talk about that later.* She threw a glance over her shoulder at Travis.

Travis moved in back of her and said, "Keep going. You're right so far. You'd gotten to where I'd chosen you as Alpha and told everyone to back the hell away from my mate."

LeAnn nodded as she felt him rub a hand down her back. "So you went to Troy and screwed with his mind and convinced him to challenge Travis."

It was a shot in the dark, but it made sense, and Alanna's widened eyes said she was right. "That's a lie!"

"Yeah, whatever. But that didn't work either. So then you killed Merilee and tried to pin it on me, which is interesting because Travis told me if you really *were* pack, you shouldn't have been able to kill her. Maybe there's an escape clause for psychopaths though. Nevertheless, that failed because everyone in the pack agreed with my opinion of you and refused to kill me when it was obvious the only one I planned on killing was *you.*

"And when all that failed, you went back to your pal Troy and told him that Merilee would still be alive if not for Travis and me. And, okay, that worked, but we wouldn't die because"—she gestured between her and the man at her side—"we're better than you."

Alanna narrowed her eyes.

"And this morning, when the sun rose, and I was still

around, you were all 'oh hell no' so you went back to my brother and told him that he needed to get me out of town because Travis was filling my head full of lies about how I needed to wipe out the entire female population of the pack. So you had my brother make that call to Travis from Troy's phone so that Travis would go all Alpha and leave me behind because…"

"I was a damn idiot," Travis supplied.

She shrugged. *No disputing that.* "Then you came here and chased me out of the lodge—which I feel stupid about and wish I hadn't brought up. My brother found me at Travis's place, drugged me, and carried me off to some old cabin of yours in the middle of the woods until he could get us out of here. And then I shot my own brother because he tried to kill Travis to get me out of the scent-match." Eventually, she'd have to deal with that emotionally, but for now, it was going in that box of things she repressed. "All of this because of you."

"None of it is true. You're a filthy, lying…"

"But here's where I run into a problem!" she said, speaking above Alanna. "Because once upon a time, you told me that Travis would never suspect you of killing Colby because he'd know that if *you* ever killed someone they'd never find the body."

"Oh," Travis and Jordan said together.

"I wondered at the context of that," Travis whispered to Jordan where he was standing behind them.

"It makes so much more sense now," Jordan whispered back.

"And it seems we have no body," LeAnn said. "So it's my word against yours that you killed her, using an injection which is, interestingly enough, the same way Colby was killed, and the way I was knocked out, despite my brother not really keeping a whole lot of syringes and drugs around, and then you also dug out her tracking tag—which I had no idea you guys even had in you." She stopped and turned to stare at Travis. "By the way, that's weird."

He raised his eyebrows and gestured at Alanna. Yeah, he had that thing where he always wanted to stay on one topic of conversation until they were done with it.

"Oh, right, so, I don't have Merilee's body…so that's a problem. It wouldn't be as much of a problem if I had my brother still alive to rant to everyone about how much you talked to him about being pack, and how you guys were such special friends that he'd swiped your lab coat to lay a false trail for that thing with Colby along with a bunch of other raunchy-smelling clothing he collected after an orgy."

"So it sounds like you have nothing," Alanna said.

"No, you're right. You've won. I can't have Travis cuff you and haul you off like I'm dying to. You'll never be charged with Merilee's murder or held accountable for poisoning my brother's mind, so you can sit there with that smirk I'd like to slap off your face—that smirk I would have slapped off last time if Travis hadn't stopped me. You can do all that because you've won."

And she waited a beat.

And Alanna continued smirking in that irritating way.

And Jordan said, "*Hm*," behind her.

"But, oh wait," LeAnn said. "You have one big problem. You're part of Rainier pack. My pack. And even if I wasn't Alpha, I could still point out pack law which says that if the majority of the pack feels like you're a threat—you know, by killing people and manipulating the criminally insane—your life is forfeit, and you'll be ripped to shreds, which I will spit on, mostly because I hate your guts."

Alanna paled.

Jordan laughed softly.

"I love this woman," Travis murmured, shaking his head. "That's damn brilliant."

"But I didn't kill Merilee, Ross did."

"Oh, I don't think so," Travis said. "There were drag marks outside Merilee's place. You were too weak to pick up Merilee's body, so you had to drag her, unlike Ross, who had no trouble at all carrying LeAnn off after he knocked her out."

The hag scowled at Travis. Okay, so she loved him a little more now that he was throwing stuff in Alanna's face. It was strange having a cop on her side—especially a smart and sexy cop.

"So which do you want, Alanna?" Leann said. "Are you going to produce Merilee's body and evidence that'll get you safely locked away in prison, or are you going to take a chance and go to a vote? Because as Troy would tell you, if he were still in one piece, the pack protects its own."

Clenching her teeth, Alanna looked over at Travis and said, "I think I'd like a lawyer before I turn over anything."

LeAnn strode forward, hauled back, and punched her right in the face.

Alanna fell back against the wall, clutching her nose.

Shaking out her fist, LeAnn said, "Damn, that felt good."

She turned, expecting to see shock on the face of the pack. Instead, she noticed first that Travis had blocked Jordan from stopping her with an arm. Though from the way

Jordan was grinning, he wouldn't have stopped her. The rest of them were facing her, but they'd dropped their chins and were looking down. Even Liam—though he was smiling as wide as Jordan while doing so. She swallowed. They were doing that thing…showing that they respected her. She was pack. She was Alpha.

"I'm accepting the scent-match," she announced. Though they'd probably guessed that.

Travis walked to her side—there was a bit of a swagger in his stride. "Liam, grab my handcuffs from my room."

"Really? In front of our pack, Travis? Kinky."

Several pack members snickered but didn't look up.

He grabbed her, pressing a quick kiss on her lips. "I'm arresting Alanna, smart-ass." Then he winked. "But I'll get them back in time for later."

"You better…because I say so, and I'm Alpha." She grinned. It sounded fantastic to say that. "And I'm getting a tattoo, but a tracker…" She wrinkled up her nose.

"That reminds me," Travis said. He yanked up Alanna's sleeve.

A thin pink line crossed her upper arm where the tracker had once been.

"A little after-hours surgery, Doctor?"

Rolling her eyes, Alanna reached into her shirt and drew the tracking tag from her bra. "A girl likes her privacy."

LeAnn snorted. "You ought to have loads of fun in prison, princess."

"How'd you know?" Jordan asked Travis.

Her mate grimaced. "Merilee's tracker never disappeared despite her killer being in the vicinity and removing it. Whoever killed her wasn't using a jammer. That left two options: it was either someone who'd never had a tracker—which I never believed"—he sent LeAnn a significant look—"or someone who'd removed it. I'd been laboring under the misconception that it was Ross, not a new…variable."

Was it wrong that she liked him calling Alanna a variable?

"A psycho variable," she added. LeAnn threw Travis a look. "Definitely not getting a tracker. No way in hell. I think it was an insane idea from the beginning."

She felt the weight as every eye in the pack swung to her. *Uh-oh.* She turned to meet Travis's gaze and swallowed. They were equals. Hopefully, she could disagree with him in front of the pack without them resorting to a battle to the death.

A smile tipped up one corner of his lips. "You don't happen to have a knife on you, do you?"

LeAnn exhaled in a huff. "No, I decided to go for the gun instead today. I feel sorta naked without *something*." Though her last experience with a gun might make her switch back to knives for a while.

There was a flare of heat in his eyes at the word "naked" that made her heart speed up.

"Why?" It didn't help her pulse that he brought up a knife right after she'd challenged him in front of everyone. That couldn't be good.

Travis shrugged. "I was going to have you dig out my tracker."

Her mouth dropped open in a soft gasp. Wow. He trusted her to do that? She probably would've hurled, but it was… nice that he'd thought of it. They didn't even make Hallmark cards with that sort of touching sentiment. She cleared her throat. "Oh, I think Alanna can do that before she goes off to spend time peeing in front of large women named Bertha. I can stand beside her *with* a knife to make sure she does a good job." She raised her eyebrows. "You're sure?"

He nodded. "And that goes for everyone. We can all get them removed." He glanced around, but the pack had returned to bowing their heads respectfully. "I'm starting to suspect that the illusion of being in control is more dangerous than being out of control."

She tilted her head. "Have you felt a little out of control lately, Sheriff?"

He snorted and shook his head. "Pretty much since you arrived in town."

"And you don't like that?"

A wide grin stretched his lips. "On the contrary, LeAnn, I'm finding some things are worth turning your world upside down for."

"Is that so?"

"Yup."

Epilogue

"Jordan said maybe I could go on patrols for our pack. He said it was possible," LeAnn said with her arms folded.

Smiling, Travis wrapped his arms around his mate, drawing her in for a kiss…while he pulled the gun from her back waistband. He had to disarm her about three times a day. She probably still had a knife on her somewhere. He'd get that away from her tonight when he dragged her to bed.

"You want to go on patrols, Mrs. Flynn?" he asked, pulling back. He loved calling her that.

"Well, Sheriff Flynn, everything is supposed to be back to normal now, and the rest of the pack is doing their usual routes." She slid her hands into his back pockets and rubbed her body against his. Usually, that would get her anything she wanted…well, it still might.

"If you shift, I'll take you on patrols." Her nightmares were getting further and further apart, and she hadn't spaced out on him for weeks. She could take on her genetic heritage with his support. She'd love running wild and free, if she could stop repressing it. He'd seen the wolf in her eyes too many times for her not to be a full-blooded Lycan.

"Jordan *said* that you take non-Lycans on patrol."

"Who died and made Jordan Alpha of my pack?" It was a legitimate question. He heard "Jordan said" far too often for his liking.

She grinned. "He called me earlier."

What? He narrowed his eyes as he stared down at his mate…his wife. "He called *you*? Not me? You?"

"He told me that he's talked to you as much as he wanted to for the rest of this year. Besides, you're actually doing your sheriff thing again, and this wasn't about something you'd know."

Not about something I'd know? What? He might have to call Jordan and tell him to worry about his own damn pack, and stop trying to horn in on his…which would sound really ridiculous this soon after their crisis, but this was his wife, and she should only be worried about what "Travis said."

At least things had calmed down within his pack enough that he could do his "sheriff thing" again. Jordan had been right about an alpha female being exactly what his pack needed. And after she'd decked Alanna, no one doubted LeAnn was Alpha. Even Liam was showing her deference, and she had him running pack errands with no complaints. So Jordan had been right. Travis wasn't about to start saying "Jordan said" all the time, though, even if he had been right on this *one* thing.

"What was it about?" he asked finally. He should have known she wouldn't volunteer the information.

"A gift for Christa."

"Oh." That was okay. That made sense. He wouldn't even know the first thing about a gift for a woman. In fact, now he was tempted to call Jordan and ask what LeAnn had recommended.

Being mated was making him insane. He made so much less sense than he had a month ago. Every impulse seemed to contradict a previous one. And half his brain seemed to be entirely LeAnn-centric. Luckily, it seemed to have the same effect on Jordan and Dane, so it wasn't just a personality flaw of his. Plus, there were perks. A lot of perks…and he had one of them in his arms—all warm and soft and smelling of honey.

She'd totally rewritten his life plan. Now it was more of a life outline—a rough outline, with room for adaptation. He'd never be as carefree as his brother Josh, but finding something worth dying for made living for the same reason as close to heaven as a man could get.

"Also, one of his clients wants a nice safe, and he wanted to run a few brands by me to see if I could break into them."

Travis frowned. He wasn't entirely comfortable with Jordan knowing her history. Partly because he liked when it was a secret between them. "I'm not sure you should have told Jordan all those…stories." Even if it'd impressed the other Alpha and left Travis feeling proud.

"I thought you wanted me to find a legitimate way to use my skills," she said. "Besides, you know how it is when you're spending the day trying to find a senile Lycan visiting Glacier Peak. There were downtimes. And I like to talk. At least it wasn't a surly bear hunt he'd brought me over there for. Plus, it really was good practice." She tucked her head under his chin.

He hugged her and kissed her forehead. She and Jordan had a weirdly fraternal relationship—which he kept reminding himself of. There was nothing to be jealous of. Jordan could replace Ross in her life. That was fine.

"So, we can go on patrol?"

The moon was full and it was night…both of which had some pull on a Lycan's shifting. In the month they'd been together, she hadn't shifted once.

Despite what Jordan had said about never speaking to Travis again, he'd called to ask about LeAnn and find out if she really was shifting. His wife was human, but had a degree in psychology and might be able to help.

If she did shift, he wasn't sure that he'd tell anyone until she was ready.

But she had to be able to shift, and the moon tonight might be enough to loosen up her control of it.

He rubbed his chin back and forth across the top of her hair. She felt so good in his arms. "We could go on patrol. Not far, though…I'm kind of tired."

She tipped back to look at him. "Really?"

"No. I'm planning on spending a good long while checking out your new tattoo. Up close and personal." Beyond it being sexy as hell, it was another sign that she belonged with him and with the pack, and he wanted to show her how much that mattered to him.

"You like where I got it?"

"Yeah, and I like that you had a female do it." He'd never known he had this jealous side to him, but he'd never had anyone he was this possessive and protective of. Maybe when more of the pack had paired off, he'd ease up.

She started unbuttoning his shirt. Her fingers were

teasingly slow, and a smile played around her lips since she knew what she was doing to his heart rate—among other things. Tugging his uniform shirt from his pants, she tossed it aside. LeAnn slid her hands under his white T-shirt, skimming her nails up his stomach and ribs until he helpfully tossed that on the floor, too. He loved the sight of her hands on him. Leaning in, she kissed the white lines of healed claw marks on his chest. Okay, he liked the sight of her mouth on him even more. Leaning to the side, she kissed the spot where he'd had the tracking chip removed.

"You've been a good Alpha," he voiced the thought aloud.

LeAnn shot him a skeptical look before going back to pressing her lips against his skin. "You don't think I contradict you too often?"

"No. You give our decisions more weight…because you think of angles I've never considered." His life was more vibrant with her opinion and emotions coloring his perspective. And the pack trusted her to have their best interests at heart. Their leadership felt balanced and complete—like he'd literally found his other half. He reined in her impulsivity, and she pushed him out of his rut. Maybe if Josh had lived, he'd have found someone to balance him out, too. "The pack looks to you to confirm or…uhh, clarify my judgments."

She laughed; her breath tickled his skin with heat. "I speak for the underdog…from a non-canine view of course." She nipped his side with her teeth in a shallow bite. All the air hissed out of his lungs. His wolf sat up and took notice as she kissed that new mark, also. "You know what I was just thinking?"

"I wouldn't even presume to guess." Well, he could hope, in light of her actions, but between her rapid subject changes and the different way she thought, it was almost guaranteed she'd keep him guessing until he was in his eighties.

She kissed down along his ribs where he had pink nicks still. Mm. Then, the one on his side that was taking much longer to heal…which considering she took the "kiss it better" approach, didn't bother him too much.

"Maybe we could take a vacation around Saint Patrick's Day. Do the honeymoon thing then."

She hadn't wanted to do a honeymoon so soon after Ross's death. He hadn't pushed it.

"You're a big celebrator of Irish holidays involving getting pinched?" Travis asked.

When she kissed the mark on his lower stomach, he was momentarily grateful her brother had given him that one before he shook off the memory of Ross.

"Honey, this is going south real fast for someone planning on going out tonight." She had about two more seconds before he threw her over his shoulder and dragged her to the bedroom.

"I like holidays involving getting pinched, but also I get a little…hot around that time of year." She looked up at him with raised eyebrows and licked her lips.

She went into heat.

He grinned. Lycan females could be insatiable when they went into heat—and it lasted three or four weeks. It was considered heaven on earth among mated men. He'd suspected her time was coming, but it was harder to sense this far in advance. It'd felt like her hormones were increasing, but he hadn't ruled out that maybe they were both making up for lost time. Her going into heat was yet another box checked on the side of her being a Lycan.

Straightening up, she unbuckled his belt.

"I'll get the time off," he said.

Cupping her face, he dipped his head to kiss her. LeAnn slipped her arms around his neck and stood on her tiptoes when she felt like he was being too soft. He bit her lower lip before kissing it better.

"Mm. I love you," she whispered against his mouth.

He slid his hands back into her hair, pulling her mouth tighter against his. The wolf in him reared up. *Mate. Mine.* And he pushed back the intense desire to possess and tame.

"I love you, too," he said, his wet lips brushing hers with each word.

Twisting, he pressed her back against his kitchen wall and pulled her legs up on his hips. Mm. They didn't have to go out. His mouth slipped down to her neck to kiss and bite as his hands explored her soft skin.

"Travis," she said, tipping her head back. "Mm. I want to go on patrol."

"Tease," he murmured.

"Stubborn Alpha."

"Mouthy brat."

"Stud."

"Sexy."

He wasn't sure why she inspired name-calling battles with everyone she met, but he'd even interrupted one between her and Jordan right before their wedding. He'd yet to find out what that was about.

"If you shift, I'll take you," he said after one last kiss to her neck.

"If you take me anyway, I'll do that thing you like with my tongue." LeAnn could negotiate like a pro. "And I'll even strip down for the patrol."

He leaned back. "Will you try to shift…for me?"

She rolled her eyes. "Fine. I will concentrate on becoming furry, but I think the closest I'll get to that is if I stop shaving my legs."

Laughing, he let her drop down against his body, enjoying every inch. This was going to be a very short patrol. The forest equivalent of around the block.

She cradled his face in her hands. "Travis, when…if I can't shift, will you be disappointed?"

He brushed his nose against hers before kissing her lightly. "You could never disappoint me."

"Jordan has this theory that if he insults your manhood enough, I'll see it as a challenge and shift just to carve him up."

Jordan was such an ass. "I've changed my mind. Now if you don't do that, I'll be disappointed."

She grinned and tugged on his belt. "You're in charge of your pants, because I don't think we'd leave if I helped you with those," she said, stepping away.

He grabbed her hand and held her gaze. "Hey, if you do shift, we'll take it slow. You and me. We'll work together on helping you get used to it."

She nodded.

A minute later, he'd shifted and was waiting on her.

She flipped off the kitchen light and stared down at him.

Mate.

Mine.

"Am I supposed to be feeling something other than silly?" she asked. She crouched in front of him. "I told you… I'd know if I turned into a wolf."

He tilted his head and waited.

"Fine. See. I tried. Now do you want to go for a run?" She yanked off her shirt and tossed it to the side before shimmying out of her pants.

He felt protective of her when she was on two feet like this, and they wouldn't be able to go as fast as he wanted. But she'd be on four feet soon enough. He could wait.

Discarding the rest of her clothes, she opened the door and stepped out into the moonlight.

Lifting her face to the moon, she inhaled. "Mm. I love the way the night feels."

He bumped his head against her hand and watched her…and waited.

And waited.

His mate was full of surprises, but this wasn't one of them. He'd known. He dipped his head down and brushed it against hers before nodding in the direction they were to go. She bolted off into the woods, moving as sleek and smooth as a river, and he chased after her.

Mate.

Mine.

Acknowledgments

Stepping outside a world I've lived in for so long is more difficult than I'd imagined. It's hard to believe this series is drawing to a close. Each of the books in this series contained characters with real issues, even if the world itself was fantasy. The time I spent inside their heads often left me dealing with emotions that seemed too strong to be fictional. Never was it more true than this final story.

Many live with post-traumatic stress disorder, and it's a daunting task to push through the days when your past is so present. My deepest respect and empathy for those who do. I'm very grateful for so many people in my life who've helped me find peace with my own struggles.

As this book brought some of my emotions to the front, I'm thankful for my friends and family who were supportive either in real life or online on days when I was…cranky as a rabid Lycan. Special thanks to: Mom, Dad, my Sparrow family, Sarah Simonsen, Heidi Ludwig, Jamie Dix, Stephanie

Summers, Amalia Dillin, Kait Nolan, Jay Donovan, Suzanne Lucero, Paul Baxter, Mary Williams, Brittany Marczak, Minerva Zimmerman, Judith Perez, Michael O'Day, Melody May, David Hickenbotham, Elizabeth Hill, Adam Hickenbotham, and Andrew Turner. I know I'm forgetting people. It's difficult to adequately acknowledge everyone when you know so many wonderful people. Acknowledgments are a good part of why I keep writing. Eventually, I will thank you all.

Erin Crum, you are the most incredible copy editor ever. In a world of typos and mistakes, you are an undervalued treasure. Thank you.

Thank you to everyone at Entangled who helped with this series—you created a dream. These characters were close to my heart, and you brought them to life. Thank you, Lewis, for all your hard work. Thank you also to Sarah Yake, my agent, for keeping me sane enough to write.

And of course, I could not leave off the most supportive person I have in my life, my husband. Thank you, honey, for never letting me give up.

About the Author

After a childhood spent wandering as a military brat, Wendy Sparrow finally found her home in Washington State. She spends her days trying to convince her two kids she actually knows how to properly parent and her nights showing her husband all the cool things romance authors know… or goofing around online…or reading, but mostly the first thing. She's active in the OCD and autism communities and writes on her blog to support awareness in both. With her whole heart, Wendy believes in happily ever afters and that everyone deserves one. If she's not writing or wrangling kids, she's on Twitter, @WendySparrow, where she'll chat with anyone about anything.

Discover the **Taming the Pack** *series...*

PAST MY DEFENSES

Vanessa is the fastest Lycan around. In wolf form, the only threat she can't outrun is her allergies. After a feline dander-bomb takes her down, she wakes up naked and in a cage, staring at a hot park ranger who had no idea what he'd trapped. When they learn that Lycans are being poached, and Vanessa is targeted, Dane will have to keep her close to protect her. But with Vanessa in heat and mad to mate, who will protect him?

THIS WEAKNESS FOR YOU

Jordan is his pack's Alpha. *The Big Bad Wolf.* When his rival's little sister—a human—comes to his door, Jordan's tasty little snack turns out to be something much, much more. To Christa, the dark shifter smells irresistibly like *forever*. But falling for a wolf who tried to kill her brother—*twice*—is bad news. Especially when in the unforgiving, shadowed world of shifters, there is no room for weakness...

Also by Wendy Sparrow...

FROSTED

ON HIS LIST

CURSED BY CUPID

Printed in Great Britain
by Amazon